Don't Tell My Mom That I Love Her

Lauren Barnett

Christmas Lake Press

Published by Christmas Lake Press 2025
www.christmaslakecreative.com
Copyright © 2025 by Lauren Barnett
ISBN 978-1-960865-30-4

Illustrations by Zoe Barnett

Interior layout by Daiana Marchesi

Don't Tell My Mom That I Love Her

Dedication

To my grandma, who always believed I could—I just wish I had hurried it up a bit. To my mom who adores me but is still skeptical that I am writing a book, and likely has some feedback. To my little sister who is my biggest fan. To my amazingly delicious, moderately unsupportive daughters, who insist this book is so embarrassing. And to my husband, who never doubted me for a second. You all made this story come to life.

Acknowledgments

Maggie is inextricably intertwined with each of the amazing young girls with whom I have worked throughout the past thirty years. This is *your* story. Thank you for letting me into your lives and being open enough to trust me to help you through the bumpy years. Thank you to my friends: the moms who, themselves, weren't afraid to admit defeat and who supported my daughters and me when we needed it most. Thank you to my nieces for always reminding me that I'm cool. Thank you to Daiana Marchesi for creating a layout that reflected my vision of Maggie's journal, and to Aaron Davis for spending many hours perfecting the cover. Finally, thank you to my amazing editors, Tom Fiffer and Julia Bobkoff, who love Maggie as much as I do, supported *Don't Tell My Mom That I Love Her* from the moment we met, and without whom I simply never would have made it to the finish line.

"What have you learned, Dorothy?"

— *The Wizard of Oz*

Author's Note

This is for all of the *Maggies* out there—even the (pretend) pretty, perfect, and popular ones who appear to have it all figured out. This is for the girls who want to fit in and belong *and* stand out as individuals; the girls who want to be seen, heard, and understood by their friends, peers, parents, and teachers. This is for the girls who still desperately crave their mother's approval and for the moms out there who miss their little girls and need a little reminder of how hard it is to be twelve today. Maggie's diary of daily dilemmas helps to provide young adolescent girls (and their totally clueless parents) with the explanations and understanding they have longed for. Maggie is raw and vulnerable, self-deprecating and funny, and has the gumption to share her woeful daily sagas so other girls realize they are not alone. She is on a quest to ease some of the pain and confusion that young girls face because they feel they are the only ones who face it. Through a careful collection of the most common themes that plague tweens and teenage girls—and their mothers—these real-life scenarios will ring true to every reader.

THIS iS PRivat!!!

All About Me

This Diary belongs
to _maggie_

* I go to _orchard elementary_ school

My teacher is
miss. lindy

And I am in _3rd_ grade

Mom's name _julie_

Dad's name _harry_

Pet's name _sprinkles_

People in my
family _mom, dad, sister charlotte_

When I grow up I want to be
a/an _bt famos_

My best friends
are _ali, Hallie, caroline_

My favorite food(s)
is/are _mac n cheese, pizza, Brokoli_

My favorite movie
is _mary poppons, parent trap_

My favorite season is
summer

My favorite holiday
is _thankgiving_

Hobbies
drawing, singing to my
favrite songs.

Dear Journal

Hello…it's me. Are you bored yet?

Welcome to my miserable existence! I know I'm not the first lost soul in the abyss of middle school and I certainly won't be the last—but for me, it just feels different and plain old worse. I can't go all *High School Musical* and scream or sing from the cafeteria tables and I can't lock myself in my room until I am 17 and fully developed and gorgeous with a boyfriend and a driver's license—so, lucky you, book of my life, you're the next best thing. So here I sit, on my purple twin bed (I hate purple) in the corner of my room. I'm exasperated (great word) and staring at my bedroom walls with remnants of tape and thumbtacks, polaroids and cool quotes I printed out. Thankfully, each piece of memorabilia is carefully (and artistically, I might add) organized to cover large blotches of my hideous floral wallpaper. I actually made my bed this morning, I am propped up on my pillows, pen in hand, and I feel very…prepared. So here goes.

To anyone who dares to open this book—DON'T. The alarm will sound and you better run and hide.

This journal belongs to ME and only ME. If you are reading it you shouldn't be and you should be prepared for it to combust in your very hands. This is my new place to voice my misery because NO ONE understands me. Forget understand me—they don't even hear me or see me most of the time. I'm totally gonna try to write in here every day. Who needs a therapist when I have you?! I am not posting any parts of this online (SUCH an attention seeking drama act) or putting it on my Snapchat story because I don't want ANYONE ELSE to read it, or comment on it, or see it, or like it, or screenshot it, or share it, or even know it exists. This is MY life and no one needs to know my business except for ME. It's ok that the rest of my life is posted, filtered, liked and shared, I mean, it's not actually ok, but what choice do I have, that's the game we all have to play. Proof of life, proof of social status and self-confidence. Ha! But not this journal—this is the unfiltered truth by me, about me, and for me, and no one needs to know (and since we are being honest, no one would care anyway) (insert "pity me" emoji). I'm basically invisible.

Let's get right to it. School sucks and I have no friends. All my friends are on other teams and I don't know anyone in my classes. I mean, we all still sit together at lunch every day, but still, I am so left out. They all have private jokes about stuff and I just pretend I get them and laugh along. Whatever. I'm so over it. They're, like, bitchy and stuff sometimes anyway. I don't even know WHAT is with Ali sometimes. She rolls her eyes at everything and everybody and always seems to whisper about me. My mom's always like *She shouldn't do that to you. You should tell her how you feel.* Really? Like my mom understands. That seriously is the dumbest idea ever. My mom is such a loser sometimes. Like any girl would ever tell someone how she really feels and like anyone would ever give a crap if she did?! She is always giving me advice, but I swear it's only what they used to do in the olden days. Anyway, Ali may actually sleep over this weekend, so it'll be fine. Holy crap this handwriting thing is exhausting. I'm literally doing hand yoga right now. So now add being out of shape to my list. I have to stretch my HAND just to complete one entry??

Sometimes Hallie and I agree that Ali is, like, weird the way she isn't into fun stuff anymore. Like all she cares about is makeup and the Kardashians. And now her mom totally buys her whatever she wants so she acts spoiled. Mom always says *maybe there is more to the story* when someone acts weird. Like *maybe something else* (like at home or whatever) *is making her mean* and *you never know what someone else is going through.* I mean, Ali's mom is kind of cool and is a personal trainer, so I don't know. How bad can her life be? Whatever, it's fine. Ali just facetimed me and we talked about soccer. (She will probably tease me about my Mia Hamm poster this weekend, but I'll deal.) Maybe I'm just overanalyzing things.

Maggie!! MAGGGIIEEEEEEEE!!! Did you finish your homework?? Did you study for math? Did you wash up yet? It's SOOOO LAATEEE! (My mom literally just screamed that to me from downstairs. Does she actually think I care?) Diary, remind me never to scream random threats to my kids when I am all the way downstairs (or ever, actually). **Ucchhhhh. She is impossible.** (I heard THAT! She mumbled that to my dad. Whatever. SHE is impossible!)

Anyway, I'm supposed to be sleeping right now it is soooooo late. I don't know why I always have so much energy at night and cannot friggen go to sleep. The mornings when my iCarly alarm clock from 3rd grade (that I can't seem to part with) goes off I wanna die and I can't move! I'm literally a zombie in the mornings. I can barely think clearly enough to pick out my outfits. My mom says *lay them out the night before*—but who has time for that? And, anyway, even if I did, I have no idea what mood I'll be in when I wake up so my whole outfit will have to change anyway so what's the point? Sometimes I just sit at my desk and stare into the mirror and get so distracted—probably because now my desk actually became a vanity covered in tubes of half-used makeup and other products instead of paper and markers from when I was young. Whenever I leave the hot-iron in my room instead of the bathroom (which makes my mom crazy) it leaves a mark on the "desk" but I want to straighten my hair before bed. Mom and Dad scream at me every day because I am late and tired. *This is why you need to go to bed earlier...* Blah blah blah!! I mean, I know, but I always make it to school on time and I've only been late like twice so who cares? But everyone is always texting and posting stuff at night so there is always so much going on that it is hard to ignore it and go to sleep. I think I have a math quiz Friday and I have no clue what is going on in math. AAAAHHHH I need to sleep but I'm way too stressed out. Anyway, goodnight Diary/Journal thing. I think this is gonna be cool. Now I can write down whatever craziness I am thinking or feeling and you won't judge me or complain back to me (like my mother)! You won't give me annoying advice and tell me to clean my room and make my bed and pick up my jeans and leggings and underwear off the floor. (It's MY room, why does everyone care so much anyway?) Perfect diary.

I have to set my alarm but I can't shake this thought… *Is it weird that I'm 12 years old and I still can't sleep without my stuffed animals from when I was a baby?* I can't help it—one is a squishy elephant that is all torn up by the feet, and my mom has resewn and patched it a million times. The other is my Bear. Yes, just Bear. Apparently my mom's best friend Jenny brought it to me in the hospital when I was born and it is just the cutest, rattiest, smushiest little thing—his nose is all squished in and one eye fell off years ago, but I don't care. (My mom still kisses me all over my face when I'm in my bed; I may as well be three years old.) OMG I am such a freak. Can you imagine if anyone in school actually knew? Here I am trying to be so cool and grown up and independent, and the truth is, I actually need my parents to kiss me goodnight. I mean, it adds up 'cause here I sit pouring my life's story and deep dark secrets into a journal I found in my nightstand drawer that I got from my grandma for my birthday when I was 8 (which, for some reason, I always kept), even though it has princesses all over the cover and little magic wands and stars all over each page. I like my own bed, and I like my dolls. I swear I feel like I am straddling two universes—one where I fully imagine myself as this sophisticated, glamourous supergirl and the other where I can't even manage to brush my own hair or part with my Shopkins collection. It's gonna be a long night.

Dear Diary

Survival of the clumsy

Sorry I haven't written in you in a few weeks! So "me" that I'm already behind, even in my own diary. School has just been so crazy! I guess just getting back into the whole routine again really took a lot out of me! It's actually exhausting—getting up at dawn, picking out a game-changing, must-blend-in-yet-look-cool outfit, doing my hair, doing my skin care and putting on makeup, refilling my water bottle for class, putting it by the door so I don't forget it, grabbing a bar as I am hauling my sweaty September ass to the bus (with all the 6th graders on it!), and, of course, finishing my homework on the bus with no wifi. It's amazing I have survived these past few weeks, when you think about it. And with no tragic zits yet, which is a small victory (the face masks totally work).

So…the worst thing in my whole life happened today so I had to tell you. First of all, in math everyone understood what the teacher was saying about fractions and stuff and I was the ONLY one who was so confused. Everyone was looking at me when I asked another question so I just pretended I got it so the teacher would move on. But I HATE math. Anyway, like that wasn't bad enough, I couldn't get my locker open when it was time for lunch so everyone went to the cafeteria without me. It only took me a few extra minutes but it felt like forever! I quickly checked in my locker mirror to confirm I was safe to continue my day, reapplied some lip balm, and grabbed a piece of gum from the shelf inside. The halls were empty. My locker sucks! It never works! Everyone else's locker is so easy, and some people even leave theirs unlocked or slightly open so they don't even care if someone steals their stuff. Anyway, Hallie said she would wait for me but I was like, don't worry about it, just go. When I got to lunch the line was sooooo long it took forever! I barely had any time to eat! And when I went to pay, someone stuck their foot out by accident and I tripped on it and my whole tray went all over the floor. I literally died! Everyone in the whole cafeteria was looking right at me. It was SO embarrassing! (I felt like I was living a nightmare in a movie or something, it was like it all happened in slow motion and like everyone was going to get up and do a slow-clap in the cafeteria). Then there was like this awkward moment of "Do I bend down and pick up my stuff or just casually walk away? Or laugh it off and stuff?" I tried to be so casual and be like, whatever I don't care, but the cafeteria lady had to come out with a mop and a bucket so my life as someone trying to blend in but be cool may as well be over. They were nice and let me get a new lunch but still.

Then I had to walk out of the food part and go over to the tables and stuff. Awkward!! 600 pairs of eyes on me when I went to sit down with my tray. All my friends were like "Oh my God, Maggie, are you ok?! That was hilarious!!" I was totally going along with it and being like "I know, can you believe?! And that forever-football-jersey (FFJ) Andrew totally tripped me!" I even think I saw Ali roll her eyes at Katie. I honestly don't know if I will ever recover from this. I might actually have to change schools. Or move. I will now always officially be known as the girl who dropped her tray and spilled it all over the floor in front of period 7 lunch. I can already see it over my senior cap and gown picture in the high school yearbook.

Now I'm worried… *Will I ever be able to shake everyone's image of me as "that" girl and have them notice me as actually even semi above average at all?* When I got home, my parents were trying to be supportive and convince me that no one even noticed. *Maggie, honey, everyone falls and everyone thinks the whole world sees it, but in reality, everyone is too selfish and preoccupied to notice or to care.* I swear, if she quotes Alexis

Rose from Schitt's Creek one more time. *Nobody cares, Mags. Nobody cares.* Get real, Mom. And did she actually just say that no one even notices me? Let this sink in—nobody cares and nobody even noticed? Now it's 9:15 p.m. and I'm supposed to be able to study after my day??!! I am never buying lunch again.

She is so clumsy and distractible. I'm worried. We should have her tested she said to my dad in the kitchen.

Great. So she lies to my face and now I have a disease.

Dearest Book of Secrets

The power of a bathroom conversation

I got a text in between classes to meet Sarah in the bathroom. We SO aren't allowed to have our phones but I stashed mine inside my boot and felt it vibrate. Sarah has dropped and cracked her phone so many times, I'm amazed it still works, let alone hasn't gotten confiscated again for the gazillionth time. Of course, it doesn't help her cause that she thinks she is super sneaky by hiding her phone in her bra, and with her mini-boobs, I'm sorry, but there is nothing there to hold her phone securely! She wanted to talk about Tyler, who she totally has a crush on, but I think Tyler likes Mandy (even though Tyler still looks 11 and Mandy looks 15). He casually took a pic with her after school yesterday and posted it, so it was so obvious (though I'm not sure Mandy was fully committed to the photo, tbh). Sarah said she was trying to learn some facts about the players on the Patriots, just so she could start a conversation. She was like "omg I hear they might make it to the playoffs." (so embarrassing, if you ask me) The girls' bathroom is like the central part of school for gossip and private talks. Sometimes you know to meet someone there because they slip you a note in class or they text you. The other day, like 11 of us all went together at lunch. I felt badly that two other girls at my lunch table didn't go, but I was SO glad I went! Some of us are totally jealous that some girls are getting asked out and stuff. Whatever. I mean, it's not like they are really hooking up or anything, they just are "together" (whatever that actually means). Actually, maybe some people are hooking up—I don't even know. I mean, I hear gossip and stuff in the halls but it's usually about the slutty girls all rotating around the same three popular boys. Can you believe they rotate and share? Spit sisters. I shouldn't judge… Beggars can't be choosers. I didn't have the heart to tell Sarah that I saw that Tyler posted it on Snapchat (the one with Mandy) so I just played dumb and wanted to be supportive. Truly, I was so distracted by her broken screen and kept thinking she was going to cut her fingers, and I couldn't get past the thought that anyone would be into little Tyler, so I guess I was kind of quiet in the bathroom and just let Sarah rant.

But Ali did tell me the other day that she had some news for me!! She heard from Will that Teddy told him that he made a bet with Alex that Alex would ask me out again! (even though I totally said no last time.) My Ariana Grande perfume must actually make me irresistible ;)

But can you believe?? He is crazy! I will SO not go out with him. And I'm like two inches taller than he is. I did use to have a crush on him in 4th grade when we both went to the same tutor, but that was forever ago. I'll let you know what happens.

I do wonder sometimes… *If I want a boyfriend so badly, is it better to wait for the right one or should I just say yes to someone because he asked me out just so I can say I have a boyfriend? And maybe it will get easier for another guy to like me if they hear I've already had a boyfriend?* (But what if that said boyfriend is so not cool or popular, and even not that cute, then I could actually be hurting my future chances of ever getting asked out by someone hot and semi-cool?) I know my mom would be like **Maggie— wait for the special boy who gives you butterflies in your stomach, don't just say yes to any boy. You are worth more than that.** Butterflies? First of all, ew. Second of all—this isn't love, Mom, it's a boyfriend and I'm 12. Really? *Isn't my reputation more important than my self-image? Like maybe I have to say yes just so I get a boyfriend and maybe move up a rung? Or would it be the opposite if that boy is Alex?* I won't tell anyone that Alex may ask me out—and Ali better not tell either!—because then I would DIE if people talked about it like in the bathroom and stuff.

Why does she have such low self-esteem? she asked my dad from the den, worried about why I was considering "settling" for a boyfriend. I swear she is embarrassed by me. My own mother!

Don't Tell My Mom That I Love Her

**Dear Diary or Journal
(I have to figure out what to call you)**

I have nothing to wear

I went to get dressed this morning and literally had nothing to wear. My mom came in and gave me major attitude 'cause I hate all my clothing and nothing fits me. So she started going through my closet and showing me all the clothes I *could* wear. *Where are the new jeans we just bought? No wonder you have nothing to wear—I don't know how you find anything in this dump of a closet.* As she is criticizing me, she begins organizing my closet, so actually, it was quite a win for me ☺ "I wore all those shirts last week!" I kept telling her. She hates when I moan and stick my neck out at her, but really, I know she was just as cranky as I was because we both hate getting up early in the morning. She bought me all these new leggings the other day because nothing fits me anymore. But now I need all new shirts. And I never have any clean clothes because my laundry is <u>never</u> done and it gets me so aggravated. Sometimes it takes a week or something for all the laundry to be done (and then, I'm not gonna lie, it usually sits on my floor in the laundry basket for a week if someone doesn't put it away for me—or until my mom comes in and tells me I'm a slob and irresponsible and it's disrespectful, or something like that). Doesn't she see that I don't have TIME!?

If I wear the same outfit again that would be so embarrassing. Everyone would be like "Um, didn't you wear that shirt *last* week?" And that would be social suicide and I can't afford another blemish on my record. I started to make a list last week of all the outfit combinations I wore each day, so I could keep track—but even that was too much work and maintenance for me. Anyway, then my mom organized my stuff in my closet (I mean, she wasn't happy about it, but she did it) and I found a pretty shirt so I was able to make a cool outfit and felt ok before I left for school. I get outfit ideas from what people wear in school or what I see on TikTok. But I want to have, like, my own sense of style. I mean, I don't want to look like a total loser, but I want to work on my image—like find a way to be unique and awesome but totally fit in at the same time. Yeah right…like that exists.

This is what I stress over… *Can I be hip and unique and start my own style but also fit in?* I guess that is what most 12-year-olds want, right? My mom is always telling me *Maggie, you look so adorable. You have such beautiful eyes. When you smile your whole face lights up.* She doesn't even notice what I'm wearing and she has no clue what is in style or not and she doesn't seem to grasp that wearing the same shirt from 5th grade is like a death sentence. And I actually think that is her passive-aggressive way of telling me I always look unhappy and I should smile more. Not sure why or how my smile and eyes are relevant when I have nothing to wear.

Maybe I'll be a fashion designer when I grow up. The thing is, even though my supergirl self has her own edgy sense of style, I need to have the same stuff as the other girls do just so I can fit in. I like the off-the-shoulder shirts but my mom always makes me wear a tank top underneath them. (not sure how I feel about taking fashion advice from a mom who thinks wearing her own college sweatshirt from, like, 50 years ago is "cute and vintage.") It's fine. I feel a little awkward when my bra straps show. And then people will probably think I am showing the straps on purpose to show off that I actually wear a bra and some girls my age don't yet. And I got these new bras because my other ones stopped fitting me. My boobs are so awkward. But the new bras have more of a cup thing or whatever so now my boobs look even bigger and everyone at school is going to think I am wearing them on PURPOSE to make my boobs look big but, really, I am not. I mean, I have boobs and a lot of girls don't even have them, and I'm kind of happy that I do, but I don't want people to know I am happy about it, you know? *Maggie, your boobs are growing and you are so beautiful but you need the right bra to make them look appropriate and you need to dress properly and I don't care what all the other girls are wearing...* It's cute how she tries to sound supportive, but really it's quite critical and judgmental, don't you think?

It's not fair because my little sister just got new black boots and I didn't. Mine are so old. I had them last year! Of course SHE got new boots, she gets whatever she wants, little goody goody ("she," of course, is Charlotte and she is totally irrelevant). Every time I ask for something new, my mom says I have to "earn" it. Really?? No one my age has to *earn* things. I make my bed almost every day! I know I could totally be more helpful with the dog and stuff, but I'm tired after school and I have homework. It's just so unfair! Oh…and I forgot to mention that the shirt I wore today…the one that was so pretty…yeah…this girl Lizzie wore the same exact shirt today! (I looked so much better in it.) But still, how embarrassing to have on the same exact shirt? People even asked us in science if we planned it. As if we would have! Like any girl ever wants to be wearing the same shirt as someone else on the same day ever. So the whole school can compare who looked better in it? So maybe the TWO most embarrassing things are: spilling a tray in the cafeteria and wearing the same outfit as someone else in school.

And also, I have the worst hair!

Why does my daughter insist on always wearing clothes that are inappropriate for her body type? my mom actually texted to her friends. I saw it. I mean, she left her phone on the kitchen counter. She is so full of shit with her *Maggie, you are so pretty* stuff. The truth comes out.

Top 10 things never to say to your 12-year-old daughter:

1. You are a tween.
2. It will get better. Trust me.
3. Just sit at a different lunch table.
4. Your little boobs are so cute.
5. Life is so simple when you're young. Enjoy it.
6. I'm sorry you feel that way.
7. Why are you in such a bad mood?
8. Well maybe you shouldn't have been talking in class?
9. Try to keep it in perspective—it's not the end of the world.
10. When I was your age...

Goodnight!

Dear private journal
(let me see how I like this title—doesn't exactly roll off the tongue)

Happy Halloween. Sort of.

OMG two days in a row! I'm gonna write so much more in you now. It's very *"cathartic"* (that's a big mental health word, I know). Adults love to say they "journal." Somehow journaling has become an activity and not just what it should be—an actual top secret DIARY (let's call it what it is) for GIRLS. Why do grown-ups have to steal all the kid things (adult coloring books? Instagram?). Anyway, getting back to my point.

I love so much about this time of year. I love the change in temperature (different outfits!), playing soccer, the changing colors in the leaves, and knowing snow and winter stuff is around the corner…but I also really hate this time of year. Halloween used to be so simple and carefree when we were young. The reason why I hate it now is because I'm not a planner, or a "plan-maker," "the one who organizes the social calendar," "the one who makes the plans for everyone else and makes all of the decisions!!" (Oops. You can tell I'm a little tense at the moment. Sorry.)

We all know that Halloween has always been about three things: trick-or-treating, candy, and costumes. But when you get older, it becomes more of a social game of "who dresses up the same as whom, how unoriginal the boys can be in the required sports jersey (well we know what Andrew and his crew will be wearing—a whole bunch of unoriginal FFJ boys) and scary masks, and how inappropriately sexy the groups of girls can be." Now, as we get deeper into middle school, we even have the added "what is the coolest neighborhood to all go to and go crazy in on Halloween?" There is actually so much pressure it's stupid. Can you believe it actually matters WHERE you go, NOT to trick-or-treat, but just to go with your grade and cause trouble instead?

I usually like to pick my costume in September. I always get so excited about all of the new costume ads and TikToks and Halloween pop-up shops—omg I'm such a dork sometimes. I never make "plans" with people for things like Halloween or sleepovers or stuff. I mean, who can think that far in advance anyway? My parents are always saying *ask "so and so" to go trick-or-treating with you.* I never ask (and sometimes I wish they would just stop asking me about everybody else's business). It's annoying when my mom tries to orchestrate my social plans in an indirect way, like she thinks she knows who won't already have plans and who might want to hang out with me. But then, I am always disappointed when a bunch of my friends already have plans to go together or to dress up together and they didn't include me (how does my mom always know what's going to happen and I don't?). I mean, why am I disappointed and why didn't they include me from the start? I don't get it. But I guess if I had asked them ahead of time, they would have?

And it makes me worry… *Is it just because they are better "planners" than I am, or are they really leaving me out?* My mom drives me crazy when she says *Maggie—if you just take the initiative and make the plans yourself, then you get to choose who you go with and where you want to go—it all ends up on your terms because you get to it first.* Is she implying that being the leader of my friend group is a small and simple task and that just anybody, even little old me, can just make the choice of their own free will and take charge of the friend-group's plans, even when said "potential leader" a) has never led the group before and b) isn't even certain she is fully accepted into said "friend-group" in the first place? But I digress… Though I hate when she says that so casually, I do see how, objectively, such leadership does seem logical—she who takes the lead gets to make the choices and is therefore cemented into the plans. I feel like I'm onto something here. Diary, remind me to come back to this mind-blowing concept. But back to the costumes, the matter at hand. I get it, I mean, we can't ALL dress up together or trick-or-treat together (at some point there are only so many angels or cowgirls or princesses), but it feels awful to be the only one not wearing the same costume as they are. Come to think of it—as I'm writing this I am realizing—why can't there always be more room for an extra cowgirl or princess? Oh right, 'cause then the group is too big and therefore doesn't appear exclusive enough and therefore is uncool.

I get so mad at myself that I didn't reach out sooner, but I guess initially I am always just really excited about the costume I already picked out and don't want to compromise what I really want to dress up as just so I can join the group. But afterwards, NOT being a part of the group always feels so awful that it makes me doubt the times that I believed I could stand on my own and be independent. Which means, if I could figure this formula out, of when to stand alone and when to join in, I could solve every girl's insecurity problem that ever existed in time and space. So I guess that would be a "no." I don't think I am quite cut out for solving the every-girl's constant struggle between fitting in and standing out. At least not just yet.

These "planners," well, they usually get together to plan their costumes weeks in advance—I have even heard that some girls discuss their costumes before summer because they want to make sure they are included when the plans begin in September!! How forward thinking! How proactive! *Maggie, it's called being proactive.* How very insane!! Then they figure out where they will trick-or-treat and if they will dress up differently during school and then again that night. The worst is when they all show up at school in matching or themed costumes. Except for me. And there is always a school costume contest or something, and there is always a prize for a group costume, and I feel so awkward not being in a theme with someone. Keep in mind, this is still kind of new for us. Up until like 4th grade, we all just got dressed up in whatever we wanted. Now, it seems personal choice and free will no longer exist. God this seems so bleak! Does it ever get better?

Diary, I think you should be aware of these social issues since you are going to be a part of my life for many years to come. There is this strange *p h e n o m e n o n* that often occurs when you are a middle school girl: when home or alone in front of the mirror, our decisions seem clear and our confidence can be high, and then when we are placed in front of our peers, our decisions get all blurry and we doubt ourselves and have regrets. I'm serious—this happens about jeans, our hairstyle, the dress we are wearing for a bar mitzvah or party, shoes, and, you guessed it, even Halloween costumes. I really thought my costume last year of a dead vampire was so cool—until I saw their super cute/borderline inappropriately sexy tutu, soccer socks, and tank top combo. So I typically go from being so totally excited to being so bummed out. What I can't figure out is, *if I know it happens and will happen, why am I always disappointed and surprised when I suddenly feel a drastic drop in my self-confidence?*

I haven't asked anyone yet what they are being for Halloween this year. I have my costume, as always, all organized in my mind. But then I have to grow up and ask myself... *Do I have to swallow my pride and whatever shred of independence I have and take the first step to join the girls (who I don't even really like) just so I don't have to be alone and feel like a loser?* I'll probably go trick-or-treating with Ali. Unless she has other plans.

She better not be home on Halloween. I have taken her trick-or-treating for 12 years. It's time she figures it out with her friends. She is too old to have me interfere. Why can't she just join the group? Maybe I should call Hallie's mom? I heard her say to her best friend on the phone. She was still on the phone when she pulled into the garage so I could hear the speaker when I was in the kitchen. I know my mom wants to go to her stupid Halloween party her friend is hosting. I promise myself I will not burden her and, god forbid, ruin her adult inappropriate immature Halloween night so she can grossly wear knee-high boots and a patriotic leotard and dress up as Wonder Woman. I don't need her help; I can figure this out myself. I'm just not sure what to do.

***this is an update and this is PRIVATE**

Caped Crusaders

****warning**—I am wallowing in my sorrow and bidding farewell to my youth—I feel this deserves the proper mature, Shakespearean Juliet monologue-esque farewell (don't tell my English teacher I liked that unit, Miss Banks would eat that up and probably call on me… I would die). So, here it is. I decided to cave on my independence because my fear of self-loathing (whatever that is) has taken over. I have packed up my pre-ordered teenage girl version of the Mad Hatter and joined the crowd instead. Under the guise of being so-called "superheroes," we are wearing capes, tank tops, and short shorts. With the obligatory knee-high schoolgirl socks (a la Britney Spears circa 1999—a real crowd pleaser) and converse sneakers. We will be unoriginal, yet cute; bordering on inappropriately sexy with just enough cuteness to appear innocent. I hereby bid my elementary school self "adieu." The shadows of innocence fade before me, as if to call out to me *You aren't ready, Maggie. You still need us!* I guess my Hermione and Princess of Darkness days are over. I pushed my Halloween individuality limits as far as I could. I am afraid I must *succumb* (we just learned that in the haiku lesson, but don't ask me what a haiku is I don't care) to the group pressure of the "collective costume." At least this way I won't be risking my reputation as a moderately unknown, dangling-ever-so-delicately-on-the-cusp-of-popularity 7th-grade girl who has mastered the art of blending in and fading out. I am afraid to admit that if I dressed in my own costume this year, I might have cursed myself and tarnished my chameleon-like reputation and labeled myself as a freak who still likes wizards and magic potions. I must check that part of myself at the middle school door and pretend I want to blend in so that everyone, including me, believes that I do. Fake it 'til you make it! That's what they say (isn't it?). I hope Hermione doesn't think I abandoned her—she is still my superhero. But even Hermione wants to fit in sometimes. So, I drink the poison from the…urn and fold my prepared costume into its original plastic wrap and tuck it away in its cellophane bag for darker times. I'm just so relieved I was included. I know Hermione would understand.

Dear top secret journal

I want braces and glasses

I know you are going to think I am so weird and freaky. (Sometimes I like being weird and freaky :-) but just secretly.) But everyone who has braces gets more attention and the girls who wear glasses look so cool and confident; like fashionable and edgy and stuff. I'm tired of being plain. I have to shake up my life somehow. My mom sometimes lets me try on her reading glasses, but then she freaks out and says ***Sweetie, take them off. They will hurt your eyes***. Uchhhhh! Chill, Mom! She is so annoying sometimes and, of course, she doesn't understand why I like to put them on. She also has these fake glasses, like, just a plastic lens with no prescription, that she bought at some cheesy eyeglass store. They are actually so much fun to wear because they don't hurt my eyes at all. I wish I could get away with wearing them to school and just be like "yeah, they are just for fun" and not be embarrassed. But if I do, everyone will know they are fake and that I am just pretending to need glasses so, therefore, that idea is out. I'm pretty sure 7th-grade girls can see through (no pun intended) the fake-glasses attention move, and no one likes a phony or a drama queen. There certainly is enough of that going around on a daily basis; I don't need to add my name into the mix.

I know eventually I'm going to get braces...but my stupid baby teeth aren't even done falling out yet! I have all these spaces in my mouth from teeth that fell out months ago and the adult teeth haven't even grown in yet. I look absolutely ridiculous. Can you imagine anything worse than having spaces in your mouth like a 7-year-old child? How is anyone supposed to take me seriously? I wear a bra, but my face looks like a little girl's face! No one is ever gonna ask me out! Not even Alex and he isn't even cool! I can't believe I actually think having braces will make me feel cooler because I'll get attention when I get them put on, and I can't believe I'd rather have a mouth full of metal than a mouth with holes from baby teeth!

Sometimes I actually shock myself… *Is this what my life has actually come to? The standard for looking and feeling cool is really this low for a 12-year-old girl that she would rather have braces and glasses than have straight teeth and 20/20 vision?* (All my parents ever say is *Ohhhhh goodness I remember when I was young and they had just invented braces and I had a mouth full of metal and they hurt so much and cut my gums and I wore my retainer and my mouthguard all day and night and I brushed my teeth in school and walked uphill to school both ways*… losers.)

I'm not really sure if real-life hallway/classroom/cafeteria 7th grader is even as important as pretend/filtered/artificial Snapchat story. We all know what really matters: what we post. That is our standard for our social status. If you don't have a pretty picture to post (whether it's your whole face or part of your face, or a full-on pose) or simply the right opportunity to post one, your life is just boring. So without a life-changing event or a forced, gleefully posed picture of myself with some friends, or an on-brand super sexy casual vacation bikini post, I have nothing on my account that says I'm cool. I'm not sure that many people are actually cool, but maybe. They spend more energy pretending so their online image at least seems cool? I'm too tired to pick out a satisfactory outfit for school; I don't have spare space to be a 7th-grade influencer. Maybe my podcast should be "Hey, I'm just over here trying to get through the day." Sounds thrilling to followers and subscribers. If I get braces, at least I can join the braces "selfie movement" and get attention and sympathy (until the next kid posts a picture of themselves getting braces for the first time, and I become old news instantaneously). I know the novelty of getting braces or glasses would wear off very quickly; I know my teeth will hurt and I will get food stuck in them and look gross. But for a few minutes, just for the moments right after I get them on and take pics from the orthodontist's chair, and for the next day in school when everyone who saw my post or story knows to look for me in school and they oooohhh and aaahhh over me for the first few periods before lunch, it will feel very cool. I'm not even asking to be tall and look like a model. In fact, I don't think I'm asking much at all. I think we can agree—I have lowered my expectations for optimal Instagram posts. All I ask is that someone just cover my teeth with metal (with a hint of color on the brackets, of course). I guess the middle school ego is so weak that even the slightest addition feels like a life-altering event. (The alternative, of course, and equally as cool if not cooler, would be if I broke my leg or tore my ACL and had to use crutches. Not that success and attention-seeking behavior has more longevity than the novelty of braces. Too bad it isn't ski season yet.)

It would be nice if my mom understood, but, instead, I keep hearing her say to my dad **How are we going to pay for braces?** I'm sure my grandma would say that my mom was a pain in the butt when she was my age, yet my mom refuses to admit it to me. Hello!! Is this uphill battle for me to climb all alone?

Diary…

I'M NOT BEING CRAZY, I'M BEING TWELVE!

I'm in no mood for formalities. Be prepared for a rant!

Sorry. It has been, like, a week since I have written in you. This just has really gotten me mad lately. I have to vent to you and I know that you won't roll your eyes at me like my mom does when I bitch to her— ***Why are you always so moody, Magpie?*** You know, I thought parents and adults were supposed to be smart. I mean, they were teenagers, or "tweens" or "pre-adolescents" whatever stupid name they are calling us 12-year-olds these days.

Someone please help me to understand… *How is it that adults have so little understanding of us and what we want and need? How do they think that YELLING at us makes us want to LISTEN to what they have to say??? How can teachers and principals and coaches and bus drivers and even parents keep screaming at us? Maybe show us a little respect and maybe we will respect you back.* We teens, or tweens—(pick a category, Diary)— we need to rebel against the clueless adults we are forced to listen to! *How about you all help us out, for a change? I mean, have you noticed that YOU are the adults and WE are the kids here?* Even when my mom has a bad day or when she is stressed from taking my grandma to another doctor's appointment, she's the first person to come home and whine that my sister and I are being insensitive and need to give her space and time to unwind. But when I feel like that practically every day of my life, no one gives me any special support! You grown-ups have lived 40, 50, 60 years and learned from those experiences and have survived these TEEN years, and some of us are just starting out… I do not see the dilemma, do you? THEY need to change to work with US. WE are just barely learning how to BE and how to survive in this insanity of middle school and all the pressures and confusion that go along with it. UGGH it makes me so mad.

They throw all these expectations at us and expect us to just behave. Sorry, when we are in a bad mood, we can't really behave if you keep pissing us off. Just leave us ALONE sometimes. Give us a break! We are doing our best! Oh, and by the way…we are friggen TIRED! I don't know why—um…maybe because school starts, like, at dawn, and we can't fall asleep until late and we have hormonal stuff going on and crazy pressures at school and TONS of homework.

It makes me wonder… *Is the reason grown-ups act this way because they forgot what it was like to be young? When we grow up, will we also forget what it was like to deal with all the ups and downs of middle school and will we act the same as our parents act now?* There is no way. Now I will have proof of the suffering. This diary will always remind me of what I lived through and endured on a daily basis and I will remember what it felt like so I won't repeat this cycle of clueless adults! The worst part is—my mom's like **We didn't forget what it was like to be young—it's because we remember that makes us strict and careful because we know the lessons you need to learn at your young age.** I'm sorry but I have to believe that we can do better. We can BE better. When we grow up, we can show our teenage kids the kind of respect we so deserved when we were teenagers! It's funny, the only normal thing my mom says sometimes is that she gets frustrated when I complain about bus drivers, or coaches, or principals or teachers and stuff screaming at us and treating us like we are animals…and my mom says **Why do people choose to work with kids if they hate kids?** I don't get it either. And, to be honest, for once I appreciated her support.

Then again, my parents chose to have kids and they yell at me all the time. **Why is she so temperamental? What is the matter with her? She can be**

such a bitch. I will never do this to my kids. I vow to always understand. And to always remember my 12-year-old self. I know making decisions is hard when you're 12, but I don't think we have much opportunity to really make that many moves on our own at all. I will let my kids pick what they want for dinner, be messy, and sleep late.

Post Halloween Diary

Thankful for my journal—express gratitude lol

Well I'm glad that's over. Not worth rehashing, really. Just relieved the big gaping hole of "what am I going to do for Halloween" is now closed until next year. Ultimately, of course, it always ends up just fine. "Fine." Not good or great, just fine. We all survived and now we all can move on. I would venture to say that even the plan-makers are exhausted and relieved. Now we turn our energy to cooler weather, warmer clothes, and Thanksgiving around the corner. I can feel my energy shifting already. Kind of like the cooler air makes me feel a bit optimistic and relieved that the start to 7th grade is done. Eyes on the next holiday… When I was little, my grandmother used to take my sister and me into the city to see the parade balloons getting blown up the night before the Thanksgiving parade in New York City. I always whined about going in because it was always after school on Wednesday and it was always cold and dark and, I don't know, for some reason I always complained about it, even though once we got off of the train and my grandma hailed a cab uptown, I always got so excited. I'm not sure, come to think of it, that I ever actually told my grandma that I was excited, but I know in my heart that I was. Of course, now when I look back on those memories I feel kind of good and I smile, but it also makes me mad at myself that I didn't appreciate it more when I had those experiences. I mean, even just that time with my grandma. We stopped going to see the balloons three years ago. The last two years we went, my mom joined us (I know I complained because I didn't want her changing the vibe that my sister and I had with our grandma, and I was always worried that having my mom around was gonna change the fun stuff like all the treats my grandma bought us, the silly and overpriced souvenirs, and the late night hot cocoa with whipped cream for the late train ride home). But I know my mom didn't want to interfere in our special experience either. Actually, maybe it truly was out of the goodness of her own heart that she came (even though we abused her for it) just so we didn't have to cancel the night altogether when my grandma started to get more forgetful. My mom didn't feel safe letting us go with her alone anymore. I wonder, come to think of it, if her joining us those years was more for my sister and me, or for my grandma. Maybe my grandma treasured it as much as we did and my mom wanted her to get a few more good years with us. In actuality, I know my mom must have loved those Wednesday nights each year…alone with my dad. She could cook and relax and know we were making awesome memories and she didn't have to deal with us for one whole night. We used to come home so wiped out from the long day and the cold air and the visions of larger-than-life sized balloons dancing through our heads. I wonder if my own mom ever told my grandma that it meant a lot to her that she did that for us every year. Maybe my grandma used to do the same thing for my mom and uncle?

Usually my grandma would sleep over that night and then the next morning, while she and my mom cooked and bickered and cooked and bickered in their robes in the kitchen, Charlotte and I would watch the parade in our pajamas and point out all of the balloons we saw and laugh at the handlers struggling to keep them afloat in the wind gusts. *Do you think it's too late to say thank you to my mom? Would she be so weirded out if I expressed some GRATITUDE (such an annoying word) as I reflect upon the special lost moments with my grandmother and know that she did what she could to help us get a few more years seeing the Thanksgiving balloons?* Here I am feeling *nostalgic* and getting a little emotional about Thanksgiving (my goodness the Halloween candy has barely even been consumed, and yet here I am, under my fuzzy blankets at the early hour of 10:23 p.m., fast-forwarding to the end of November). I think I'm evolving. Maybe when my mom comes upstairs to kiss me goodnight (and to yell at me that I am not asleep yet) I will say thank you. Maybe ;)

Dear Diary

BFF day

Ali called me and said tomorrow is "dress like your BFF day." (I think whoever started this is actually calling it Twin Day for Spirit Week, but everyone knows what that means.) I am so psyched. We have matching BFF necklaces that we got when we were, like, in 3rd grade and we planned our whole outfit. Wacky socks, our black boots, a plaid flannel shirt, a neon tank top underneath, the necklace (obvs), and our hair worn down and blown straight. We are gonna look AWESOME! But then the craziest thing happened. Right after I hung up the phone with her and she facetimed me (on my stupid old phone that BARELY works), I realized it would SO suck for Sarah and Hallie and, like, Maya and Bree and they would feel so bad. It would be awkward to be at the lunch table dressed as twins and have them be like "Oh. We didn't know it was BFF day" and then they would feel so left out. I mean, I felt so awful when I was "left out" on Halloween. And even though Ali and I are best friends, we are all kind of one big group. Ahhhhhhh this is so stupid! I am so excited to dress up but now I feel so bad. And it's, like, so late at night so I can't even call or text them (well, Sarah isn't even allowed to have her phone at night in her room) to let them know so we can all do it together. If they showed up as twins and I didn't know I would be SO embarrassed. I need to call Ali…

Ok. I did it. I checked with Ali (I kinda feel like she is in charge and I don't know why I feel like I have to get her approval). She was like "Oh come on, it's just for fun, we can just do it alone, but I totally get it." So now we are going to do it alone, but maybe dial it down just a little bit so maybe it isn't quite as obvious that we are twinning—wear the wacky socks and our boots and our BFF necklaces, just not the same shirt, so it totally won't be obvious or in their faces, but at least we are doing something. Anyway, we have had these necklaces since we were 8 so it's just funny. But the weird thing with these "theme" days is that someone just randomly posts it online and not everyone even finds out about it. So when we show up to school tomorrow I am sure not a lot of people will even be dressed up. *OMG what if we are the only freaks dressed as twins and people think WE are crazy?* (so annoying 'cause my mom keeps telling me **Dress up and have fun with it and don't worry about what everyone else thinks.**) I need to go to sleep. I am so wired and awake… My mom is freaking out at me from the other room. She is taking out all her stress on me—just because she is tired from "her long day." Every night she is on the phone now and she rushes through all of our conversations and just wants me to go to bed.

We keep giving her all these privileges and she continues to prove to us that she is not mature enough to handle even her most basic responsibilities. (Whining to my grandma on the phone from her room.) She gets to vent to her mom, but when I vent to her, she just says "suck it up"? I'm trying not to listen through the walls, but how can I help it? It's not spying; it's not as if she is whispering. I wonder if they had phones in the olden days when my mom was growing up and if she ever overheard my grandmother venting to my great grandma…*tales of intergenerational gossip*…(and now I hear the soap opera theme music)…such a crazy thought.

She doesn't even know I didn't even finish my social studies homework. And Quarter One just ended and Mr. Lowe will say something on my report card about how distracted I am in class. It's so late. OMG. How could I be expected to focus on homework when I have to deal with this whole outfit and "including everyone" drama? Mr. Lowe has no idea how important this is, and he was never even a girl so he DEFINITELY has no clue. He is one of those teachers that was born a boring grown-up and was never actually a kid. Literally everyone in the world who is normal would agree that successfully navigating Twin Day without offending anyone whilst *simultaneously* remaining cool far surpasses the global trade policy or whatever. I have to shower and blow out my hair tonight, too. This conversation with my mom should be fun :-)

Dear Diary

I am a leader…but I have no followers

I am pretty proud of myself that I like to do my own thing sometimes. I am an individual and that's cool. I don't actually LIKE to be alone, it's just that sometimes no one is around so if I have to be somewhere I have no choice. Being a part of a group of friends gives me a sense of security, and believe me, as you know, I don't even like my friends half the time. I'm sorry—I admit it! Even though every day it seems that my group changes just a little bit, and even though I sometimes freak out at home when I feel hurt by them or left out of things, I guess my group always comes back to me and I go back to them. But, even though I know it doesn't seem like it (Halloween—GULP), I like that sometimes I am really ok with making my own decisions, even despite the fact that I have an (albeit moderately unsatisfying) group of friends. *But if I really am ok with my choices, why do I doubt myself and doubt those same decisions because without a crowd backing me up, it feels like my decision must be wrong?* I guess I don't want to be like them and give up any independence I have (though each day it seems I give up more and more of my independence and individuality), but it would be nice to have a small crowd who agrees with me and likes to be around <u>me</u> all the time—a crowd who validates my decisions. I usually am fine being the leader of myself, and sometimes even feel comfortable in the role I play with my group of friends. I feel comfortable with how I look and dress and stuff most of the time. But even though I have a lot of friends, no one "follows" me and I don't get why.

I like Mandy and Ruby and a lot of other girls…when they hang out with me alone or hang out with me and Maya and Ali and Hallie. But when girls like Katie and Ruby sometimes hang out with Kaia and Josie and all the other girls from JFK, they are SO annoying to be around so I just walk away. I can't really figure out what it is about Kaia and Josie and why they always have so many girls following them. These girls are, literally, always attached at the hip or shoulders. Shoulder to shoulder down the halls. Tweedle Dee, Tweedle Dum, and all their minions. All the girls from JFK Elementary are so obnoxious and such show-offs. They do talk about boys a lot, so maybe that's why people follow them? *Then I think to myself (and convince myself because I feel like such a loser)—maybe the other girls who follow them around and copy their behaviors are actually just scared of them?* My mom sometimes says **maybe they are actually nice, but that we all think they aren't because they travel in this big clique so we all are uncomfortable around them (so we assume they are bitches because we are just intimidated by them).** I can't believe my mom just called Kaia a bitch. That was a pleasant surprise during her morning advice column! But how would I ever get to know them, anyway, and be able to decide for myself? It's like there is a wall around these girls and I can't get over it. *Maybe they are actually even more insecure than I am and that is why they can never be seen alone?* Boy, wouldn't that be ironic.

I want to be popular. I mean, who doesn't? But I am not even sure what that word means. *Does popular mean having a crowd following you? That boys like you? To be popular do you have to look and dress a certain way so you all look the same? Is popularity using intimidation? Maybe popularity is about instilling fear? Or is popularity the opposite—that you don't care what other people think of you? That you are so confident people are just drawn to you? Is being liked and being admired the same thing? Maybe we "like" the regular people but admire the popular people?* Whatever it is, it does sound glorious.

I feel like I am a hypocrite for claiming I like to be an individual, yet I am most comfortable in a group. *Do you think it is even possible to be a leader, an individual, popular, and part of a group all while NOT being mean to anyone? I could ask Mr. Lowe during our lesson on world leaders, but I'm certain he will go off on a tangent and I will be asleep before the conversation even gets started. That was my intellectual inquiry for the day.* I think I am getting carried away here. (Today surely is a day of a lot of unanswered questions!) I'm sure there are many popular people who are nice. Right? Well maybe not when you're 12, that's for sure. I guess I will figure out all these answers someday—though I don't think I am the first to ask these questions. *I wonder if a person can be popular if they stand by their own beliefs and aren't afraid to think independently?* Again, not while they are my age. But maybe they can when they are in high school, or are an adult. That's when things will change. God, I can't wait!

What is she waiting for? An invitation?? Doesn't she know she has to learn to make her own decisions? She is wasting her time analyzing everything. Meanwhile she is failing school and she is too distracted. I think my first quarter report card must have just been emailed. For the record, I am not failing. Perhaps I could be just a bit…more…focused? Why is my mom in such a bad mood anyway? She should just quit her job so she can just take care of us (and, I guess, take care of my grandma now). She just always seems stressed because she has no free time.

Notice my dad never responds. He probably knows I am always listening. He is probably putting Charlotte to bed (sometimes I wonder if he does that because he doesn't know how to talk to me or just wants to give my mom some alone time?) and is ignoring my mom's rant. Why is she so supportive when she is with me, but behind closed doors she rips me apart? Maybe her supportive words are just bullshit to get me to go to sleep. The many sides of Julie. She wears many hats…critic, therapist, night-time snuggler, caretaker, evil witch, mediocre chef… She is so *multifaceted*. Can't she tell I have a great deal to contemplate?

I have a quiz tomorrow and my tutor came today. It would make for a great piece of juicy storytelling and fantasy if my tutor were a sexy, nerdy 23-year-old college graduate just making some extra cash before he travels the world and then settles down into his lucrative career as a philosopher and film critic, yet instead, I have Mrs. Blanche, a 66-year-old retired math teacher. Enough said. I am still having soccer practice, even though it is November! And I am tired!

You are so lucky you are not a real person and you don't have to think about all of these confusing thoughts and questions all the time. It's exhausting to always have to analyze things—especially every night at bedtime! My head is spinning.

Dear Popularity God

Popularity and Power…the popularity pyramid

It's all about popular. I've been thinking a lot about what we talked about the other day. LOL, what I talked about. I keep analyzing what this whole popularity thing really means and why everyone is always focused on it. I have a lot of questions (and I don't even think my mom knows the answers!). I mean, popularity isn't the biggest thing in the world, but sometimes it really feels like it is. Right? *Popularity means having power.* And, I guess, maybe all this power gets confusing to the popular girls so they become mean…or are they mean to start with so it gives them the power? The school counselors always tell us that if the popular girls get popular by leaving people out all the time (they like to use the word "excluding"), then, eventually, they will be all alone because they will have befriended and then kicked out every girl along the way to the top of the pyramid. But I never saw a popular girl who wasn't at the top of the middle school pyramid, and she is certainly never alone. Ever. And I don't think it is because she is being "inclusive" (that word is so annoying, I swear). *If you aren't "at the top," can you even still be popular?* But here's another thought—*are they popular because people _want_ to be their friend?* Because that is what we used to think popularity was when we were young…everyone wanting to be their friend. But I think they are popular because *maybe people are afraid NOT to be their friend.* They are scared to stand against them. Or, in another way, scared NOT to be friends with them because then it appears you are against them just by default! So I can't stop thinking that this means we are stuck without much choice at all. STUCK. Trapped in this *labyrinth* with morals and individuality at one end and queens and ladies-in-waiting at the other. *On Wednesdays We Wear Pink. If we want the girls to like us and to think we are cool and if we want the boys to like us and to think we are pretty and even just to notice us, then do we have to follow the popular girls whether we agree with them or not?*

What are you planning to do? Ignore all of your ideals and values just so people notice you? Is that what you've worked so hard for in life? It kills me that I know she has a point. And it did kind of blow my mind that she said I have strong ideals and values… I feel like I just sat up a little taller. I'm lying in bed and puffing out my chest like a proud bird or a lion (just to give you a visual, Diary). I guess I'm not brave enough to test out the idea of compromising it all just to get noticed—but is anyone brave enough…or foolish enough? I think we all know that answer. Girls are afraid to go against the crowd, or the flock. God, it does seem cool to be popular (sigh).

Wait—maybe there is hope for people like me. Maybe there are different types of popularity. (Is this my "aha" moment?) Maybe the popular girls who have all the power and get all of the attention are the *leaders*—the ones that are at the top with the crowd always around them. They are the ones people crowd around because they are afraid not to be their friends. They are the ones that hook up with the boys and the ones that everyone in town knows—even all of the moms. The ones with a reputation. *That Nicki girl is so promiscuous! Have you heard about her? Her older brother is the one who has all the parties–remember their mom, Debbie? She has had so much Botox and plastic surgery she is unrecognizable… I feel sorry for that poor girl. No wonder.* (Out of the mouth of my very own mother talking to her friend at the diner last week when we saw Nicki at a different table. I was mortified.) But there are also the girls that are popular because we really do want to be their friends. I think I know some really nice girls (or I know *of* them)—and I don't think they are sluts or bitches at all. (Sorry, that was a bit harsh. Let me rephrase.) They aren't solely focused on hooking up or pushing people down and making people feel bad. And they have a lot of friends. And people can even consider them popular, but it is such a different kind. The really nice girls who have tons of friends are popular because they are *confident* and secure. As I sit here and procrastinate even more, and instead of doing my science homework and lab report while I am trying to solve the dilemma for every 12-year-old girl, I think, simply, "popularity" has such a positive and negative meaning at the same time. I have a feeling I'm not going to be able to figure this out tonight. My mom is stomping upstairs heading towards my room as we speak. Gotta go!

Dearest Diary my only friend

I hate my parents

I mean, doesn't everyone? They are so annoying. Even as I am writing this, my mom keeps knocking on my door and huffing and puffing about how I have to organize my stuff and clean up my room and do my homework and get to bed and shower…blah blah blah. I mean, doesn't she know I just tune her out after a while? I literally don't even hear the words she is saying. It is noise. She is so noisy sometimes. And it's my room. I can keep my stuff anywhere (and everywhere :)) I want to. *Mags, your room looks great. I'm so glad we paid for carpeting when we can't even see it!*—she always says a version of that sarcastically when she is forced to enter the jungle of my room. It's my problem when I can't find things—not hers (though I know she will disagree 'cause I certainly do freak out like my dad when I can't find things, and then she totally does have to help me find it and calm me down…she is good like that). So she does help <u>sometimes</u> but she is still a total pain in the butt. My dad? To be fair, I don't actually think you two were ever properly introduced. He is Harry. He doesn't come into my room much. I think he is scared of it, quite frankly, and even a little scared of me. I'm unpredictable, and that is a lot for a boy's brain to handle so he manages to stay far away, and I guess that works best for both of us. But we both do love going to our favorite deli together on the weekends—they make the best breakfast sandwiches—and I always feel like when we are eating or driving or out running errands, we always have fun and it seems super normal. But entering my room after the sun sets, that is not within his comfort zone. He prefers to hang with Charlotte because "she needs his help with her homework." I'm fine with it. It works for the whole family dynamic. I'm, well, complicated…or maybe the word COMPLEX is better, and

Charlotte is just boring. Sometimes, when Harry has had just enough of our bickering and stress, he just screams every fourth day, decides to take a stand and be the involved, opinionated Dad, and then he is done and retreats to the couch. And then I cry. That really throws him. He doesn't understand me and he certainly doesn't understand girls. He tries to bond with us, he will ask us about our friends and our weekend plans, he keeps us up to date with his latest work projects and golf game stats (if that is what they're called), but mostly, it seems, he is still trying to understand my own mother.

I wonder if a mom can be a good mom if she isn't always trying to set rules and enforce them and teach me and lecture me all the time? Can a mom just be a normal person??! Can't she just be cool? Does cool mean she has to let me do whatever I want whenever I want? And God forbid I have friends in the car or she is with us after soccer practice or driving us to the mall—she is always trying to be cool and chill and chatty with everyone—it is SO embarrassing. The other day when she dropped me off at Starbucks she actually PARKED and WALKED ME IN and bought us all lemonades and then SAT DOWN for a few minutes to CATCH UP!! Let that sink in for a second. She was one small step away from ordering a round of shots like Regina George's mom. You may wonder why most moms aren't even side characters in teen movies. The scenes where they turn around in the front seat of the car to ask the girls in the back a question…so cringy. I do think maybe a mom could be cool*er* if she spends time with her kids but doesn't hover and if she sets rules and boundaries but allows her kids to make the ultimate decisions, and if she lets me live in my messy room and just shuts my door. I'm grown-up enough that eventually I will get sick of living like a pig, right? Can't I be left to decide when to clean my own room? (Apparently not—I can't find anything and my mom *does* tell me I have to clean it!)

UGH!!! It just feels like my parents don't even try to understand me. Even when I really want them to know what I'm thinking and feeling because I haven't been able to figure it out for myself yet. Like, I know I'm in a bad mood and want privacy, but they should be able to see beneath my door slamming and yelling and just know that I'm going through some hard stuff that I can't quite discuss or verbalize or even figure out right now. Why do they have to argue back to me? That is just mean! And then they punish me for my bad attitude or for missing the bus because I overslept! That isn't my fault and punishing me only makes me angry! **I think it is very fair that we hold her accountable for her things and for keeping her room clean, as well as getting enough sleep so she can wake up for school. She has to know we have expectations. We are teaching her responsibility and accountability!**—she will say to my grandma on the phone. (I can only hope my grandma is responding with a snarky comment about how my mother was a lazy slob when *she* was a teenager and how quickly she forgot.) I wonder if my mom was accountable when she was my age. I wish I could pick up the other landline phone and listen in, or beg my grandma to call my mom out! If only Grandma weren't losing her memory—this is when I need her on my side the very most! I loved the days when I was a little younger and Grandma would give my mom crap about her dinner not being flavorful enough or her living room pillows not being puffy enough. Come to think of it, I think I felt badly for my mom during those times. Maybe she doesn't remember how it felt to be criticized by her mom and that's why she does it to me? Maybe, just maybe, when she complains to my grandma about me on the phone, she is actually longing for the comfort of a good verbal shape-up, rather than what she has now, which is much softer and gentler…yet, I guess, "neutral"… Like, I don't think my grandma knows how to respond at all any more ☹ I think I miss her and she isn't even…gone.

I am trying to write down everything I hear my mom say to my dad downstairs as fast as I can . . .

I think I'm having a harder time with this than I thought. I know (my dad said). It's just...hard. I'm used to calling her and getting her opinions and having her tell me all the nonsense about her canasta and Friday night dinner and the "ladies" and her aggravations. And now she just... listens on the other end of the phone. It's just me talking and she is, like, lost in space. Where is she? And, as awful as it sounds, where is she going?

AND THEN SHE STARTED TO CRY.

It's going to be hard for a long time, Jules (my dad said).

And tonight (she went on)... Yes, I know, he said.

Tonight (my mom kept saying)...was always such a special night for us, and for the girls, and my mom and I always argued about it for days leading up to it... The weather, the train time, the girls' Wednesday schedules, the prep for dinner Thursday, my brother for being a pain in the ass, yet now I miss those fights because I think it was all just so wrapped up in the tradition of Thanksgiving and the balloons and the girls' memories with their grandma. And I kind of liked that she got to be the good guy and I didn't mind being the humbug and telling her not to give them too much candy and to be home at a reasonable hour. And now we are just...home. The girls are in their rooms and here we sit. I'm sorry, Harry, I'm kind of a mess.

It's ok, honey. It's ok.

And then I cried. I grabbed Bear like a little girl, I curled up in my dumb twin bed in the corner of my room, turned off the lights (except the rainbow fairy lights on my ceiling), and I just sat there. Sad. What does all of this mean?

Thanksgiving day:

It's weird writing in this diary in the middle of the day…in daylight. I feel so exposed. But I feel like I have weird emotions on my brain and my chest feels kind of heavy. My uncle Robby is picking up my grandparents from their condo and bringing them later for an early dinner, but it's just not the same. My mom being sad and unhinged just really feels unsettling to me, like I feel like the ground is shaking. I'm sitting on top of my covers (of course my mom made me make my bed early because of Thanksgiving, as if anyone is going to come upstairs to my room?!) and I'm dressed in "holiday stuff" (so awkward) and I feel weird. Charlotte and I watched the parade on TV, but it was boring. My grandparents used to wait to go down to Florida until after Thanksgiving because it was such a fun tradition for us to watch them blow up the balloons, but this year they aren't going down at all 'cause of my grandma's health. I came upstairs this afternoon because I felt like I was wandering around my own house. I saw my mom go into her room and pull out a box from under her bed. I was gonna go in there and see if I could play around in her closet to distract myself, but when I saw her do that, I kind of tucked behind the doorway and slipped into my room. She seems really off today, too. Like she is in some kind of cloudy haze. I wonder what was in that box?

Anyway, I think I'll hide in here for a while, until someone yells at me or notices that I'm gone. Maybe my cousins will be here soon—I guess I'm that desperate for a distraction. I don't feel like putting on music and dancing around my room, I don't feel like crying, I just…I guess I just don't want to start Thanksgiving.

Dear Diary

The pressure of a plan

The weeks are going so fast. Well sometimes. Other times they drag and I want to die! But sorry I haven't been writing lately. I guess Thanksgiving was good. My grandma really seemed different, so it is really bumming out my mom and grandpa. She had cancer a few years ago, but she had been better for a while. But now she just acts weird and keeps forgetting random things so it makes me uncomfortable to speak to her. I wanted to talk to her about the parade and the balloons and floats but I kind of felt like she was only pretend-remembering, but I still tried to keep the conversation going. My mom made place tags for the table and she sat me next to my grandma. I guess she always had a soft spot for me (she always had great taste in grandchildren) and maybe my mom thought it would make my grandma happy to be seated next to me? I kept the chatter light with my grandma, and at one point, she even grabbed my hand and held it and rubbed it gently. Even though it was days ago, and I'm so tired from boring school today, I keep remembering the feeling of how soft and fragile her skin felt. I played with her bracelets like I used to when I was little. For as long as I can remember, she has always worn three silver bangle bracelets and they each have different colored stones in them. They really aren't that special or valuable, I'm sure, but they always remind me of my grandmother and it kept my hands busy during the appetizers and her arm felt so wrinkly in mine. It was a good distraction to avoid deep and awkward forced family thanksgiving conversation, all of the "How's school going," and "What are you studying," and "Can you believe what the President said"… So I found myself talking to my grandma about her bracelets and where she got them (I realized I had never actually asked, and, of course, I'm not even sure if she knew the answer anymore, but it kept her busy to tell me a story, so we both benefited). She ended up lighting up a little, like a spark plug went off in her mind, and she started to smile and tell me about the time that she was shopping with my grandpa many years ago and that *we were in London because your grandfather was traveling for business so I tagged along. And we were at Harrods (or something) and I had seen my very glamorous fancy British friend Eliza wearing these same bracelets, so when we got to Harrods your grandpa surprised me with them and bought them at the jewelry counter.* I was trying hard to pay attention but my mind started to wander to London and then what I was going to eat for dinner because I really hate turkey. I was, like, nodding to my grandma (still holding her hand) and telling her that was such a cool story and told her I couldn't wait to go to London someday and asked her if maybe she would take me. (Of course, I knew that she couldn't, which made me sad, but it felt good at the moment to make her feel happy.) At one point I caught my mother's eye across the table and she gave me this very soft smile and a little wink, and then she actually mouthed, "She got them at Bloomingdale's," and I got it. Like, "Just let Grandma keep storytelling, and thank you." I'm not sure why my mom or grandpa didn't correct her (they seem to be doing that a lot lately), but it was probably because it was a holiday dinner and they were on their best behavior, and, truthfully, my grandpa was just busy talking to my uncle about the Cowboys game so…maybe he needed the break, too. Talking to my annoying cousins is far worse, so I joined my grandma on our fantasy trip to the jewelry shop in London. It was delightful, as, of course, London was back in the olden days.

My grandma's name is Rose. I'm actually named after my grandma's dad, Martin, 'cause he died right before I was born and I guess my mom was really close with him (some stuff about her being his first granddaughter or whatever). My Grandma Rose and I used to be pretty close. She and my Grandpa Burt used to stay over a lot on the weekends when I was younger before they started spending more and more time in Florida. I liked when they were here visiting, especially when they babysat 'cause it meant my grandma would take me shopping and we would dress up and have fancy dinners at nice restaurants. She loved it when my sister and I would put on our "party shoes" and try to act really grown-up at the nice restaurants, but, really, we just ordered noodles. I know she was tough on my mom, and even sometimes tough on Charlotte and me, but mostly it was cool because she would wink at me when my mom was being annoying. Like *"I got you, Maggie. I know your mother can be a pain in the ass."* Which was so cool.

When my parents were home, she and my mom would always be off in her room somewhere, or whispering in the corner speaking their own language, so, I don't know, I guess I just let them have their time together and stayed with my dad and grandpa. But after a while we only saw them a few times a year. I guess I feel kind of bad 'cause now she is sick and my parents keep talking about the fact that my grandparents can't go back to Florida anymore because my grandpa needs more help taking care of my grandma because of her memory loss, or something. Anyway, I'm glad they're back.

Anyway, the other day I was so upset because I wanted to go see the high school play but no one invited me to go. It was Shrek. I may as well be Fiona. So, like, I'm basically a troll. Maybe I'm too hard on myself. (Well, she does kind of get her "prince" anyway, so maybe troll-life isn't so bad after all.) My mom kept bugging me about calling or texting someone to come with me, but I felt so awkward. They probably all already went! They aren't going to want to go again! Mom kept saying *Maggie, why do you always close the doors before you even try to open them? You will never know until you ask them!* or something weird like that. It's just that, like I said, I am not comfortable making plans. Sorry! I do love when people call me and invite me, though. And I totally saw a few people posting pics when they were at the show. Then again, they weren't really my good friends, but still, they went together. Weird how I feel left out and I don't even like them! I'm so weird.

It sucks to always have to stare at everyone else having fun wherever they are ('cause what else is there to do when you are home but look at people's Snapchat stories and check Instagram) when you are never there with them. Everyone else always seems so busy and so social and so happy. Is that just the way they want others to perceive them, so they are careful about what they post? Or, could I be equally busy and happy if I just came up with the ideas myself (and then posted pics and videos)? *It makes me wonder—do people make plans to actually have fun or just so they can post pictures so people _think_ they are having fun?* As much as I know how orchestrated it all is, it still feels so shitty not to be a part of the orchestration.

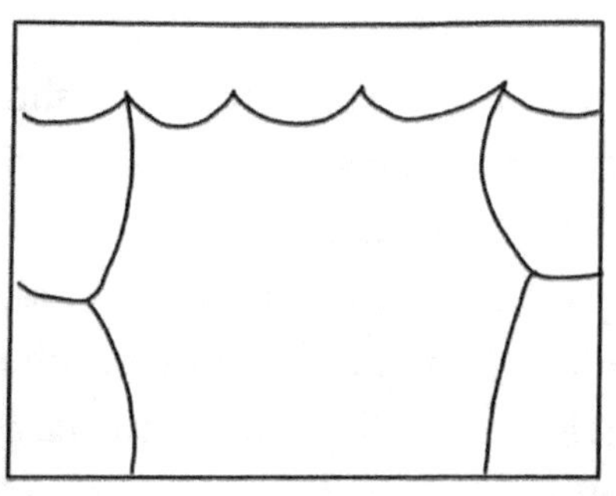

My mom eventually realized that I just needed her to make the plans for me (I just couldn't really ask her). **Obviously she needs my help, she just hasn't**

figured out how to put herself out there yet she said to my dad when he asked why she does "everything" for me. It turns out, Ali and Sarah wanted to go, too, and they were sitting home just like me. We are all such dorks. But we went and had a great time! We put it on our Snapchat story.

Dear Diary

I hate my friends

I don't know. I'm just not happy with them. I know the other day I was fine with them but now I'm not. Maybe I need to change friend groups. Why do they like all these "new" girls from the other schools? Those other girls are awful. They aren't even nice, and they travel like a herd and are always talking about boys and hooking up and TikToks that only *they* have seen together. And their private jokes and all the stuff they did together when they hung out, like "that was SO funny" and "omigod remember that time…" Sometimes I want all new friends. Throw all the game pieces back and collect a fresh new set. Send back my dinner and get a whole new plate. "Excuse me, waiter? I've changed my mind altogether. I now only eat vegetables and fish harvested off the coast of Japan. I'll need to see the menu and start this order from scratch." I want to have private jokes, too, but not with girls like Kaia and Josie. I don't even know what my other options are, though. Who else could I even be friends with? I literally don't even know where I would go. Everyone already has their group. And every time I even try to hang out with or sit with or talk to other people, first, I feel guilty, like I am betraying my real friends, and second, my friends always say, like, "Maggie, you ditched us at lunch" and I'm like "It's ok, I just want a change but you guys are still my friends." (Yeah right. Like I could ever say that. No one would ever say that. Maybe a grown-up, but not a girl.) *Could you imagine if free will actually existed in a middle school cafeteria? Girls just sitting where they want whenever they want?* HA! Utter chaos I tell you. So what I really say to them is "What? I couldn't find you guys. I got here late because Mrs. Rydelle was talking my head off after class it was so awful." Like the only way around acting on my own free will is to make up a stupid lie to get out of it. Of course, my mom's theory is so delusional and unrealistic. *You should be able to sit with whomever you want whenever you want to—establish yourself as a free agent and no one will wonder anymore. It's when you lock yourself into a group that you get stuck there.* STUCK. There's that word again. I swear sometimes I feel like she lives in a fantasy world. So here I remain—stuck with a group of friends I am bored with—with nowhere to go.

But the truly big news, and this is so beyond super top-secret military operation magical mystery alert 007 agent action…code word…(code word to be determined)… My mom couldn't pick me up after school today so I had to take the bus home. I don't know if I actually really hate the bus, or just want my mom to pick me up, because in reality (even though I could never tell my parents this) the bus isn't really THAT bad. My ride isn't as long as you would think and there are actually some random nice people on it, even though everyone is just sitting alone scrolling. Anyway, when I got home, even Charlotte wasn't home and my mom and dad were still at work. And (I've been bursting to tell you, Diary, all afternoon!) I finally remembered I had the chance to go look under my parents' bed and see what that mystery box was that I saw my mom looking at over Thanksgiving. I was shitting my pants, but I felt this pull to go do some digging. I was so scared I was going to get in trouble. The thing is, I really don't think my parents have any secrets from us and I'm sure if I had asked, my mom would have told me and showed it to me, but instead I decided (perhaps foolishly) to make this a covert operation, and, Diary, now that I have, I truly can never give it away. My mom must have picked the box of stuff up when visiting my grandparents' condo. It was stuff from her own childhood…mostly old pictures and souvenirs and keepsakes of random junk. But also, her diary. <u>My mom had her own diary.</u> I was literally shaking when I saw it. I mean, how could I rationalize opening and reading her diary when I would DIE if she read mine?! I struggled with that for a hot second and then flipped through quickly. I accidentally stumbled across a part where my mom said something about my grandma, and that definitely *piqued* my interest, and in another entry she was writing about her friends (I even recognized some of the names), but I swore I wouldn't read it—I would never want to break her trust like that. I quickly threw it all back in the box and replaced it as it was, tucked and folded under their bed. But now it is haunting me. Knowing the possible key to my mom's past lies nicely just down the hall, handwritten in her beautiful *script penmanship from the olden days* in her leather-bound baby pink "My Very Own Diary" Barbie diary.

Mondays suck. I have a test Thursday and a quiz Friday. So much to look forward to. Ugh! I have to go to sleep. I have to go in early tomorrow… not even normal to have to wake up at 6 a.m. Ridiculous. **Maybe if she spent a little less time worrying about where she sits in the cafeteria and a little more time studying, she would get more sleep** was the last thing I heard through my walls before I dozed off.

December 8th

Dear Diary
Dear Diary
Dear journal

Sorry. There is no more room.

The cafeteria is its own little world. Thank goodness I have friends and options of places to sit. Who cares that I don't even like them?! I feel so badly for those poor kids who walk out with their trays and have nowhere to sit. The crazy thing is that sometimes there will be, like, 27 girls squeezed into a table meant for 18, and next to that table there will be a table of three girls. These girls at the crowded table always squeeze and shift over for another "cool" girl, but if anyone else comes over, they will totally say "Sorry, we have no more room." The movie "Mean Girls" in real life. It's legit. I wonder if that movie actually made us behave even meaner! Like "You don't even go here." I swear there are even T-shirts that say that and kids wear them to school. In what other universe would such unfairness even happen? Middle school is its own universe, its own planet; we make our own rules here about acceptable ways to treat other people. I should be thankful I have a seat and a table that I belong at. Being a cafeteria nomad is no life for me. *Am I just exhausting myself trying to change the system? I guess I should just appreciate my friends for who they are and stop trying to be happier somewhere else. They aren't mean to me, so I should just be thankful and stay put. Right?* I really don't think it is worth the risk. I have already suffered the greatest cafeteria embarrassment a student should ever have to face—I don't think I can handle wandering around going table to table asking people if there is room for me all because I am a little bored with my friend group. I am clearly expecting too much from them and I am asking for trouble. ***The grass isn't always greener on the other side, Maggie.*** Is she trying to tell me to stay where I am and settle for less even though I'm not happy? Sometimes I wonder if she is protecting me or teaching me to expect less so I'm not alone in this world. **Yes, Maggie still has her core group from elementary school. It really is so nice how they have all grown up together**, she will exclaim to her friends. It's as if she is more insecure about my insecurities than I am!

December 9th

Dear Diary I'm just practicing my small handwriting

I AM NOT IN A BAD MOOD!

Sometimes I go from being in a great mood to being in the worst mood, and I literally have no idea why. Something will set me off and I become a crazy woman (not that I would ever admit that to anyone but you, Diary)! I mean, one nasty look from one kid in school can set me off for a week. I will spend all my waking hours trying to figure out why she gave me that look. Was she mad at me? Was it my big ears or my outfit? It was my hair, I know it was my hair. Maybe I had a huge zit and didn't even notice? *Why are you so upset, sweetheart? You are so cranky lately* both my parents will say, and then my little sister will annoy and tease me about it—as if she could possibly understand. She has it so easy. Wish I could be 8 again. She loves to get the extra attention from my parents when I am always the one to complain and throw fits about no one giving me privacy or leaving me alone. But I really never know why I feel that way. I just know I'm miserable. So everybody constantly asking me and bugging me about it obviously just makes me feel worse. Maybe if they just left me alone and picked me up after school like a good mom and then let me come home and eat my snack, scroll through my phone endlessly, and watch Netflix and relax after my long day—then I would start to feel better. It's embarrassing to admit, but sometimes I just even want a hug from my mom and I don't want her advice or opinion. If she jumps in and gives me her thoughts, then I just snap at her like this angry psycho person and then she yells at me for snapping and, of course, it turns into this big mess and I feel worse. Sometimes I truly do feel like I am not even in control of myself. Like my emotions just come in these waves and I am a slave to them. I swear it's an out-of-body experience. *Why do my emotions get the best of me? Will I ever be able to admit how I really feel and say I'm sorry for acting like this out-of-control lunatic?* I don't even expect that I will be able to change how I behave. I'm too angry to and no one even cares. But I just want to admit that I know I'm being crazy so everyone just backs off. It's the idea that admitting it somehow seems to acknowledge that I know I am wrong, but that's just the thing, I think I am actually right and it's everyone else out there who just doesn't get it.

Word to the wise…if you have a daughter who gets into a bad mood, just give her a cookie and give her some space (I hope my mom reads that part). If you give a girl a cookie… I used to love that book :-) If you give your daughter a cookie, she will smile and say thank you, and then she will ask you for some milk. And then when she has her milk she will feel grateful. And then you will ask her what's wrong and why she is upset and then she will spill the milk and leave her plate full of crumbs on the table and run upstairs frustrated and scream she hates cookies and her mom will never offer her cookies again. *Have a snack and take some time to think about what you just said.* Well, it's a little different than "Here's a cookie, sweetie, you look like you need some space" but I'll take it. Maybe my mom is so upset and she can't figure out how to express herself honestly either. Come to think of it, she has been doing a lot of the same door-slamming and grumpy groans as me, and, quite frankly, it is pissing me off. This is my time to be a moody teen (almost teen) and she already had her turn. Maybe she is getting her period… like every day! Maybe since she has been stressed out lately because of my grandma, my moods are actually really HER fault! *She is making me so stressed out and I am already stressed out enough.* Well, there you have it. Apparently, as per usual, it's all my fault.

Diary, I hereby declare that taking a quick glance at maybe one or two entries of my mom's Barbie diary will be forgiven because my intentions are noble and she would totally let me read it anyway if I just asked. Tomorrow will be operation true confidential crime (code word) **BARBIE.**

December 10th

Dearest Diary

I love my friends

I'm feeling particularly sane right now. Like actually zen. I don't know if I'll ever admit this to my mom, but after yesterday I think I feel kind of bad that she has to deal with me and also my grandma. Anyway—I'm going to enjoy this fleeting moment of clarity. It feels good to be calm. Since I'm always obsessing over my friend group and deciding where I stand, I decided to see if I could figure out why everyone else just seems satisfied and happy with the status quo and I'm over here doing jumping jacks just to be noticed or to change things up. If you actually try to think about what you want in a friend, I guess it means something different to everybody. I figured out what is important to me in a friend, *in my quest to overanalyze my life and drain the carefree youth from my soul as I enter the darkness of my adolescence* (that was my dramatic handwriting). The qualities I think I look for in a friend are trust, a sense of humor, and acceptance. (But I guess it could depend on the day you ask me this question—maybe sometimes my answer would be different.) But being liked (and maybe even appreciated) for who I am is probably important no matter what. I mean, they have to actually like ME! (I'm not certain that is an actual character trait or quality, but whatever, it's really important.) I want to feel like they want to be with me and that they <u>want</u> to be my friend. And, of course, that feeling needs to be mutual. I guess that is belonging. Maybe belonging is a step above acceptance. It's security in knowing who your friends are. It's fitting in like a piece of a puzzle. Being needed as part of their group. My own group of Dancing Queens, my own sisterhood, a club with its own handshake…

It's also comforting finding a friend or a group of friends who all kind of feel the same way about things or want the same thing. (In middle school that usually just means having the same sense of style and having the same opinion about the other girls and cliques in our grade.) It helps with all of this self-doubt I always have. Someone who will move over for me at a table; someone I can look for in a crowded room. I've had a lot of the same friends since I was pretty little, so I guess we must like each other. I went to elementary school with Ali, Hallie, Sarah, and Bree. I don't know why I complain about them so much. My mom has had the same best friends since she was in 4th grade. That much I know because she always talks about it—even when they fight. Actually, I don't think they fight, it's kind of strange. They have come in and out over the years, but they have always been a constant in our house. Claire, Diane, Jennifer, and Jeanie, and then Wendy was her friend from camp. Claire moved to LA when she got married so we only see her like once a year, but the other four don't live too far away. (I feel like Wendy was a little crunchy weird and moved to Vermont for a while.) *Your friends are a sisterhood—never take them for granted.* Her friend Jenny came over last week to help my mom figure some stuff out about my grandma but I don't know what. I saw them hug when she left so it must have meant a lot to my mom. But then right after that she was like ***Maggie, have you studied?? Did you clear your plate? Why is it that you don't lift a finger around here?*** So maybe she really was mad at Jenny after all? She totally took it out on me and was in a really bad mood.

This is absolutely forbidden against all rules terrible I'm ashamed of myself, but I took a picture of an entry in my mom's…err…in BARBIE today (as promised)… I was simply too terrified to plant myself on the floor in her bedroom for an extended period of time, knowing full well that I would get sucked down the rabbit hole of her uneventful adolescence and then get caught snooping and grounded for life. I suppose, as suspected, it was nothing earth-shattering (like my diary) but it made me smile…

Dear Diary

I feel so gross and ugly, even though Diane swore she loved my new Naf Naf shirt I wore to school today. I'm so awkward and when Danny said "hey" to me by our lockers I barely was able to mutter "hey" back. Diane was cool and was waiting for me in the cafeteria because she knew Danny and I were going to meet by the lockers. I was giggling but so embarrassed that I didn't even talk to him. My one chance! I'm hiding in my room and blasting my old favorite Madonna CD (it always puts me in a good mood) and do not want to go downstairs for dinner and have to face Mom and talk about my day. I hate that! And Robby is so lucky he is always out late for basketball so it's just me and my parents. And it's beef stew for dinner and I HATE beef stew. I can't make my stereo too loud or my mom will yell at me, but thank god for Madonna right now.

Gotta go…

xo

The more I think about it, the more I realize friendships go up and down day by day, but overall true friendships last throughout time. Like Diane. I don't know why I expected my mom's diary to be interesting, it was actually kind of boring. It didn't even sound like it was from the early 1900s, which sort of threw me off, to be honest. It sounded like…I am trying to put my finger on it…omg it sounded like me.

Maybe I just need a fresh start because my friends know me so well and I know them so well? And I'm already kinda bored with myself so maybe that's why I am bored with them. I have this craving to reinvent myself. Not necessarily turn from a peasant to a princess reinvent myself, but more "13 Going on 30" "Who do I want to be when I look back" (not who do I want to be when I grow up—that's a little intense even for me). I am trying to get to know Ava and Alix more, and am beginning to feel more comfortable with other girls in some of my classes, but still, it isn't easy to start from scratch. Maybe I should try to focus less on all of the superficial stress of being popular and wanting more and just accept the stability that I have in my old friends? Is that what my mom meant? I think I can trust my friends, well at least today I feel like I can trust them. And we do act like total freaks together sometimes, so we laugh a lot. I love that part. When we are all together, we have fun. But sometimes when we are in smaller groups, it isn't that much fun, because now some are starting to whisper behind others' backs. Even I do it sometimes and I hate to admit it. Maybe it is from boredom, or, like, we are giving up on the need to make an effort with one another because it is so comfortable? Either way—that's not good. *Why can't I just be satisfied and happy right where I am (hi I'm Moana :-)? Is it wrong to want more and to expect more from people? Or will that search just make me more unhappy? Should I be working more on acceptance and less on change? Are the girls that are (or seem?) happy just more boring in general so they want (settle for) less, or are they more confident so they don't care?*

The popular girls either like to have followers who morph to be like them, or they like to be with the girls who are trendsetters and leaders so they all can be cool and popular together. Their standards are "my friends have to look and be cool." Pink Ladies' Code! Maybe the popular girls are leaders because they are independent and don't care what people think about them. Maybe the top of the food chain actually doesn't give it much thought at all? (Actually—I am fairly certain that the top of the food chain *very carefully* got themselves there.) Since they are so confident, other girls admire them and want to be like them and so they are drawn to them, and they have an instant friend group. Sigh. Instafriends. They are so lucky. I think we covered this in the "popularity chapter" a few weeks back, at the beginning of my deep dive into my *existential* crisis and goals for (middle school) life, yet here we are again, still trying to uncover the overarching theme of girl life and what makes someone have main character energy and all the rest of us the side or supporting characters.

Dear Evan Hansen

The magic of the illusion

I guess I'm back to the tortuous popularity dilemma. So when you really think about friendship and popularity, you realize they are sort of related because popularity couldn't even exist without friendship, or the <u>illusion</u> of friendship. What I mean is, *do you really think the crowd of girls that follow the most popular girls are truly their friends? Do they really ever KNOW each other or protect one another? And, to be honest, would I even really want that in the first place?* Popular people have a lot of friends. That much I know for certain. But maybe those are not the types of friendships that would work for me. Trust, laughter, acceptance… Makes me want to ask the queen bees what qualities they look for in a friend. Probably loyalty, convenience (like they are always available and up for anything), and willingness to be a chameleon and blend in and look and act like everyone else that day or week or year ("Mean Girls" has stood the test of time for a reason). Say hello to the plastics. When I say it that way, it makes the popular girls seem so unoriginal and so boring—but it feels so different at school or on social media. There, they always seem so happy and so, well, COOL! I know for sure, when you are in 6th grade or 7th grade, all that matters is WHO your friends are, not how many you have. I mean, come on, cafeteria tables are filled with gaggles of girls, but could you really even name them all? But you could probably predict the assigned seats of the girls who crowd around the popular table.

I think I changed my mind. My most important characteristic for a true friend is that they are nice. Plain and simple. If they are not nice, forget them. No time, no interest. Maybe that is more important to me than acceptance, trust, and laughter. They have to be a good person. Sometimes Mom is like **Why are you not hanging out with so-and-so** *anymore?* and I try to explain that she bothered me so I left. I stopped hanging out with her. I don't sit with her anymore. She became annoying and insecure and it wasn't fun to be with her anymore. She started to talk badly about other people. It all boils down to she wasn't nice anymore. I guess I'd rather have no friends than be friends with people who aren't nice to me? I really don't mind being alone. Sometimes I have momentary confidence. It fades, don't worry. That's why God invented Netflix.

Anyway, my friends are cool (most of the time). I wonder if my mom ever dumped an old friend and gave herself a fresh start? I wonder if she was popular or where she stood in her circles or if she always had a seat at the cafeteria table? There simply has to be more juicy stuff in there. Maybe just one more glance tomorrow after school. It's truly for research purposes, and I'm sure, in fact, my mom would be relieved to not have me bother her with more of my "drama'" if I could just get her advice straight from her very own teenaged mouth!

**random thought. I forgot to tell you…wait for it…I GOT A NEW iPHONE!!!!!! Finally!! I was like the last person in the whole grade to get a new one! I had my mom's old one for, like, ever. And now I also have this super cute purple case! I facetimed Ali right away to tell her!!!! I'll be so pissed if they give my old phone to Charlotte. I had to wait years for a new phone and certainly didn't have any phone until 5th grade. Charlotte will have to wait like I did. She better start with a used one, too, or that would be so unfair!

Dear non-electronic diary

If it isn't posted, it didn't happen

Everyone has Instagram and Snapchat, obviously. I have like 350 followers. I keep trying to make my Insta feed look artsy or stay like in one color theme, but it never looks cool or natural. I feel sort of grown-up (like a teenager) when I get just the right pose. Snapchat is just a quicker way to talk to my friends—you never have to worry about your feed or what you look like, it's supposed to look and feel more natural and less filtered. *Why must you send all of those pictures of yourself to everyone you know every day when the picture of you looks the same every day—I don't understand it!* (she really doesn't—that much is true). My mom really doesn't get the difference between the Snapchat pictures and the Instagram pictures. It is like having two totally different identities. Anyway, posting and looking at other posts is fun. But I do sometimes feel like some people just post everything they do to sort of show off, like to prove it happened. Everywhere they go and everyone they hang out with. Seems like certain people go everywhere together. Sometimes when I do have plans, all we really do is look at our photos, take more photos, and edit them and share them. We always do photoshoots—if it's a group of us, then everyone has to pose with each person in the group. The thing is, when you think about it, all of our pictures are so posed. They aren't even natural or real. So, I can't help but wonder, is anything we see on social media actually real even at all?? This is sort of sad to admit, but I don't really remember a time lately that I went out with friends and we <u>didn't</u> post a picture of what we did. It's like a diary, but a fake one. And then who do you take the pic with and which one do you ultimately post and who do you tag? *Social media has **capitalized** on all of our 12-year-old insecurities and made it even worse by asking "How do you want to tell* *the fake, edited, photoshopped version of your real, actually boring miserable awkward life?"*

And the crazier thing is—our days and our moods are totally shaped by what we see on Instagram and TikTok; how the girl(s) looked, was I there, where they went without me, where we went together, how gorgeous all of the celebrities are, how talented everyone else is but me. When we all hang out somewhere, no one even puts their phones away for a second. I know I'm guilty of the same, but now, it's as if no one we are with really even wants to be there in the first place because all everyone is doing is reading their Instagram and faceting or snapchatting other friends… They are hiding in their phones, escaping from the discomfort of actually having to have a real conversation or *talk* to each other. AND THAT IS WHEN WE ARE WITH OUR ACTUAL FRIENDS IN THE SAME PLACE DOING SOMETHING TOGETHER THAT WE ACTUALLY MADE A LOT OF EFFORT TO PLAN! Seems kinda hopeless for our future as civilized people. All we want is to be included in plans, and then when we are, we aren't even with the people we are actually with—get it? *Confounding* (insert obligatory new vocabulary term). Maybe this is why the middle school cafeteria is so awkward, because no one knows how to have an actual conversation for 45 minutes without a phone! Ohmygoooood what if it is just ME that no one wants to talk to and that is why everyone I hang out with is always on their phone??

It is funny how we all feel so good when we get another follower or if someone comments on our pics. It's an online popularity contest. I guess it's like Facebook friends, but no one I know has Facebook 'cause it's for old people. **If everyone just put down their stupid phones for once and looked up, they would learn to actually communicate with one another!! We used to have to TALK to each other when we were their age, not hide behind our phones and computers all day** (she says in her daily fit of aggravation over today's "youth" and frustration over everything "me" in general). Good luck changing society as it exists today, Mom. My mom is always on her phone. Maybe she is hiding from the hard conversations with me.

Shamefully, when I got home from school yesterday and my mom was at work, I covert mission impossibled kim possible austin powered power rangered avengered my way into her bedroom once again. Heart racing, riddled with guilt, yet thrilled at my top secret lavagirl mission, I swiftly slithered under the bed and snapped a few more quick pics of random pages of the **Barbie Book**. Accidentally, I noticed one of those vintage black and white photobooth pics slide out—I had no idea from what page, so I got nervous and shoved it back in randomly, but I did catch a glimpse and my superpowers noticed that it was my mom, Diane, and Claire from some arcade or something. They were actually so cute it made me smile. Like it was timeless and, strangely, literally could have been a pic of me, Ali, and Hallie, which then made me a little sad. On the back of the photo, scribbled in the hardest-to-read-ever script, were their three names, the name of the arcade or restaurant (or whatever), and the year—it looked like 1992, so basically it was ancient.

As I lie here in bed, I keep feeling tempted to scroll through my phone and read the diary entries, yet at the same time I keep thinking how ironic it is that I was feeling so frustrated with all of the social media nonsense and just want to get OFF my phone for a bit, so I'm torn. (I also do have to finish my homework and watch a video on photosynthesis or something.)

Dear diary continued

Twilight and other fairy tales

Ahhh the holidays. Sort of feeling bummed out for myself right now 'cause I celebrate Hanukkah and it is, like, super boring. Christmas is so much more fun. And it stinks even more because I guess I've gotten a lot of stuff lately (like my iPhone and stuff), which I know is awesome and I should be totally grateful and appreciative, but now for Hanukkah my parents are like *You already got so much that you wanted and we spent a lot of money,* blah blah blah. What about the fact that I had to "earn" that stuff? Remember? They made such a big deal about the fact that I had to earn it with good behavior and treating my sister nicely and getting enough sleep. So I worked SO hard and I did, but now I don't get real Hanukkah gifts? Unfair.

Sorry, I totally got off topic. But sometimes the holidays make me sort of dream about having a boyfriend. Is that so weird? I'm a freak, I know. But some people have boyfriends and I know they will exchange gifts, and it makes me jealous and a little lonely. Is it wrong to dream about the fairy tale? And dancing with a boy? And kissing? I have no idea what that must be like (gross!) and every time there's a kiss on tv my mom is like *this show is inappropriate you are too young to watch this* and I have to change the channel. (Ha! If she only knew what I see on "The Bachelor" and "Love Island"! Who needs Mr. Dumbleface's health class or any sex ed!) But even though seeing all those girls on tv make out and have sex is just gross, when I saw "Twilight," I got this really strange feeling inside when I saw Edward and Bella kissing (and doing a lot more!). OMG!! Edward is SO hot! The honeymoon scene was so awkward but so awesome to watch I couldn't turn it off. I was so embarrassed and there wasn't even anyone else in the room with me—my god if there were I would have DIED! Is it so creepy that I think this vampire is hot? I don't expect to fall in love with a vampire, I'm not a total idiot, but he does seem totally perfect. I just get lost in my own thoughts wondering… *When will this happen to me? Why can't it happen to me?* It will never happen for me :-(

Is that what kissing is like? It's probably nothing like the movies and is so totally gross. Maybe.

Journal/Diary… *Can you imagine how strange it will be when I DO get a boyfriend and all I can compare him to is Edward, Jacob, Thor, all things Ryan Gosling, Mr. Romantic from "The Fault In Our Stars," Chandler and Joey, "The Bachelor," shirtless guys on "Survivor," every hot guy in "Riverdale" and "Gossip Girl," anything bad boy Chad Michael Murray, Timothy Chalamet, the cute romantic guy who sings in "Pitch Perfect" (I forgot his name), and, maybe, Prince Charming (better yet, Prince Eric is much hotter)?* The future of my potential relationships looks bleak—and doomed right from the start. Boyfriends on tv and in the movies who fly through the air, save lives in a heartbeat, sweep girls off their feet (literally), have magical powers, lead a kingdom, sing, and fall in love at first sight? Those are some pretty tough acts to follow. How will any guy be able to match up to that? I want to be accident-prone like Bella and locked in a tower like Cinderella and have him save me in his arms (like seven times in two hours :-)). Oh my—lying in bed all day on a weekend is dangerous stuff. ***Honey, it's ok to dream but that is not reality*** (here she goes encouraging me to settle for less, again). ***All girls and women dream of the fairy tale and want the perfect love story. We allllll want to be the Disney princess and have our happily ever after, but…*** God she is miserable sometimes. Is that supposed to give me hope? I know once my dad did try to play along and picked her up once in his arms and then he fell and dropped her. (I'm sure that was a fun few hours for my dad after that one.) My dad is no Edward or Prince Charming, but I know he totally loves my mom. But that is boring. Maybe actual true love is boring. I wouldn't call my parents' love story worthy of royalty or film, just your basic, classic Emily Gilmore we-met-in-the-law-school-library story. Do you think my dad was *ever* romantic? Harry, a romantic? Eww did my mom even want that? I wonder if they had any real Broadway-ballad-like moments, or if their dating relationship was always budgeting and scheduling and doing the dishes and couch-sitting. I should ask them one day. Definitely not today—my parents have been fighting so much more lately. I'm sure it is all my fault. Maybe love is overrated.

I think I really want a boyfriend! But, actually, right now most boys are such dorks and losers, I really don't want a boyfriend. I wonder what ever happened with my mom and Danny-by-the-lockers. (I just realized I never even read the covert **Barbie Book** entries on my phone! What if they accidentally upload to the family iCloud or something? Is it worse if my mom reads my diary or if she reads my phone and finds out I'm reading HER diary? Omg this is too much for me to figure out. I need to read them and delete them ASAP.) (Suddenly I'm lying here petrified at the thought that she already has secretly read my phone and now knows I have secretly been reading her diary and she is just waiting for the right moment to use it against me.)

I still have a little crush on you-know-who. FFJ Andrew…sshhhhhhh **She really needs to get a little perspective and stop holding her head in the clouds.** (My dad didn't even comment after she said that. Probably either because he was glued to the tv and didn't hear her, or, maybe, just maybe, he really feels I should dream because it is who I am and he doesn't think anyone will ever be good enough for his little princess). Maybe my mom used to be a dreamer like me and he misses that girl and he sees all of that great stuff in his thoughtful introspective over-analytical high-bar-setting complicated complex awkwardly stunning groundbreaking middle-school-cafeteria-hierarchy-overturning 12-year-old daughter.

I think I'll actually laugh myself to sleep with those thoughts of my father :-). Oh Harry.

'Night.

Dear Diary

Can you keep a secret? Don't tell ANYONE!

I know I should totally be asleep. It's gonna hurt in the morning, but I can't go to sleep. I'm NOT tired. I want to be able to fall asleep so badly and I can't. Sunday scaries. So frustrating! So I thought I may as well tell you a school story. A story about secrets. The ones people can't keep. They say they can…ooh, everyone says "I promise"—but they never can. People love the attention (I guess I am speaking mostly about girls, cause I really don't hang out much with boys, nor do I feel like they have secrets). Actually, that is dumb, I'm sure they do, and I KNOW they can keep a secret because they are dumber and less attention-seeking than girls and they probably forget what the secret was or who it was about right after the girl whispers it into their ears. Right? (I know you agree.)

Oh. Anyway. Sorry I got off topic. Every time someone has juicy gossip or even some really personal private information, they always feel the need to tell someone. Actually, everything private just <u>becomes</u> gossip because everyone shares it! The hallway can sometimes be a whisper fest. I know my mom thinks it's crazy that people (girls) are always surprised and upset when people gossip about them. She is always genuinely shocked at girls being so naïve—*why do people tell their deep dark secrets to people if they don't want them to tell anyone??* Oh, I know, because they tell their best friend because they <u>trust</u> their best friend. Right? Well sadly, they shouldn't. Trust no one. The more secret it is, the juicier it shall be. This didn't happen to me, don't worry. I can totally trust my BFF. (But I don't have anything awesome and private to share with her, even though I KNOW she would keep it a secret.) (I think Ali is my BFF.)

It's actually a boring story of a girl in 8ᵗʰ grade who hu'ed with two guys at one party and she told them both not to tell anyone and one of them was her boyfriend. The other one told his one friend not to tell anyone ('cause, rumor is, he actually really likes this girl), and the friend promised he wouldn't tell—but this girl from his social studies class was also at the party and she saw them talking and when she told her friend what she saw, the friend said she heard that guy liked that other girl and then another friend said she saw them walk outside to the backyard by the trampoline earlier in the night (even though it was freezing out!)… and then we all found out by homeroom this morning.

Can you imagine what it was like in the cafeteria? You have no idea! I felt bad for the girl—but she's gross. I also felt bad for the guys. *Am I crazy to say that if someone told me something I would keep it a secret? I think I am trustworthy?? But doesn't everyone say they are trustworthy even when obviously they are not?* Because girls feel so cool when someone says "Hey, did you hear about…" and then the other girl can say "Yes! And by the way did you ALSO know…" So not only does she feel cool that she already knew the information and was not left out of the gossip, but now she has MORE information, which makes her feel even cooler and more popular. Information is like gold to these freaky chicks! Information----> power----> popularity. Hmmmmm. Kinda gets me thinkin'…

Ok. To be continued. My dad just came in and threatened me with my life. (JK, but he did yell at me.) Downstairs, he and my mom had a huge blow-up fight. From my bed all I could hear was **how could you possibly understand what my days are like? You are at work all day and come home and expect me to be up for conversation when all I have is conversation all day long—at the supermarket, on work calls, on the carpool lines, with my mother's impossibly long list of unresponsive doctors, with the schools…the list goes on. I'm exhausted! No one in this family seems to care and all I do is care about everyone else in this** house. Please! I just need a break and I know you are trying to help by asking, but you're not. I guess she has the Sunday scaries, too. Clearly my mom is simply too busy to care about anything or anyone but herself right now. She is so moody lately—so short-tempered. (She is acting like she is 12 years old!) She actually sounds really upset, but still, Julie, get it together, you are a grown-up! And I feel bad for my dad who just got mowed over, but he didn't have to take it out on me. Why can't they yell at Charlotte tonight! Of course Charlotte is already asleep, so it is always about me and how they can blame me for their grown-up problems. I just hope I can sleep after all that tumult and yelling. My god, it is almost 11, I can't believe how loud they are being. Goodnight!

December 14th

Dear Mondays are the Worst Diary

We NEVER exaggerate

I know I told you I would continue the "gossip" story today after last night, but I already got bored of it, and it's old news and today I kind of got to thinking. Aside from not being able to EVER keep a secret, girls my age always make bigger deals out of things than we need to. Like, he is the HOTTEST or she is the MOST popular girl in the whole school. Middle schoolers know EVERYTHING—that's why we like to use superlatives. Well, maybe they aren't even *superlatives* (I mean, who really cares what they are called? It's just some stupid grammar term we learned in Ms. Hughes' 5th grade class). I am the ONLY one who feels this way, of course, because everyone else is SO stupid. Like sometimes I have the BEST day EVER and then the next day it can be the WORST day ever. And each feeling we have feels like it's going to last FOREVER! It's like, when we are in that mood and in that moment, there is no end to it. *You girls are being crazy and not thinking clearly. You are being a tad bit dramatic, don't ya think? I mean, let's not get carried away here.* Well, we don't see things any other way. I don't know why, it is just the way we are, I guess. Grown-ups like to just label us ALL the time as being dramatic. *So, what's the latest drama these days?* my mom will ask. (Come to think of it, she hasn't asked me that lately and it used to bother me when she did, like she was bored and wanted to enter the soap opera of my daily life, but she stopped asking.) But anyway, really to me, drama is causing a total scene and fight for no real reason. We "tween" girls are not faking it for attention, we ACTUALLY feel the way we say we do. At that moment in time, it really IS the BEST or WORST moment of our lives (for example). Wait… *Does that mean we are terrible judges of our own feelings? That we blow everything out of proportion and have a warped sense of reality because we are too young to have clarity?* If so, then we have NO idea and that is the CRAZIEST thing I have ever thought of. *Isn't it weird to think that generations of almost-teenage girls have been misjudging and misunderstanding the reality of their own lives?* YES! It is the MOST ridiculous thing I have ever heard because our thoughts about our lives ARE our lives. You can't tell us (well not you, but grown-ups) that we are ALL wrong! Don't you think when grown-ups turn 100 or something really old that they will also look back at their 40-year-old selves and think the decisions they made then were also crazy? It's these feelings and actions that help us survive this WORST, BEST, UGLIEST, PRETTIEST, LEAST CONFIDENT, HAPPIEST, BESTEST, MOST TRAUMATIZING AND MOST EMBARRASSING, MOODIEST time of our lives. We are very black and white. Our world is extreme. Extreme with no in-between. But we are so in-between. I guess that's what my English teacher has been saying irony is.

And you know what else is funny? The more people believe something negative about themselves, the more it becomes true, right? So, the more "dramatic" we are told we are being, the more dramatic we become. Maybe that only works with negative things like all the mean things adults call kids and teenagers (shall I mention a few? loud, disrespectful, rude, disorganized, immature…shall I go on?). We can call it "anti-manifesting." Almost as if to say, why bother trying, ladies, the world hates you anyway. It's a hard knock life for us. We keep hearing these harsh character traits that, apparently, we all embody, so we just behave that way because we feel it is what we are supposed to do as "tween girls." I totally have to come up with a different word for girls my age. I hate the word tweens. It's like we don't have our own identity because we are <u>between</u> some things. What are we between? I am simply very 100% 12. I'm not just waiting here in between 11 and 13. I'm just upstairs waiting for dinner! I'm starving. I haven't eaten ALL day. And now my mom is on her phone. AGAIN! She is ALWAYS on her phone. **R O S E. Yes. Tomorrow? 3:30 p.m.? Ok.**

Great. Another afternoon I have to take the stupid bus home because my mom will be too busy to pick me up. If I don't starve to death before tomorrow, that is. This whole thing is so unfair.

Dear Diary

Friends are good for something but not everything

Sometimes I feel closer to Ali and sometimes I feel closer to Maya. I guess we can't be BFFs with someone every day all the time. But it really makes me sad and hurts my feelings when Ali isn't 100% nice to me. Maybe I am being extra sensitive? But then other times she totally includes me and I feel so good again. But other times Maya makes me laugh and she is easier to be around. *Mags, my love, friendships change as you grow up and it's ok.* But then in the same breath she will say *True friendships should be easy and shouldn't be too much work.* Really? Was it always easy, like the sepia-toned ancient photo of my mom and her friends that day at the sock-hop? (I kind of made myself chuckle with that one, even I know the '90s weren't as ancient as poodle skirts and Elvis.) Sometimes things with my friends are easy and relaxed but other times my mom is bugging me to call them and make plans because I'm complaining that I'm bored or alone, blah blah blah. Then I start to ask myself—*Do the real, true friendships require the most effort or should they need the least amount of work? I mean, why am I trying so hard, anyway? Is work the same thing as effort?*

Each friend is good for different things she will also say. Not exactly sure what that means. But I guess some you want to tell your deep dark secrets to, others you like to have sleepovers with, and some you act like a lunatic with. Maybe that's what she means? Anyway. I don't really care why; I just know I had a really lousy day in school and feel pretty sorry for myself tonight. I'll consider this moment of sad lying-in-bed self-indulgence a little nod to my own self-care. It's hard to say if something specific happened, because I can't really recall anything like that, but I know when I walked over to the table with my lunch there was no more room for me. Gulp. Heart in stomach. Blushing. Awkward moment. (Maybe I'm not actually hungry and I should leave.) I wanted to run and hide. Without hesitation, instantly transformed into a middle school superhero kicked into survival mode, I quickly scanned the cafeteria for available seating, and I saw Neha see me and smile (she was in my gym class last year and we take the bus home together when my mom is too busy to pick me up). Anyway, it wasn't like they said, "There's no more room" (thank god, 'cause I would have died), but there just wasn't any physical room. They ended up (probably *reluctantly*) moving over, though, and I squeezed in. I just felt like I was annoying them and they didn't want to be with me. *What would I do if I was annoying my friends?? Would they ever tell me? Maybe if they told me that would be even worse? Maybe I should live in denial and believe they like me?* Maybe I'm not cool enough. Not sure what they want from me. Lately they have been having some other girls at our table at lunch. Today Alix and Meghan were at the table. They are nice, but I feel like they were in my seat. I'm exhausting myself—maybe I'm exhausting them, too?

The worst part was that tonight when I was in a bad mood my mom didn't even care. She was ignoring me and she should have helped me. She was way too busy texting her friends and doing the dishes to even notice that my whole life was falling apart. And I shouldn't have to be the bigger person and tell her I need her. That's HER job. She IS, in the truest sense of the word, the bigger person, so it is HER job to just know. But instead, I got this, muttered under her breath while she slammed the frying pans back into the drawers… **The whole world doesn't revolve around you, Maggie. Nor does this house. Do your homework, get off your phone, stop overanalyzing your life, and go to sleep.**

Mom of the year, for sure. Wow. She is supposed to be able to read my mind and help me. Meredith Blake Evil Stepmother. She isn't listening to me and she is so disrespectful of my needs. She always ignores me, and, clearly, she is too preoccupied to care. Sometimes I feel like I'm not even there. Everyone else is important to her except for me. It's not fair. Why won't she help me?

I picked up my phone and scrolled back a few (hundred) photos till I found the **Barbie** entries... The time had come. This particular one caught my eye...

Dear Diary,

Sometimes it feels like I'm all alone in this world—or, at least, in this house! I had a fight with Diane today and my mom was just going on and on about her tennis game and how I need to improve my grades and not be so preoccupied with boys and my "silly friendships." Silly Friendships?!! These friendships happen to be my LIFE and Diane is one of my best friends ever and I am sure at one point Miss Perfect Mama Rose (ha!) had her own fair share of fights with Carol or Edith or Peggy over dumb things like who was getting pinned or going rollerskating, or whatever they used to do in the 1800s. I'm very upset and my very own mother is too busy worrying about my grades and her perfect son Robert, and she doesn't even realize that being 13 is, most definitely, just impossible, and everyone in the world has their ears pierced and is allowed to wear mascara except for me!

ARRGGHHHH I just want to scream!

Now my head is totally spinning. I feel like I'm whirling in a time-travel tornado or something, and everything feels alice-in-wonderland topsy turvy. So am I supposed to feel sorry for my mom or worse for me? Am I supposed to be upset with my grandma for ignoring my mom's essential adolescent needs or furious at my mom for being angry with my perfect sweet grandma just because my mother was being a self-absorbed teenager? This is all too much. Maybe I wasn't meant to read her diary for this very reason (um, in fact I KNOW I wasn't supposed to read the diary at all). But now I can't unsee it. I'm so mixed up. And now it's my turn to be a moody (almost) teen, and I'm wasting precious energy worried about my mom now?

I can't wait till Christmas vacation. I need a break.

Dear Diary

The game of telephone

I'm sitting here in the kitchen eating my snack all alone, so I thought I would catch you up. Remember the other day when I wrote in you and talked about secrets and gossip? Well, here is an update… I call it "the game of telephone." Remember the game we all liked to play when we were little (actually we still do play it sometimes, but now we add other rules and play "broken telephone" just to mix it up and have more fun)? Anyway, sorry, I get off topic because I get distracted (lol, my parents tell me that all the time).

So today this girl Christine told Georgia that she may go to private school, but she told her not to tell anyone (well, at least that's what I heard). Anyway, by the time we all got to lunch (there was a seat for me today, btw, phew!) all the girls at my table were talking about it. But I heard her parents were getting divorced. I admit I felt sort of good to be included in the conversation rather than say what I should have—"Guys, we shouldn't be talking about this it's not nice." But the thing is, I don't know who Christine's friends really are or anything, but Georgia (I heard) only told this other girl Emma because Emma heard them whispering in the halls and thought it was about her. So, when Emma pulled Georgia aside and asked her what she was saying about her, Georgia swore to Emma that it wasn't about her but that she was sworn to secrecy. Obviously, Emma didn't believe her and felt totally insecure about the fact that the girls were talking about her in the hallway and that they were now mad at her and hated her outfit (that's the way girls think…exhausting, right?). Finally, Georgia caved and told her it was about Christine dand made her swear to secrecy. Emma felt better and relieved and promised she would never tell. But at 3rd period math someone asked Emma if she knew why Christine went to the guidance counselor earlier and Emma, being totally responsible, said she couldn't tell. Then a boy in class chimed in and said he heard it was because her parents were getting divorced. And Emma, who thought she was protecting Christine from that rumor about her parents (which, as it turns out, was not true), said "No, it's because she may go to private school." I heard at lunch that her parents were pulling her out of our school because they didn't like the "crowd" she was hanging with here. I have no idea why.

Operator?

I'm not sure what my point is here but, *are we always obligated to stop gossip or is it ok to save face by playing along? I feel a bit badly that it was a little entertaining to watch this all play out, and, quite frankly, mesmerized by the fact that I can sit here over my afternoon snack of hummus and pretzels (I'm so healthy) with a side of Doritos and a chocolate chip muffin that I brought home from the cafeteria today, and recall every last detail of this game of telephone (and the fact that I saw Emma wearing a cute pink hoodie today that now I feel the need to find online somewhere), yet somehow forget to bring my dumb math textbook home multiple times a week.*

Dear Diary Again

Allies vs. Switzerland

I finished my homework. We don't have a lot because it is almost vacation!! Woo-hoo! And actually, I took the bus home again today and saw that girl Neha, and we actually smiled at each other and said "hey," so that made the bus trip more bearable. Clearly she hates the bus, too.

Girls like to help each other out. Sometimes. But we also like to help *ourselves* out...if you know what I mean.

On the lunch line I heard a girl I didn't know say to her friend Alisha "Oh, I overheard Serena talking about you. She was being so mean. She told so-and-so (a guy—I didn't catch his name) that she didn't like you because last time you guys hung out you told her you liked Anthony, and she used to like Anthony when she was in 5th grade."

Alisha was horrified (I noticed as I was waiting for my sandwich and my iced tea). "What?!" she said to this girl. "Why?! I can't believe she was talking about me behind my back! She was just at my house last week and she said she totally didn't care that I liked him!" And then I saw Alisha get tears in her eyes and I felt bad. But I kept listening (how could I not?). Anyway, I was still in line behind them so where was I supposed to go? Then the other girl (I think her name is Sofia) said "Yeah, we are in art together and she sits at my table. We were all talking about the graduation party you had in 5th grade." Then the sad girl, Alisha, said to Sofia "But what did you say when you heard Serena say she didn't like me?" Sofia replied "Nothing. She really was just talking to (the guy, I forgot his name). I just wanted you to know she was talking about you. She is so mean."

I like to call this girl "Switzerland." In this case, Sofia is Switzerland. She never stands up for anyone. She never confronts anyone. But she is super smart because no one is ever against her because she always sides with whomever she is with at the time. (It certainly doesn't hurt that she is cute and smart and sporty.) Watch out for her. I'm sure there is one in every grade. She is the smartest girl in the room. Cunningly manipulative, yet so discreet no one even realizes it's happening. Never *devious*, never *polarizing*. The perfectly honed skill of blending into the background just enough, yet upbeat enough that everyone loves being around her. She doesn't get much screentime. No spotlight 11 o'clock solos, but gets to wear the pink lady jacket and always has a seat at the table.

Switzerland never said anything in art class to that girl at the table like "Oh I like (Alisha). She is so funny, and she sometimes just acts silly, whatever, I'm sure she didn't mean to do that." Bottom line is she never stuck up for her friend. She didn't have her back at all. But she THINKS she had her back by telling her that the mean girl was talking about her during 2nd period art yesterday. Like THAT is supposed to make her feel better? I would be like "Wow. Thanks for the help. 'Friend.'"

I try to stick up for people when I can. But it isn't easy 'cause it can be pretty embarrassing. I mean *who wants to take the risk and put themselves out there and step in the middle of a conflict that they are probably so relieved they are not involved in in the first place?* Switzerland is the easy way out. It is a carefully honed skill of being comfortable avoiding conflict and stepping over doing what is right to maintain a very specific role in the middle school food chain. It doesn't take a genius to know, though, that the easy way out isn't always the right thing to do. But, shoot! It surely does help you become popular. Switzerland is always on everyone's side.

I didn't tell my mom about this gossip. It did feel kinda strange when she came upstairs and I was just like "good" when she asked about my day. *Oh, I'm so glad you had a good day.* It was so obvious she was testing me. Usually, even when I try not to tell her, 'cause I like to feel like I am strong enough to withhold information from my opinionated, advice-giving mother, I cave like a small child who ate a cookie in her bed. But this time—not this time. She doesn't deserve the details today. I'm gonna keep all this juicy stuff to myself. I don't need her advice or criticism today. Plus, she was mad at my grandma once when she was 13, so I'm still mad at her for that. I have this one all figured out. I am ok with my passive involvement in gossip-girl-land, and I may have almost met a new friend on the bus but cannot tell her lest she think it's ok to never pick me up again. When my dad got home and asked my mom how I was (he asked about Charlotte and me, of course), I was just coming downstairs to eat and heard her say **Fine. I guess they are fine. Go ask them yourself, I'm not the only parent around here.**

I think my mom is upset with her mom—she is upset that my grandma is sick. She is angry at my grandma for doing this to her. I guess it is super complicated. Maybe she feels ignored by my grandma now the same way I sometimes feel my mom ignores my needs, except my grandma has an excuse. Maybe my mom does, too?

Dear Diary

A better day

This isn't even an official entry. I just got home from school, but something has been on my mind all day. Sometimes my parents surprise me. Today my mom did. I feel bad sometimes (like last night, even though she was very clearly having a bad day herself, when she tried to help me with my math homework even after I eliminated her opportunity for maternal caution and counsel when I got home from school). I give her a really hard time a lot and I know I can be so obnoxious sometimes (and you know what's weird? I can't stop myself even though I know I'm being mean). She says I treat her like a punching bag sometimes (but that's not the point right now). Last night, as you know, I blew her off. And she was pissed—but she still offered to help me?

Anyway, I'm rambling… This morning I was rushing and running late (what else is new) and I didn't have time to put on a cute outfit because I never put my laundry away (which is so unfair and I HATE doing it and no one else I know has to do it). And I hated what I was wearing and felt awful and super down. But I didn't have time to change, and my mom was like *We have to GO!* 'cause I missed the bus because it comes so friggen early! So, in the car on the way to school, she totally saved my day. I've been into her clothes lately (because I'm almost her height!) and she must have known (maybe by my cranky miserable attitude in the car) that my day was off to the worst start ever and that I might never recover. She took off her vintage cozy college sweatshirt at the stoplight and told me to take off my awful, 2-sizes-too-small shirt and she gave me *her* sweatshirt to wear. Right there in the car. She didn't ask me any questions, she didn't tell me I was being awful, she didn't give me her adult perspective, she just stripped down to her sports bra and saved my day. Is it wrong that afterwards I made her duck down low (in hindsight, it probably was not the best gesture of gratitude that I screamed DUCK) as we pulled up the hill into school because I was casually embarrassed—though incredibly shocked and grateful by her gesture—because she was driving in a sports bra? I can't remember if I even said thank you. But I feel like she knew what it meant to me. What if she only did it because she hated my outfit? *Wow. Am I really that cynical and negative? Maybe deep down it was her way of admitting she's been wrong for all these years? And that she felt badly that she didn't put away my laundry and thereby forced me to wear such an awful shirt? Or maybe she really was just feeling my 12-year-old pain because for a split second she remembered what it felt like. Would she forgive my tantrum if she knew how vulnerable I felt? If she found out the truth, she would know I was just a weak, exhausted pre-teen, in-betweener, upside down mess of a 12-year-old tween-age girl.*

(later tonight!)

For the first time in a while, the voice I heard from my bed was my mom speaking in a totally calm voice to my dad on the couch. Weirdly enough, it made me realize I haven't heard that softness in her tone in a while and it kind of made me sad to think about it. She was actually telling my dad (really quietly so I had to turn off my music and TikTok to hear it) that she was really touched by what happened in the car this morning. She didn't even bring up the fact that I so horridly screamed at her to DUCK after she literally gave me the shirt off her back. She got it. Without my snarky grumpy teen-ish self being able to find it in my heart and cold soul to say two simple words, "Thanks, Mom," she still got it. She knew that what she had done changed the course of my day. Maybe she feels it's a turning point in our relationship. Maybe this kinder, gentler mom is my new mom? I find myself now bursting with the inner conflict of guilt and thinking I should say thank you, or maybe that ship has sailed and it is too late to go back. I think I will be happy when she comes in later to kiss me goodnight. I kind of want a hug. Maybe my mom needs a hug…

Strangely, when she came upstairs later, I found myself feeling awkward even in my own bed with my own mom. It was as if I had forgotten how to let her in and just be a kid. I think I got so used to always having a set of armor on. I was glad when she got into bed next to me and kissed me on the forehead. I leaned in. Then she glanced over at my floor and saw, crumpled up in an inside-out ball next to my cascading backpack, charging cords, and a scented candle (gross) my secret santa gave me today—the very vintage college sweatshirt she had saved my life with. *Is that my sweatshirt?* she asked. I could barely speak and just froze and looked up at her behind me on my pillow. I felt all of the good stuff that had happened between us today suddenly flash before me and hated myself for being so careless. *It looked cute on you. You can borrow it.* I felt like I was being tested. Thank you, I said quietly. *Sweet dreams, Mags.*

Maybe she knows I read her diary? Should I give her some motherly advice? Maybe she needs that from me right now, like kind of a—*I know you are going through a difficult time with Grandma right now so maybe you should do something nice for yourself to take your mind off of the stress for a little bit?* I didn't say it, though. But that was a crazy Freaky-Friday feeling! It kind of gave me the chills and sent a little dramatic Lindsay Lohan shiver down my spine. I'm going to sleep.

December 21st

Dear Diary

Three's a crowd

I know I'm on vacation and I am supposed to feel so relaxed and happy. But the other day Ali asked me to go into town with her and I was so excited. I know I should have called her 'cause I was so bored, but I was so psyched when she called to invite me. Sometimes I think she doesn't want to be my friend anymore, and then she calls and I feel so stupid 'cause of course we are friends. *You see? You sit around and wait for someone to call you and they are all just sitting home waiting for the same thing! Silly girl!* God I hate it when she is right.

Anyway, she told me Maya was coming too, so I thought, cool. But it wasn't so cool. I never thought I could feel so left out with my two close friends. But I did. It was such a bummer. I was actually embarrassed and felt like they didn't include me. It was like there were so many private jokes (probably from the cafeteria table and all the things they now do together that they leave me out of). I was, like, awkwardly laughing along with it even though I had no clue. Sometimes I would be like, "What are you guys talking about" and then they would be like, "Oh don't worry about it, it's no big deal" and they would continue. Private jokes hurt so much—even when they aren't even really about anything important. Sometimes girls think that as long as the joke is about something trivial, then it isn't worth explaining—but I'm here to tell you: if a few girls are laughing about a story about black leggings, it seems to be the most top secret story in the universe if you aren't in on the leggings. Yeah, for them it's not a big deal, but for me, it was everything and it ruined my whole day. I mean, I got cute earrings and we went out for ice cream, but I didn't really have fun. Feeling sort of sorry for myself right now. And pretty angry. Now I'm angry at myself that I didn't make my own plans and that way I would have been in charge of who came and of what we did and of the conversations. When break is over, that's it. I'm taking chances. I'm starting with my new bus friend Neha. She was always nice to me in gym class and she seems nice and chill on the bus and we sort of live near each other so it's convenient. It's official. Tomorrow is the new me (well, January, to play it safe). Calling, planning, posting, tagging, and I'm gonna start working out and eating healthy. I'll make a smoothie every morning before school and lay out my clothes the night before.

And here I was feeling like my mom totally got me, until I heard her talking to my grandma on the phone. **When she doesn't have plans, she mopes and complains, and when she finally does have plans, she is never happy. I'm at a total loss. Mom? Maggie, Mom, I'm talking about Maggie!** Why did she have to keep saying my name? I don't think my grandma remembers me?? Whenever my mom gets off the phone with her she is even more grumpy. It feels like she is just so used to having her in every aspect of her life, that now when she tries to include her in the daily stuff, it frustrates her so much that my grandma can't keep up. I wish I could tell my grandma how sad my mom is, but I also want to tell her how annoyed I am with my mom, 'cause she would get it.

December 23ʳᵈ

Dear Diary

In Summerrrrrrrrr

My Dearest Diary,

I'm trying to write fancy in script. I know you won't judge me (that's why I have you, sometimes you are my only friend)…but am I a total freak that I'm already counting down for camp? 179 days, but whatever. I'm not even saying this because I am upset. I really am in a good mood today. I'm over the whole Ali-in-town-thing. I slept really late and woke up to snow on the ground, which I LOVE. My mom made chocolate chip pancakes for breakfast—well, brunch—and I've been sitting in my pjs all day watching "Friends" and she doesn't even care (she probably feels guilty because my parents haven't taken us away on a vacation in years). I have no homework and no pressure to do anything or go anywhere because of the snow—so that is a relief. It's like an excuse not to have to make plans because no one would drive anyway. I know the Insta posts suck from everyone on their airplanes off to exotic, beautiful, warm beaches and I'm stuck in Boringtown. And even though so many girls are away together on vacation making TikToks from the airport, here I am on my couch—look at me—I'm rising above it and I am happy in my pjs at 3 p.m. I'm trying not to feel sorry for myself that Christmas is in two days and we don't celebrate Christmas and every year we beg my parents for a tree. And, of course, every year they say no. Just like that. *We don't celebrate Christmas, we are Jewish.* Just like that. How unfair is that?! So basically everyone in the world goes to the beach for vacation or celebrates Christmas and gets, like, a gazillion presents, and all we get is Chinese food and the movies on Christmas day? You know what, I'm not gonna let myself spiral into the grinch. I feel like I'm growing… today. Today is a good day. Who needs Christmas? And presents, and twinkle lights, and caroling, and ornaments and presents, and matching Christmas pajamas and a boyfriend…oh wait, I mean presents.

Before I break into my summer sonnet, I feel I must share my big new-me accomplishment today (I figured I should give January-me a head start). Feeling my best self today (I mean, it's 3 p.m. and I practically just woke up but still). I DM'ed Neha and said hey. She is home, too, this break and I made some lame comment like "at least we aren't on the bus" and she lol'ed. I'm branching out and living on the edge.

Sometimes I miss my summers at camp more when I'm happy. My mind just starts to wander, and I'm back in my summer home just feeling free. And in my memories of camp, I feel the weight lifted—the weight that is always pressing on me every day at home. Sometimes this weight just comes from my parents, or the constant burden of knowing I have responsibilities at home to behave and clean up and be respectful; the burden of getting up every day and putting on a brave face to greet the day and whatever nonsense it will bring; the burden of homework and a social life. The stress of acting and looking a certain way every day in school, the stress of TikTok trends and keeping up with Snapchat and Instagram. At home (as I'm sure you've figured out by now) I'm constantly analyzing my social status and my friendships. But I just love my camp friends. And at camp there just aren't any burdens. It's just a feeling—I guess like what childhood must feel like before you have to grow up and go to middle school. No social media. It's like the perfect paradise of an ice cream melting on a hot summer day. My camp friends just know me and understand me more than my home friends sometimes. I guess I feel like I can just be more myself there. Like sometimes at school I am not sure who I am, but at camp I always know. *Maybe it is all of these burdens of getting through each day at home that prevent us from feeling free enough to be ourselves? Is it simply because we aren't relaxed (and not entirely due to a total lack of self-esteem) that makes being 12 so unbearable? Is that why only in summer, when we are truly relaxed, we are free to be whatever and whoever we want? Or is it actually being away at camp that brings all that good out in us?*

The weird thing is, my mom is always like *call your camp friends, I'll drive you, invite them over, meet them for lunch or at the mall* when I get home from camp, but I never do. It's like, if I am not at camp in that special place, then the friendship doesn't feel the same. Is that so weird? The real world just infiltrates my soul and prevents me from being the person I am with my camp friends—so maybe I am afraid to call them because they will know I'm not the same person. I don't want to give away my secret and then they might see right through me and not trust the "summer me" anymore. I simply just can't risk it. I guess I feel I need to preserve that image they have of me being happy and wacky and confident. I wonder if I am my true self at camp or my best self—and if that version of me could ever exist in any aspect of my real life. And what if I do accept the vulnerability of taking that risk and they reject me 'cause they have other plans?? At camp WE NEVER HAVE TO MAKE PLANS!!! Camp is BUILT-IN plans! That is why we are all free and relaxed. And there is no Instagram so you don't even have to WATCH OTHER PEOPLE'S PLANS. If you took all of us out of the camp environment, we all know deep down we would not all be friends. But without the outside pressures of MAKING STUPID PLANS we don't have to worry. But if I call them now—they would have plans and then I would feel alone and things would be different.

It would just be the best if camp could be all year round. Life would be perfect then. Never having to make plans and always having built-in friendships. No judgments or pressure. No phones. If only. *But if camp were all year round, then wouldn't my camp friends morph into my real life/home friends and then change everything? Maybe the short blissful summer is what allows us to be free of all the insecurities that control the rest of our reality?* I wish she could just be at camp. (she wants to get rid of me) I wish *I could just be at camp*, she said on the phone to *her* best friend from camp, Wendy. Seems like we have that in common. My mom still (yes, STILL) talks about the glory days of camp. She has been teaching us her camp cheers since we were babies. Charlotte and I used to tease her all the time in the car when she would sing at the top of her lungs when one of her old songs would come on the radio. Thankfully Charlotte and I have our own songs from our own camp—it's actually one of the only things she and I have in common. Anyway, why is she even missing her childhood days? She is a grown-up and her life is so easy now! She doesn't even have to work that hard or have any stress about what she looks like every day! She gets to do whatever she wants all the time!!! Charlotte is so easy it's actually gross. My dad just is happy to be around her so no complaints there. That leaves me. My grandma and me—her only real burdens. I know I will be so much happier when I grow up. I'll even be so much happier when I go to high school and college and when I get to move out on my own.

But here's a horrifying thought… What if this really is it for me? What if my happy, carefree times at camp is really it and my mom knows it? She has seen the future and it isn't all it's cracked up to be and that's why she tries so hard to make me get the most out of my excruciating adolescence. Maybe this is, like, the only thing my mom actually understands about me. I'll take it for what it is. I started out so happy and now I've fully exhausted myself. "MOM!!!!!" (I yelled) (I'm starving and if I don't eat soon I might die).

Dear Diary

Period…

Weird. Gross. Go away. Ewww. Not sure what is happening. GROSS! I mean, I knew one of these days it was bound to happen but, really? And of course, I'm surrounded by my whole family and I'm so embarrassed. (I guess it is better than getting it in school. What would I even do if I did?) My mom and I have discussed what I would do if I ever did get it in school, like *go to the nurse's office or go to the bathroom and make sure you have pads and extra underwear in your locker*, but then everyone would know why I'm leaving class and I'm not even allowed to leave class to go to the nurse so that would never work. And then what would I do—change into a backup pair of pants and then everyone in class would ask me why I changed my pants and then they would all know I got my period in school and they would all be laughing at me. I'm freaking out a little bit, I'm not gonna lie. I mean, I literally have been waiting for this moment my whole life and now it is here?

I really can't believe this is happening. So much for that TWEEN nonsense. *If you get your period, does THAT mean you aren't "tween" anything anymore but you are legit?* Currently I don't feel tween—or teen—I just feel disgusting and creepy and uncomfortable and like my whole secret world of privacy has been blown open for all to see. Soon my dad will know and my little sister will nag me about it and ask a gazillion questions and my mom will tell my aunt and my grandma and I just want this to go away so I can pretend it never happened.

I called for my mom when I went to the bathroom and then she gave me this little pad thing. I will not use it. I can't believe I have to put on snowpants and this pad thing to ski! I feel like an Oompa Loompa!

My mom was fine about it and didn't make a big deal out of it, which I guess was cool. I don't even know if any of my friends have gotten their periods. I don't even know if I got mine?? There was just this dark brown spot in my underwear. This is so weird. Am I young? Am I old? Ahhhh. Sometimes I feel like I just need to scream. I am so glad I have you, Diary, because I cannot talk to ANYONE about this. Honestly, I feel fine, I don't even know if I got it. I probably didn't. I feel like I'm ready, but maybe not. Come to think of it, I have been in a bad mood lately. Does that have anything to do with it? My mom sometimes says that when she has hers or is getting hers she feels crappy and cranky. And she certainly eats like a pig when she is getting her period. Have I been hungrier these past few days? I guess I thought I was tired, but I really have been cranky? I was even too embarrassed to text Ali, and she got hers like four months ago.

I'm starving. Maybe Ishould eat
something. Should I? AHHHHHHH
HHHHHHHHHHHHHHHHHH!!!!!!!!!!!!!!

Ok. I'll keep you posted.

Later on…

I cried today. I didn't cry a lot, but I
don't know why I even cried. I just cried.
And then my stomach hurt and I got a
headache. I can't fall asleep. My mom had
to give me some medicine. I'm so uncomfortable.
She actually was really nice about it, like we
could relate to each other about this 'cause we
are both women now. Thank god I don't have
school tomorrow. We took a family trip to
some lame mountain in Massachusetts to
have some "quality family time"

since my mom has been, like, so unavailable lately 'cause she has been taking my grandma to so many doctors. And we all know how well "forced family bonding time" goes anyway. The ski conditions sucked today, too. I'm just happy to be curled up in bed (even though the ski condo is so gross and I'm stuck sharing a pull-out couch with my sister) with my headphones on. **Well, at least we know why she has been such a bitch lately.** I guess she doesn't realize I CAN HEAR EVEN WITH HEADPHONES ON. My dad actually agreed, too. As if he even understands how much pain my body is in right now. Boys have it so easy. Charlotte didn't have headphones on and she heard my mom say that about me. She is asleep now so I'm using the light of my phone as I write, but it was actually kind of sweet…when Charlotte heard that, she rolled over and gave me a hug and said "Congrats on your period, Maggie. Is it gross? Are you ok?" and I thought it was super sweet of her, even though she probably doesn't even know what a period is. It was just nice, like, to have a sister on my side.

Dear Diary

She wasn't invited

I feel bad. I got invited to Maya's birthday party, but Sarah didn't. It's in January and it's gonna be so much fun because we are going into the city to go ice skating and then to The Candy Shoppe (it's a trend) and then back to her house for a sleepover. (I probably won't sleep over because I really just like my own bed so my mom might pick me up around 10 p.m.) But she can only invite a certain number of people because we are driving in. But I don't know what to do. I mean should I not go because I feel bad that Sarah will be left out? But I really want to go. Is that so selfish of me?

It's so hard, because if I were on the other side, I would feel so bummed if all my close friends had this awesome time together and I weren't included. But would I expect them not to go in protest? I mean, her mom said she had to limit it to eight girls and I get it. I know Sarah understands that, but I know when everyone gets back to school we are all going to be talking about it at lunch and stuff and then it will make it worse for Sarah. And there is literally no way to avoid posting pictures and making TikToks. Well, I'll just make sure we don't talk about it. Right? Not everyone can be included for everything all the time. And I guess maybe Maya and Sarah haven't been that close lately. Maya is allowed to invite whoever she wants, right? I mean, it is HER birthday. My mom doesn't make me invite certain people to mine if I don't want to, but she does say *Be careful because sometimes hurting their feelings is harder to deal with than just including them.* I guess that is the dilemma. But we always hear this message of "always surround yourself with the people that make you happy," so *why do we then hear "include everyone so their feelings don't get hurt"? Are their feelings more important than ours? Why should we have to invite people if we are not friends with them???*

The thing is, I know Sarah is planning her Bat Mitzvah and now that she is so hurt by Maya, she will totally not invite Maya, and then it never ends. And at my Bat Mitzvah party I am NOT going to want to invite Kaia or Josie, even though my friends are becoming friends with them. Do I have to? They are so dramatic and always steal the attention away from everyone. They, like, always have to be the center of everything. It will be my special day (even though it is months away and it will probably get canceled because I don't know my Torah portion and I never practice and I hate Hebrew school) and I will not want that. I'm not even sure about Katie and Ruby because every time they are around them they turn into these followers. It is so annoying. I don't even know why I started talking about my birthday or my Bat Mitzvah… Thankfully I have a while to figure it out. Right now I just feel bad for Sarah. But I really want to go to the party.

I guess one of the things that makes it so hard to be a "tween/pre-teen/young teenager/in-betweener…girl my age" is that we are stuck. Yeah that's it. We are stuck. I've said it before and I'll say it again (and no, Ferris Bueller, life moves like molasses). Stuck. We want to have the freedom to choose who we want to be friends with, and we should have the freedom. But when we choose, and thereby limit and exclude, we then become left out ourselves. Because most of the time, the other girls our age are not making those decisions yet, so they are just following everyone and going along with everything and they don't think for themselves. Switzerland. So, if you want to make your own choices, you could be called a leader. But if no one backs you up, you are alone. So…we are stuck without choices or we suffer the consequences of payback. So, unless we are the most popular girls (here I go again) who can make their own decisions and exclude people whenever they want, we are all just stuck? Well that sucks! I want to be able to choose my friends, but when I decide not to sit at the same cafeteria table every day, I don't want them to leave me out of the private jokes and plans the next day. What if January-me is ready to make a new friend—will I lose my old ones? I really am stuck. *Are we all trapped between having to do something we don't want to and wanting to do what we can't?*

It's weird. When we got home from skiing my mom went to stay with my grandma. So, she isn't home tonight. I don't know what to say to Sarah or Maya. I'll just text my mom. Hope she doesn't get pissed because it's so late and I'm still up.

…she didn't respond. I'm so annoyed. And now I'm upset. She usually has some wise words. I really needed her advice.

Reluctantly, I ended up scrolling through my phone again and stumbled on another pic of my mom's diary. I only took a few that day, but I guess I never read this one.

Dear Diary,

Diane and I made up, of course, I could never stay mad at her for long. My mom always likes to remind me that friendships aren't always easy but that some friends aren't worth getting all worked up about because the "relationship runs deeper than that" or something like that. Anyway, my mom decided she wanted to "spend some time with me" this weekend and she told me she would take Diane and me to the mall. (I'm actually excited to get some new clothes because it feels like nothing fits right anymore.) Diane's mom never takes her shopping so I'm glad

Mom is letting me bring her along (plus, Mom and I would kill each other after a few hours). I hope I can find a cute pair of jeans. And she better let us listen to our own music in the car and not force us to listen to some hippie stuff it's so weird.

Gotta go xoxo

I guess in a weird way, I forgive my mom for not answering my text tonight.

'night

dear diary

The love triangle

Well, maybe life doesn't move pretty fast, but vacation sure does. We are back to school. School vacation was fine. I guess it was fun. I skied a few times, which was cool. I may or may not have had one total meltdown because of the possibility that I may or may not have gotten my period for the first time, but I would prefer not to even go there. I guess it's ok to be back at school. Getting up this morning pretty much sucked. My dad actually drove me because my mom said she didn't feel like fighting with me on the first day back. I think she needs a vacation (that was intended to be ironic). One day back from break and I'm already tired and up way too late. I haven't even started my homework (can you believe Mr. Addison assigned two chapters on the first day back?! Dial it down, Addison, we are 12!).

Anyway, this is what's really getting to me. I heard at lunch today (I sat at my "regular table," of course, and we all just kind of caught up about break and all of the awesome new clothes everyone (except me) was wearing from their Christmas gifts) that Alex was going to ask Ali out. So weird. I mean I don't like him, but I thought he liked me. And Ali was so casual about saying she is debating saying yes? So now no one has a crush on me? Figures. No one ever does. And I still have a crush on you-know-who but I won't ever tell him or ANYONE! But if he doesn't ever ask me out, whatever, I won't care. But really it would be so cool if he did. I mean it would sort of make me feel good if I got a little attention that way. I learned how to straighten my hair really well over break (I had nothing else to do) and got the new straightener that was sold out forever when Kylie (or was it Kendall?) posted it in September. I guess it was a productive week off.

So lame that I am asking for attention. I'm kind of tired of always blending into the background. But everyone always talks about the people who have boyfriends and stuff, so I can't imagine if I actually had a boyfriend. Would he really like me? Maybe I am better off just biting my tongue and staying friends with Ali and all the girls I grew up with because at least it is safe and they sort of like me—so if I stand a chance of any guy asking me out, I'm better off being surrounded by a group of "friends" rather than be the freaky girl who stands on her own two feet. Maybe it is too risky to leave this friend group. I know I said I was ready to move on, but then I risk being alone. I think it is safe to say that being alone in a middle school cafeteria could be the scariest venture in the universe. I understand why so many of us accept the mediocrity and phoniness of our existence because the alternative is just too dangerous. I wonder if Neha is also bored with her friends and her middle school existence.

The weird thing is, shouldn't I be angry that Ali is even contemplating saying yes to Alex? I mean, *isn't she supposed to say no because friends are always supposed to come before guys?* At least, that's what I thought the mantra was. **Don't ever let a guy come between you and a friend** or **Guys come and go, but friends are forever**… I think that's what my mom has always said now that I have been talking about boys more at home? Ironically, I don't know if I would do the same for Ali. I'm not even sure we really are friends at all lately. Maybe the new me would worry less about struggling to keep a friend who doesn't have my back, and decide to look out for myself instead? Maybe Ali is the smart one here and is carefully calculating her way to the top. I am actually giggling to myself thinking maybe Ali has the same New Year, New Me mantra as I do. She is putting herself first and her social status will join it. Me? Well, I'm still over here liking the wrong boys and wanting more from friendships, wishing things were different but not taking any steps to change them. I'm not saying I'm willing to Regina George myself and take a dark turn. In fact, I'm fairly certain Ali is turning to the dark side, and, although a small cold piece of me might envy it, I know the real me wants no part of it.

This is my new year—the year I will finally turn 13. A real, live teenager. No more in-between. I want it to be a fresh start for me. It's a new beginning. Maybe black is this year's pink. Maybe I can try to find my individuality, my voice, my free will, my cool sense of style, a new makeup routine, my confidence, my happiness, my prince, and my best friends this year. I can almost hear the theme music now. Percussion… tension building…the lights dim…popcorn is eaten. Perhaps I am aiming too high—I should lower my expectations. Perhaps just a small costume change will do it, or even just a new shade of lip gloss. Maybe I should just focus on the little and important things like trying to care less about Instagram and the jeans I really need, and more about getting ready for my Bat Mitzvah. My priorities are so backwards. Notice that "learning more and getting good grades" are not on my agenda at all :-) **She is gonna burn the house down with that stupid hot hair iron dryer!!** HA! That was actually my dad! He is so clueless he doesn't even know what it is called, or how incredibly essential it is to have straight hair, but I'm working on lowering my expectations so let's not get crazy here. If I'm lowering my expectations, then I should be happy that any male, even my father, notices my hair is straight at all. **Oh, honey, it's fine. Aren't you happy Maggie is at least beginning to care about what she looks like before she leaves for school in the mornings?** Omg—I actually thought she was sticking up for me, until she dropped that little super passive-aggressive comment while they argued and my dad watched football. On that note, goodnight. I have to get to sleep. New me shouldn't agonize over Ali or Alex. Tomorrow I will tell Ali she should go for it. Fake it till you make it—I'll convince myself that I don't care, and then, apparently, eventually I won't. I'll figure it out. If Ali were really concerned she would have called me after school to discuss. So if she doesn't care, why should I? I can feel the spotlight now…it's my big solo. **Lights!**

104

Dear Diary

The truth comes out

Today was fine. I did say to Ali she should totally go out with him, but she was like, "I don't even know if I like him," so it was kind of a dead issue before it even started. At least I said something to her, it felt kind of good. But when I came home I needed to discuss and process all of this. I wanted my mom to back me up and validate (*validate*). I feel like the more I need answers, the more frustrated she gets with me. It's like, she was such a better mom when I was in 3rd grade when everything was so easy. She was so caring, and always was up in the mornings to make my lunch and snack and to drive me to school and was always home when I got home from school to make me a snack and stuff. Now? Forget it. Even though I like having more independence when I get home and I can just do whatever I want and eat whatever I want when she isn't home, it is still so annoying walking into an empty house. I mean, what is she so busy doing? I know my grandma needs her more now, but aren't we allowed to need her, too? This is kind of <u>her job</u>, right? Now I'm all Sandra-Dee-ing and trying to start anew and figure out middle school once and for all—and that is no easy task—and my mom is always too annoyed with me to help me. Sometimes I actually legitimately lose my mind and she is just like *Maggie, you really need to calm down and speak to me respectfully if you want me to help you.* WHAT?? She is my MOM. *Isn't she supposed to help me no matter what? How am I supposed to speak calmly when I have nothing to wear, I didn't get to go on vacation, my best friend likes the guy who is supposed to have a crush on me, I have a zit on my forehead that won't go away, and the mean teachers keep piling on stupid homework and projects like they don't even care about us?*

I don't know how to talk to you anymore. You are so unreasonable, Maggie she said as she walked away in a huff and her voice trailed off.

And there it was, plain as the zit on my face. She doesn't understand me and she doesn't care. I didn't have to overhear that one or read that in a text. She just flat out said it directly to my face. That one hit me hard. Am I being unreasonable? Is she? Between a hormonal 12-year-old with all of life's ups and downs happening, seemingly minute to minute, and a mom who is clearly hormonal herself, hot and cold with her moods and her body temperature at any given moment, who is to say who is more unreasonable here? To be fair, I win. I'm the kid, so by default I win. I don't mean I win because I am more unreasonable, because I most certainly am not. I mean I win because I am the child and it is in my job description to be unreasonable and it's not my fault. Actually, it's my *responsibility* to behave this way in order to raise good parents and solidify this family and pave the way for Charlotte. THAT WAS SO MEAN, MOM! YOU DON'T EVEN UNDERSTAND ME OR CARE ABOUT ME! I had to write that down 'cause I feel kind of badly that I actually screamed that to her from upstairs and I think it was maybe one of the first times I said such harsh things to her, but you know what, Diary? I felt it. When I was brushing my teeth tonight, Charlotte was standing next to me washing her face (her beautiful, youthful, zit-free face) and she said "Sorry Mom has been cranky lately, Mags. I guess work and Grandma are really stressing her out but still. And I like your hair straight, you look pretty." She is so cute. I told Charlotte she looked pretty, too, and told her she could borrow my vintage Led Zeppelin T-shirt since it's so cool (I mean, I'm not into their music) and she was psyched 'cause my mom won't buy her stuff like that.

I'll be sure to make the bus tomorrow—I don't even want to see Mom in the morning.

Dear Diaryyyyyyyyyyy

School gets in the way of my social time

I know it sounds sort of ridiculous. But lunch isn't long enough. We have to wait in line and then pick out our food and then I have to figure out where I want to sit on that particular day—even though ultimately I always end up at the same table, in the same seat, with the same friends. But Dear Diary, I ask you, what stupid grown-up decided that 22 minutes was enough time for us to do all that AND have fun?! I will tell you…a grown-up like all the other grown-ups who decide we need to be in school for like 11 hours and still be focused and paying attention and organized. All we really want to do is talk to each other! There is so much drama going on at all times, we need time to talk it out and figure it all out! How can you expect us to do that when we have math, then LA, then science, then general music, blah blah blah and only, like, three minutes to get to each class AND go to our lockers. As it is we are racing upstairs to the other end of the building to go to some classes, I practically have to carry all my books with me because I have <u>no</u> time to go to my locker. How can we keep the friends we have, keep up with all of the gossip, and try to make new friends when there is no time at all? But when the teachers say we have to be quiet in class, it's like, really? How? We have so much to discuss and no time to discuss it. And then they say that the socializing is interfering with our academics and our learning. But that is actually hilarious. I think school is literally interfering with all the time we need to figure out all the friend stuff and boyfriend drama and talk about birthdays and plans and the latest gossip and joke around and stuff. *How come in class I always have so many things I want to ask the girls and so many funny stories to tell, but at lunch, when I finally do sit down, sometimes it is even a little awkward to figure out what to talk about?*

Without our Snapchat filter, or TikToks in the palms of our hands, why does actual, free flowing conversation feel so forced? The other day when I got into trouble for talking in class, my mom was like **Why don't you have these conversations at lunch when you have the time and not during math class?** My answer is always that we don't have enough time to talk about all of these important things at lunch, but maybe the truth is that we are all just so uncomfortable, forced to sit there and make conversation with the girls directly next to us at the table. It is really only when I'm not supposed to be talking at all (in class) that I think of the very essential things I was supposed to discuss earlier at lunch! Oh and I sat next to Neha on the bus home. It didn't even really bother me that my mom couldn't pick me up because we still needed to cool off from our big fight the other night (I think she is getting ready to apologize) and I wanted to hang with Neha anyway 'cause new-year-new-friends.

Tonight downstairs my parents were arguing more about money and the cost of all the medical appointments for my grandma and stuff about insurance and then she dropped the bomb on my dad. **So as if my week weren't bad enough, I received an email from Maggie's math teacher the other day...** I thought she was being cool about it, but she was just saving it up for a rainy day. I hate Mrs. Rydelle for telling on me. I have to go to sleep before my dad comes charging up the stairs.

January 8th

Dear Diary

Arms folded

My parents hate when I fold my arms. But when I fold my arms, it usually goes hand in hand with a nasty pout and scowl on my face. I get it. Bad "body language." Whatever. Obviously if my arms are folded and I have a frown on my face I'm miserable or bored and I don't want to talk about it. Like when my parents make me go somewhere or do something that I don't want to do. It really isn't fair. They usually say stupid things like **we always do things for you so sometimes you need to do things for us.** Some nonsense about reciprocity. Like I owe it to them to behave because they always do things for me? *Isn't doing things for me their job as parents? Why do I always have to appreciate it and feel like they are doing me a favor and going so out of their way for me and making so many sacrifices for my sister and me?* (Anyway, the truth is, I actually do really feel bad tonight. I was a major biatch to my parents and I knew I was doing it, but I just couldn't stop.) They dragged us out for dinner to the worst restaurant on the planet. All I wanted was pizza but no one even cared. I was even more grumpy because I couldn't find anything to eat on the menu and it was freezing in the restaurant and Charlotte was driving me crazy and kept wanting to play on my phone and I wanted to just be on my phone but my parents wouldn't let me. It's a weird feeling to know I am acting selfishly but I can't stop even when my parents get angry at me. And even though we already had plans with another family tonight, and I'm kind of friends with their son, even though he is a year younger than I am. Like I knew it was so rude of me, and poor Brian was just trying to make simple conversation and I had zero interest. After all, he literally has no idea what I'm going through. He has it so easy—he is a boy and he is 11. I'm a little embarrassed I threw such a fit—even when the waiter came over I couldn't even manage to be polite. I just grunted my order and was shot a look across the table that I haven't seen since I was a toddler. I guess I deserved it. I will apologize in the morning. I guess I really did have a bad attitude tonight. But the restaurant was SO boring. And it's a Friday night! (Not that I had any other options.) And then when we got home, I went on Instagram and saw a pic of Maya, Ali, and Josie all together. So, then I felt even more like crap. How did Josie get into the mix? I think they all play basketball together or something, but still they didn't even ask if I was free (even though I wasn't free). Those girls didn't know that I was busy, and they still didn't invite me. I know—I shouldn't have to be invited to everything all of the time, but it still sucks to come home and see it rubbed in my face on their story. I don't really expect my parents to understand, but at the same time—*why can't they understand? They lived through this already.* I know, in the olden days there was no social media or even phones or stuff, but surely some adolescent things have remained the same—and I'm pretty sure feeling left out, being stuck with your parents on a Friday night, and being in a bad mood have pretty much been the make-up of a girl's bad day since the beginning of time! For, like, ever!! **You should see Maggie's amazing English report on "Lord of the Flies," Mom. She really is a great writer— she must take after her grandmother. Yes, I read that book, Mom, don't you remember? And Robby had to show me his book report because I couldn't write the paper on it, remember? Charlotte likes to read like Dad... Well, we had lovely family plans tonight but Maggie was in a mood. I don't think I *ever* did that to you, did I, Mom?** she said to my grandma on the phone tonight. She has to call her every night nowadays, but does my bad attitude have to be the topic of conversation? I wish I could have heard what my grandma said in response. A few years ago, the "old" Grandma would have said something awesome and sharp like "Julie, you most certainly did and you were impossible, too, now maybe send Maggie to me for a few days." But now, I'm sure she doesn't say much at all, which I guess sucks too. Even though I'm sure my mom hated that my grandma called her out, she probably also hates the alternative of her own mom slipping away. Ugh that does sound awful. Sometimes it feels like this eternal mother-daughter conflict (well, at least it feels eternal) is part of our hard-wiring and we can't break the patterns, which means, strangely, that maybe it is necessary for our survival and even sense of who we are? Like, if we always kind of view ourselves through the lens of our mom's opinions of us, then what happens when our moms stop fighting with us altogether like my grandma is now? Maybe without the constant tug-of-war, my mom feels she is missing a chunk of her own soul? That's very deep—ugh that's enough for now.

Dear Diary

Drama, defined

There really is a difference between drama and being dramatic. Drama is real. It is the lives we live and the crap that happens, truly, every day… changing cafeteria tables, hurting people's feelings, being broken up with, wearing the same shirt as someone else to school, getting a C on a quiz when everyone else got an A, not being invited to a party, seeing someone whisper about your eyebrows from across the hall, absolutely needing something that your parents won't buy for you that everyone else has. That kind of stuff. It creates drama because it is really serious and sometimes gut-wrenching, and because it involves more than just one person. Being <u>dramatic</u>, well, that is a whole different story. I have no patience for that stuff. That is when a girl gets dumped and everyone has to <u>hear</u> her <u>whole</u> story about the phone call and the text messages because she just loooooves everyone crowding around her and feeling sorry for her. Being dramatic is making a big deal out of everything just for attention. Like a girl will get upset at lunch and all the girls around her will rush her to the bathroom. (I am not typically the girl who runs to go with her. I mean I would go to her if she needed me, but I'm not into the "clump" of girls following her. I hate giving in to drama. Maybe my old self would have wanted to follow the crowd to the bathroom, but the new Taylor Swift me is comfortable just waiting to hear about it afterwards.) (By the way—Switzerland is never dramatic. If she were, that would mean letting her emotions get the best of her and strongly having an opinion and she is way too careful to do that. But she is involved in every girl's drama story, <u>ooohhhing</u> and <u>aaaahhhhing</u> and having her back in every situation. She agrees with everyone's advice—she is not the voice of reason, but the cheerleader.) *That Sofia sure seems sweet.*

Switzerland even has the moms fooled. She is sweet, for sure, but please tell me she has a dark side, low self-esteem, or a strong opinion hiding somewhere! Honestly, if she didn't that does sound kind of lame. Actually boring. Then again, I have faith that Swiss Miss is quite exhausted from morphing into everyone's friend all day long and suppressing her true opinions. She'll implode one of these days…oh she will implooooode.

I guess you can say I don't really have the patience for dramatic girls. I hate when my parents call me dramatic, or a drama queen. They have no idea how sane and reasonable I actually am. Ha! The other night they might have sung a different tune, but in the scheme of things I am the most level-headed of this wacky bunch, I'll tell you that! The only one who gets sucked into my drama is ME! I leave alllll this crazy for myself…and you, dear journal. Nobody needs to hear all of this! I mean, I do get upset about stuff, but I don't want everyone involved or giving me their opinions and thoughts and feelings. Sometimes people talk about how upset they are, and they really just want a little bit of sympathy or support. I guess I'm ok with that. I'm just the kind of person who will always say "I'm fine" even if I'm not. I don't like to get attention that way. But, to be honest, it would make me feel better sometimes if my friends or family just knew when I was upset and took care of me, without my having to be dramatic and over-the-top about the day's crisis. *Is there a way to get attention and support but not be dramatic in order to get it? If there aren't red flags and sirens blaring and tears streaming and screenshots taken of nasty texts, then will other 12-year-olds even pick up on the subtle clues that there is a friend in need?* I certainly haven't figured out that magical formula yet. I don't think anyone really has. If a girl gets attention, you can be pretty damn sure she has asked for it. And not usually in a good way. On the bus home Neha and I started talking about all the drama at lunch today. It's funny, she kind of said the same thing about not wanting to feel left out but also hating all of the drama. And then she told me this story about her friend group and her one drama-queen friend Rory and how Rory always makes everything about her and always causes a scene and everyone has always walked on eggshells around Rory and then Neha said she was so tired of it. I know that girl Rory! She is in my second semester art class now with Neha and me! I'm so excited to watch this all unfold and watch the show. It sucks that Neha feels stuck with that girl. I asked her on the bus why she still hung out with her. "It's complicated" she told me, and I smiled back—as if to say, tell me something I don't already know—and then we both rolled our eyes and went back on TikTok. Anyway, I'm getting into trouble again it's practically 11 p.m. and my room is a total disaster. **Can you please go tell Mags to turn off her light and go to sleep on time for once and to put away that stupid diary!** My dad was totally begrudgingly (*begrudgingly*) making his way up the stairs to my room. I felt his "I really don't care how late she stays up but I'm not gonna fight with Julie on this one" attitude emanating e m a n a t i n g through the halls. My mom has been so cranky these past few days and weeks. Maybe she is getting her period! Gotta go!!!

Dearest Gentle Reader,

The Common Enemy

Sometimes I wish I could write and speak in a beautiful British accent. There are a few things that bind us together…bind friends together, I mean. There are bonds we have that can never be broken. Like, for example, a private joke. An inside joke that no one else understands. Something that happened at a sleepover or in 2nd grade or at camp. The kind of joke that makes you look at your friend at a random time and remember…and then burst out laughing in front of everyone. And everyone around you is like "what is so funny," and you and your friend just look at each other and say "Nothing. You wouldn't understand."

A shared boyfriend. That's another bond. Not that I would know, but I can imagine. And I've seen it in the movies and stuff, where one girl dates a guy and is totally over him (she has to be totally over him or it would be the opposite of a bond, it would destroy their friendship)… and then her friend dates him later and she ALSO is so over him. That seems cool 'cause they get to laugh about him and what a dork he is/was and stuff. Well it works in the movies, at least. I guess there is a fine line between sharing something and actually competing over it. Like having the same new haircut or wearing the same new outfit, or having the same crush. These are delicate, potential bond-breaking dealbreakers in a friendship. Sometimes the safest things for girls to have in common with their friends are the things that aren't too personal to begin with.

I'm sort of off topic. I really wanted to talk about another fun thing to bring friends together—the common enemy. The one awful girl who you guys both don't get along with. The one awkward boy who likes you both and always embarrasses you but really embarrasses himself all the time.

The attention-seeking girl in your class who always fakes injuries and shows off like a 5-year-old. That is the common enemy. It is so awesome to share that bond with a friend. It's like a private joke. It gives you power when you need it. Boosts you up with a smile when you are feeling down. Reminds you that you have a friend when you feel alone and it is an easy, built-in topic for conversation. There is a girl in my gym class; she is torture. Every day she has a new injury or fake story. Mandy and I always just look at each other when she walks in. It's like we are both waiting for her story. It is comforting, I'm not gonna lie, to have that bond. And it is funny! And it feels cool to have this common understanding with Mandy because she and I really never hang out outside of gym class. The girl, Susan, totally deserves it anyway. Talk about asking for attention. In this situation she fakes it so much and is SO dramatic that it actually works against her. Kind of interesting because it makes you think that *maybe even being dramatic has a very delicate balance—if you go too big too soon, is it true that you lose all of the attention you were so desperately trying to get in the first place?* **Maybe Susan just needs a friend, Maggie, and that is why she is crying out for attention. Maybe it really is a cry for help?** Oh, please, Mom. Stop being so dramatic.

After dinner I went upstairs as per my usual routine. I write in you as I always do—to hyper-analyze my life and to avoid homework and family interaction at all costs. Tonight, however, during my mother's nightly call with her mother, she said **I'm not being dramatic, Mom, I really am worried about you and you don't get it.** So who is the drama queen now??!

I'm kind of worried about my mom and my grandma, but I feel pretty uncomfortable talking about it. And besides, my mom doesn't need my help or my sympathy anyway. I'm just a kid, or whatever, and she doesn't seem too thrilled with me lately so I'm probably just better off staying out of her way, except when I need her to drive me places and stuff.

But lately she has made comments like *Maggie, not everything has to be about you all the time. You aren't the only person in this house who is going through a difficult time and you are just being so selfish.* Selfish?? I'm so confused but I don't know how to explain it. Like, am I supposed to take care of her now? But I don't even know how to and I have so much going on in my own life. She doesn't even understand my life and how hard things are every day. I kinda feel like she is being selfish. She is my mom; I am not hers. And she thinks she gets it all, but she was 12, like, 100 years ago in another century and times have changed. Wake up, Mom! Being in 7th grade is so much harder for us than it was for you guys. And you just have to deal with it. I don't need your advice. Half the time you don't even know what you are talking about! I just want your support!!! And now she is telling me I have to support her? But I have homework to do!! Argghhhh! Sometimes I just want to screeeeaammmm! But then I would get yelled at for screaming. FINE! I'll just take care of myself.

Dear Diary

Rejection…

SUUUUCKS! Just want to put it out there. It sucks. When the boy you like doesn't like you. (Sigh. Andrew.) When you audition for the lead and you get a lame part instead in the stupid chorus. When you go to sit down at lunch and the table you want to sit at has no more room. When you don't get to play on the team you think you are good enough to play on. When you don't get the solo and the same girl gets it…again! When you are supposed to break into teams or partners and no one chooses you. Sometimes it really feels like life is so unfair and everyone is out to get you. And sometimes it feels like things will never turn around and you will never get what you want or what you deserve. And it feels like the same people always get everything—all the good stuff. Over and over. Maybe I need to explore this bitter side of me more deeply. Maybe this is the edge I need, the kick in the January-ass I have been searching for, the pre-intermission belter. No matter how hard you try or how good you are or how pretty you feel or look on the one awesome day when you wore your brand-new sweater, we always get beat out. That one girl is always a better singer or athlete or prettier or has a better body. Or she is smarter or is a better studier so she gets better grades. Or she is stronger or more focused so she tries harder or practices more or is more motivated, so the coach or the teacher or the counselor notices and rewards her and recognizes her. *What if I just really want it? Doesn't that count for something? Do I have to be the absolute very best or try the very hardest? Can't I JUST WIN SOMETIMES JUST BECAUSE IT FEELS LIKE IT SHOULD JUST BE MY TURN? When's it my turn? (she sings to herself) Haven't I paid my dues?* Who am I kidding? An average, moderately motivated underachiever like me never wins. Maybe there is hope for me in college. (That took a bit of a turn, I fully realize that was a little dramatic…rein it in, Maggie.)

Don't worry, nothing really specific happened. Just your basic stuff like getting passed over by the chorus teacher, the cute boy, and the cool girls. Just an average day in paradise. My mom knew I was in one of those moods today after school. Unfortunately for me, this awareness did not play out in good advice delivery on her part. I believe her words to me were *Mags, I'm sorry you are disappointed about the solo in the concert.* (No she isn't—stop lying.) *The teacher just needs to choose the singer with the best voice. That's life. We can't all be the best at everything.* This is what I'm saying. Is that actually supposed to make me feel better? And what, exactly, am I the best at since you just made it clear to me that it isn't singing? Do I have a hidden talent I have yet to discover? That's life? So life is just one big colossal unfair rejection letter unless you are perfectly popular in every way? And easy for you to say, Mom, what have you tried out for lately and been rejected from? You don't even like leaving the house in your gym clothes and no makeup. You do well at the magazine (come to think of it, I have absolutely no idea how she performs at work). Whatever, why can't you just back me up? Why can't you be like "I'm gonna call that teacher right now and give her a piece of my mind" even though you and I both know that would not help or be appropriate. Just say what I want to hear—even if you are lying and I know you are lying. It still would make me feel better. A girl needs her mom to support her no matter what! I couldn't really express myself to her that way or find the words to say or the courage to say it calmly. I wish I could have, but instead I just got so upset with her rejection of me after my full day of my own rejection, I think I just yelled something crazy like "You don't even care about me and all the other moms care more than you!!!" She tried to tell me how absurd that accusation was, but I didn't care. Sometimes the truth is just a feeling and not the facts. (That's actually quite brilliant of me, I think. *Prophetic.* Is that the word? I saw her text she sent to her best friend tonight. **I'm beginning to think I am failing at this motherhood thing.** And then I felt awful. Did I just make her feel rejected just because I felt rejected? Maybe subconsciously I wanted her to feel like shit just 'cause I did.

Dear Diary

The Upside Down

This world of in-between land feels like the Upside Down. Not with scary demons and stuff, but where everything looks normal on the surface, but is a mess on the inside. Roaming the halls of school, you would never see the demons we all have swirling in our heads. We all live in our own Upside Down. We have the self we show the world and the self we hide away. And at the same time we are straddling childhood and adulthood on very unsteady ground. What a balancing act! *Maybe this really is the hardest time of our lives and this is what the grown-ups mean? It's like every day we are experts in our own circus acts. We are in disguise, balancing on high tightropes and jumping through hoops of fire all while trying to wear the cutest outfit and do our homework. That really does take talent!* I mean, really? How friggen old AM I? Talk about stuck between two worlds. Here I am with my stupid period for the second time and I lose a tooth!! (I mean the tooth fairy came and I got 10 bucks, so obviously, that was cool.) But am I a kid or am I a teenager? I guess that is why they call us that god-awful word: TWEENS. For one of the first real times, I really feel stuck in between different parts of my life. Sometimes I feel like I'm having real grown-up issues and problems (like the friends, and with my parents, all that stuff). But then I feel like such a child (like when I lose a tooth at age 12) and do things like cry to my parents when I'm upset or throw a tantrum when I'm tired (I know, can you believe I still do that? It's like an out-of-body experience…like I watch myself acting like a toddler, but I literally cannot control it).

The other day I had a complete and total meltdown (maybe it is because I had my period?). *You can blame anything you want on your period while you have it, it is one of the secret privileges of being a woman!* So that's cool. I can be a total bitch and eat whatever I want and cry and whine and be a hater and then be like "Oh, sorry. It's 'cause I have my period" lol. (*maybe I can say that in school if I forget my homework!!) HA!! As if!

I did like losing a tooth because I really do want all my baby teeth gone already. I have a little kid's mouth, that's for sure. No braces yet, a palate expander (which is totally for 3rd graders), and holes in my mouth from lost teeth over the summer. I may as well be 8 years old. Officially a total dork.

But on the bright side, I did buy some makeup with my tooth fairy money. I actually took the bus home to Neha's house for the first time. We had talked about doing it for a few days when we were in art and this tooth fairy money gave me the excuse. Her mom drove us and waited outside (a little bit overprotective, but whatever I was just grateful to be there with Neha) and then she dropped me off at home afterwards. My mom won't let me wear it, she said the mascara was way too dark and "grown-up," but I might put it on in school and then she will never know. I am always the last person to be allowed to do *anything!* I feel like just proving to her that I can do what I want. I mean, it is my choice if I want to wear makeup. I can decide what is right for me. I know when I am tired, I know when I am hungry, I know how to wear an appropriate amount of makeup and I know how to straighten my hair and I should be allowed to make these decisions when I want and how I want. I'm just not sure it is worth the risk of having her take away my phone if she finds out. Like besides looking like I'm 8 years old, I have to get punished like I'm 8 years old? I'm so mixed up inside and out, and I don't know when this feeling will end. Is anyone else feeling this way? Is this what all girls go through and what generations of girls went through before me? But why does my mom act like she never did? And then the strangest thing happened, in my own Upside Down... **She's like a lost puppy right now, honey. Be patient with her. It isn't easy.** Why did she say that to my dad? I know he doesn't get me, but since when does she? Maybe it was a momentary lapse of judgment or an overall lack of energy to fight any more because she is so drained, but why can't she say it to me? Do I have to pretend I didn't hear it? If she found out that I overhear her deep dark opinions through the walls each night, then I may never know the truth. Her truth. Sort of diary-truth-serum truth. Even worse, what if through the walls was always her intention of having me truly listen? Maybe the two of us just can't speak face to face. But why is it so hard for us to be honest to each other? Maybe the more that she is feeling undone and upside down, the closer to understanding me she is actually getting. Why is she softening up? Falling apart? Breaking down? Getting more frustrated? I don't have the energy to worry about her right now. I can barely find time to brush my newly toothless mouth.

January 26th

Dear Diary

The leader of the pack

I figured it out. My lifelong struggle. My goal in life. My dreams and aspirations. Here it is. Are you ready, Diary? You have been with me for quite some time now. I'm 12 and a half, and I know I complain a lot (A LOT), but it really hasn't all been that bad. Maybe you know me so well that this won't even be a surprise to you, but I guess it was a surprise to me when it hit me like a ton of bricks today in school. We had a Cultural Arts assembly, so, naturally, I spent my 45 minutes watching everyone sitting around me with their friends. They were all whispering and giggling and texting, and I was just sitting there with my friends. So bored. I don't think anyone behind me was looking at me in my row. I WANT ATTENTION!! I WANT PEOPLE TO NOTICE ME!! (I thought maybe if I screamed it out in caps that it would seem louder and someone would hear.)

Seriously, I know some girls my age want to hide and not come out until they are 18 and gorgeous, but not me. (What? I AM gorgeous? Why thank you!) I don't want to hide, I want to scream and shout "I'm here!! Hello!" like in "Horton Hears a Who." But the thing is, even though I am nice and respectful, and I follow all the rules and I include people and I dress nicely but appropriately, and I am sort of cute and sort of smart…nobody sees me. Maybe I'm boring. Or annoying. Or, worse than that, *unoriginal*. But really, *how do you fit in and stand out at the very same time?* I know this isn't a new question to you. I've asked it in many forms, but it keeps creeping up on me. I guess some girls have mastered it: the leaders. They get all the attention. The popular ones. The ones with all the right clothes, the most money, and the perfect personality to go with it. They are the athletes and the stars. The people who get the solos and the parts and make the teams. But *what is it, really, that makes them have this perfect personality?* They aren't any funnier or louder or nicer than I am. Well maybe they are louder so they seem funnier? Is it their confidence? They have an "essence," the "It factor"—it's a gift. I'm still not sure if they are born with it or if it is a carefully honed skill. I'm sorry—I know you are disappointed in me because I have been doing my research this year and I should have figured it out by now, but I haven't. I guess it just isn't that simple.

These girls who have the attention of others also get the attention of the boys. Are the girls who are popular only popular <u>because</u> the boys notice them? *Can a girl be popular with girls if the boys don't notice her?* And, here's a thought, sometimes girls who do get all of the attention from the boys are actually less popular because they are trying too hard. I think there are girls that are popular because they are just plain happy and smiling all the time—they are easy to be around and non-threatening. Everyone likes them. Even boys. Even boys like a girl who smiles. Sometimes—and this may really come as a shock to you—they aren't even the prettiest. These are the girls who are born with confidence. People like me (most people) are insecure but otherwise happy, yet we have a quiet way about us because we are always observing and analyzing and trying to find ourselves and figure stuff out all the time. I think we are the basic middle schooler. Then there are the other popular people—the stand-outs: the ones who command and demand attention, sometimes even by making other people afraid not to follow them. They might not even be confident or happy on the inside, but they have mastered the art of getting attention and you have to admire that. This is the skill. And, truthfully, I think for these stand-out people the attention might not last. It just takes too much work for them to keep this up day in and day out. *Since I was not born with this intrinsic confidence, and I'm not a star athlete and I don't have a beaming smile all the time, no real skills to make me stand out, what shot do I have at grasping a piece of the attention?* **Just be yourself, Magpie. People who peak in middle school have a looooong road ahead** *of them. Your time will come.* I'm still wondering what that even means. My whole life is <u>right now</u>—I'm not exactly concerned with the future when the present is so difficult. It's hard to wrap my head around having all the right qualities that will (may) make me a better grown-up, when I know those qualities might hold me back from thriving until then. I'm not sure I'm really buying that theory.

As I was saying, there is even another way people get attention in middle school and it is if they have a broken leg or a sprained ankle, or something. Because then everyone has to help them with their books, or with the elevator, or carry their lunch. I really must be one crazy girl that I actually have been jealous of broken bones and crutches. (Maybe if I happen to turn my ski the wrong way next week ever so slightly… oh my god I am a sick chick.) Oh, and birthdays. That is another way people get attention. For that one day that is yours. The ONE day a year that I will get attention. It has to be perfect. My birthday isn't until June, though. Anyway, back to wanting attention but not wanting to be the attention-seeking annoying girl. OH MY GOD am I the attention-seeking annoying girl?? DIARY! I'm even irritating myself. I don't want to be the girl on the outside looking in. I am clawing my way in, desperately trying to get in, pathetically even joking about breaking my own leg. What has my life come to? "MOOOOMMMMM!! I'm gonna fail my test tomorrow." I don't know why I called her. It was a foolish attempt to get out of my own head. I should have known that when she came upstairs at 10:15 p.m. she was going to be less than thrilled with me. *Maggie, you are a growing girl and you need your sleep! And why do you always wait until the last minute to study? I hope you are planning on doing better next time. When will you learn that this is a pattern for you?* I wonder what she will say through the walls later tonight. I won't know, I guess, because my pre-teenage upside down brain will finally be asleep. I realize that girls all around me are doing the same thing, trying anything to get attention and to join the crowd…it's just that no one would dare admit it. But why are 90% of the girls trying to get attention while 10% have all the attention? That just seems so unfair and so unbalanced. Sometimes I feel like the difference between us and them is that we are waiting for things to happen TO us, and they are MAKING it happen. Maybe I'm just crippled with indecision. My mom is so indecisive, too. I hope I don't inherit this from her. But my dad isn't. He just decides and does. He makes up his mind and goes. Is Charlotte more like my dad? She isn't as complicated as I am, but then again, she is practically a toddler, so what does she know. My brain is cloudy because of puberty, I remember learning that in health class or something. So maybe it isn't entirely my fault. Maybe my mom is indecisive because her brain is cloudy with…I have no idea.

It is time for me to make things happen. I will not be like the 90%. The pathetic clawing girls. I will be original and I will be me. (Oh my god I hope I can pull this off.) This is BIG. I'm Wonder Woman! (Even Wonder Woman's mother wanted to protect her and didn't believe in her and she had to, like, run away to break free of her reign and stuff.) Somebody grab my lasso.

But seriously, do you think I can pull this off? I mean I can't change my whole wardrobe (my mom would never allow it, nor would she pay for it), but I suppose I can change things up a bit? Maybe I can change things on the inside a little. I guess I just feel like I'm always sitting with other people in the cafeteria…and they are never really sitting with me. Does that make sense? That really seems sad. I want people to want to sit with me! What kind of friendship is imbalanced, after all? Doesn't a friendship have to be equal on both sides—I keep picturing a seesaw. Like if one person is trying too hard they end up on a totally different level than the person who doesn't care as much—one all the way up to the sky and the other, exhausted, treading water, sitting with her butt all the way weighted on the ground. Tomorrow I'm gonna say hi to my friends at the table and then I'll sit with Neha and her friends. There it is. Wish me luck. Tomorrow is another day!

Dear Diary

Small moves, big changes

On Wednesdays we switch things up. Well it might not have moved mountains for the rest of the cafeteria, or sent the shockwaves I had anticipated and feared, but my new table was a big move for me and for my new gameplan. I hate to admit to my mom that she was right (but she was right). Nobody really cared. I know Ali and Maya noticed and thought it was odd, but it wasn't like they asked me why or said they missed me. (I mean, what am I waiting for, a farewell party?) I am really trying to be ok with this and not get in my head about my "old" table's lack of overall concern, and I'm just living in the moment and being overall happy I have a new friend and even, maybe soon, a broader friend group (will it even be a "friend group" at all) or just new options and fresh conversations. I even came home on the bus today and didn't complain and when my mom asked, I actually said my day was good. To which she abruptly spun around from the kitchen window and looked at me with a smile (which was nice to see) and said *What did you just say? Am I mistaken, Miss Maggie, or did you just openly, and without bribery or manipulation, admit with no hesitation (and with a smile, I might add) that you had a GOOD day?* I had to chuckle to myself, as she did have a point. But of course I replied s n a r k i l y (is snarkily a word) "Well, Mom, did YOU have a good day, too?" and I kind of ruined the moment. (It was nice to see her smile, too, even if it was at my expense. Just don't tell her I said that.)

The funny thing was—she actually answered me. *My day was fine, thank you for asking. A bit frustrating with work because I have to work with this new woman on an account I have been working on for months and now I have to include some of her ideas and train her at the same time, and to be honest (tbh)*—she winked at me (omg it's so embarrassing when moms try to speak in text terms like when they say "hashtag brb," but that's for another conversation—I had to stay focused on my mom's rant and I was so bored I was catching every 3rd word)… *and the account people really trust me* (I think that's what she said) *and they are less than thrilled that I had to include Harley—can you even believe her name is HARLEY?!* That part I remember because it cracked me up inside. I didn't want to tell my mom I know two Harleys. *And overall it just sucks because if I didn't have to keep leaving early to take Grandma to her appointments then I wouldn't have to work with HarleyQuinn or whatever her stupid name is, but instead, I have to be appreciative that my boss is so flexible and understanding with what is going on with Grandma so what choice do I have?* Someone really needed to vent! But, like, really?? I had a great day and she sucked the life out of me with that one.

Dear Dumpy

Dumped

Sorry I have been out of the loop lately. Remember those big plans I had? Changing the world? Being a new person? Well, minor setback. I guess I was pretty traumatized by being dumped. I know, you are probably thinking "But you don't have a boyfriend, Maggie?" Yep. That's right. God forbid I actually have a boyfriend. This is way worse. I never even knew such a thing was possible. But I got dumped by a friend. She had been totally ignoring me lately and was also not responding to my texts and was always posting pics of herself with, like, everyone else in the grade except for me. When I went to try to sit near her at lunch a few days ago she would totally turn her head. I was feeling so uncomfortable. I finally was like "Did I do something? Are you mad at me?" and she said "no. it's fine." But then Maya told Josie that Sarah didn't want to be my friend anymore. I didn't even know that was possible. One second you are friends and next second you aren't? I know that sometimes we grow in and out of friendships and we get closer with some people and sometimes friends change. But I didn't know it was literally possible to end a friendship just like that because one person decides they are done. *Am I supposed to fight for the friendship because of our long history together or just let it go like she did? Maybe she did me a favor?* I'm feeling so confused right now—like I'm angry, and hurt, and sad, but also I don't really care I'm just embarrassed, and definitely self-conscious about the fact that I could be the type of person that someone wouldn't like, when all I do is try to make sure everyone always likes me... Like I feel physically uncomfortable in my own skin—kind of itchy and I want to change into softer pajamas. I hate these pajamas anyway they are so old and are from, like, 5th grade and the pants are too short anyway.

And anyway, what did I do to her? And now I am so embarrassed because everyone is talking about it. And Sarah won't even talk to me. I literally am freaking out. What is the matter with me?????? Why wouldn't she want to be my friend? We have known each other for so many years and stuff. I tried texting her and she is still on my private story and I DM'ed her. But I totally don't want to be a stalker. But this is so weird!! I don't think I was mean. Was I? Does she like Alex? Does she think I like Tyler even though I know she likes Tyler?

My mom knew I was upset and she just came into my room. I quickly threw this diary under my pillow. She actually said she was glad I was able to let my feelings out in my diary 'cause it is a good way to process all of my thoughts and feelings. (I knew she knew I had a diary, but I guess it was always a little unspoken truth.) Then she told me she used to keep a diary when she was my age and that it always helped her a lot. At this point, I didn't think she was testing me to see if I had seen her diary (even though I know she wouldn't have cared if had). I found myself almost telling her that I knew she also kept a diary, but I quickly decided against it. Regardless, I was glad she told me. (We have more in common than I would like to admit. Yikes.) My mom sat down on my bed and weirdly just started to spill her guts a bit…lots about remembering when my grandma told her she was glad my mom had her own diary so she had a safe place for her thoughts and how it's hard sometimes for moms to understand their daughters and that it's not easy to express how we need our moms sometimes…and the whole time she was sort of in-a-trance-like gazing around my room at my makeup table (desk) and mirror and messy floor and I wasn't sure if she was talking about me or really about herself but it didn't really matter.

…

She finally texted me back. I hated to interrupt my mom's trip down memory/therapy lane, but when I told her it snapped her out of it. Sarah said she wasn't mad at me. *You don't deserve to be treated this way, Maggie. You have too big of a heart.* A lot of good the size of my heart does me. She just doesn't think we should be friends anymore. Well that's fine, because I didn't want to be her friend anymore either. She is boring and my new, attention-grabbing self has no time to be slowed down. I need excitement, and spontaneity, and glamour. I don't need drama. And to think I went to bat for her when she wasn't invited to Maya's party. I should have looked after myself first. Anyone else would have. I have no time to waste. When Mom went back downstairs she said to my dad **Do you think I should say something to Carol?** As if my dad heard her when she asked him, or would even know what to do about this girl stuff. I really hope my mom doesn't call Sarah's mom. It was nice to hear that for once she had my back, but that would absolutely mortify me and make things, like, a thousand times worse. I know it won't be easy, but sometimes we in-beTWEENers just need to figure this stuff out on our own. I knew what to do. I had this one covered. **You know what, Harry, I think Maggie has got this one all figured out.**

Dear Diary

InstaDone

All it does is make me feel badly about myself. All I see is the stuff I'm missing out on. All the time. So why do I put myself through it and read it all the time? *Is it better to be in the loop and feel like crap or to be out of the loop but not know what you are missing in the first place?* **Maggie, that phone is literally sucking your brain cells away. Can't you please just put it down?** I like all of the funny accounts and the memes and the celebrities. It's true, my For You page is addicting. But anyway, I'm taking a stand and deleting it. (I'll leave Snapchat for now.) It's self-care—it will only make me feel happier and stronger and more independent. I won't be bogged down and can focus on all of the new things in my life that make me feel good. Here I go. Who needs it, really? Every vacation they are on, every shopping trip they take, every sleepover they have, every yummy food they order or eat, every birthday party they go to, every Bat Mitzvah. All the beautiful, perfect people. All the trends and the body I don't have and the fashion I can't afford. I'm over it. Done. Saving myself from the boredom and loneliness of feeling left out. These uber-edited filtered photos will stalk me no more. I am singlehandedly preserving my very own self-worth. I deserve more. I want to see people for who they really are. Less time on my phone and more freedom to do the things that make me happy. Come to think of it, what does make me happy? Well now I will have so much more time to find a hobby or to work out and be healthy or dance in my room because I won't be wasting away on Instagram. **She needs a hobby besides that stupid phone!** One simple deleted app can change it all… I feel so powerful. Taking charge. DELETE! The New Me doesn't need social mediaaaaaaaaa it's toxiccccccccccccc I am so confident and above it all!! (me shouting from the rooftops…very quietly)

DEEP BREATHS!

Oh my god. What have I done? I'm so bored. Uploading. Hurry up!! I won't allow myself to feel badly. I will set realistic limits and I will change my Insta image. It will take some work, but I am committed to the change. It is entertaining after all. I'm totally fine with it. Literally.

D.D.

Back on track

Sometimes my self-pity drains me. I actually feel good about myself today and about my body and about my looks. I mean, I need my mom to take me shopping and stuff, but, still. Things are good. I am happy with my friends—it's weird, ever since I started to sit at Neha's table, it's like it gave me the opportunity to talk to the friends (at my original table) in more real ways and not just as this huge group crammed into one long cafeteria table. And I kind of think they are a little envious that I was comfortable making the change and not making a big awkward thing about it (not sure why everyone makes such a big deal about cafeteria tables anyway!). I'm bonding with some new friends and am making an effort (with the good ones) to stay close with my old friends. I realize now I have to run my own life. Watching everyone live their lives around me and in front of me (well, in front of everyone) is enough to make a person crazy insecure. If I keep watching from the outside and keep waiting for things to happen to me, I will just turn into an ordinary girl, and I know I don't want to be that girl. But I want it to be real. Funny thing is, maybe I have to fake the new me on my social media so people start to believe it. So, I can combine my real life change with my artificial self change and, together, maybe one will influence the other in the right direction! *Don't you think it's strange that at our most awkward, insecure, vulnerable time, we spend 90% of our waking hours taking pictures of ourselves and publicly posting them or putting them on our story?* (Then, of course, we edit them and add effects and filters to make ourselves look better so the picture isn't actually even real, if you really think about it.) It is a full-time commitment to look (appear) this good! But I do truly believe it is all a way to show everyone in school that we are not loners and that we do have friends. Even though, actually, that doesn't make sense 'cause half their pictures are selfies. Funny and ironic, if you think about it. It's like "Look at me I'm gorgeous and in a bikini and having the best time…by myself in front of my mirror." It's like we are all the modern day Snow Whites, except instead of vulnerably asking the evil vacuum of the mirror, we pretend we feel the fairest of them all and decide that the best way to let the people of the kingdom know is to put a bathing suit on and share the photo with 1,300 people our age. So…

It's hard not to get jealous and spiral into self-hatred by comparing myself to everyone all the time. I guess if I were detached like Switzerland I wouldn't care so much. But I am opinionated and smart and that makes things that much harder. I actually care. *Sometimes the right decision is the harder one.* Or is it *Sometimes the harder choice is the right one.* Either way, it goes something like that. I know what my mom means. It doesn't make it easier to hear, but that saying is meant for people like me who always try to do the right thing and who always overanalyze their lives. No one really knows how, I think, except for me. My friends may just see me as bubbly and happy Maggie. Rarely do I let my guard down in front of them, I think as a way of protecting myself because the truth is, they aren't really good at supporting me. Well sometimes they do, but really, they are all secretly dealing with their own in-betweener worries; how could they possibly help me with mine? Come to think of it, ever since Neha and I have been talking on the bus rides, it's like I forgot that I usually pretend to be a different person 'cause I'm not trying to be anything but me. That sounds so cliché, but when I think about it, it's kind of true. Like there is no agenda (or social media world) with us—we are just two kids stuck on the bus making the best of the ride home as we vent about our long days in school. **Mom, I'll see you tomorrow. I know.**

Yes, this is the doctor I told you about. Mom, we already went through this! Yes, at noon tomorrow. Yes, the children are great. He's fine, too. Ok, I love you, too. Sometimes I kinda wish I couldn't hear through the walls. Now I'm all distracted. Every day things get a little harder for my mom and grandma, and all it does is make my mom even more stressed which really sucks for us. I just realized I haven't really spoken to my grandma since Thanksgiving. I can't believe she bought this diary for me when I was so little, and now it's hard to remember those days when she used to be so much fun. I guess I'm on my own again after school tomorrow and Mom won't be home even after I get off the bus. I try to be understanding, but it does suck. When Charlotte gets off the bus and my mom isn't home, I always have to be in charge of her and her snack and homework and stuff. So frustrating. Neha has a little sister, too, so she gets it. At least we can share Rory stories on the ride home. Rory threw a total tantrum in art Tuesday when one of the boys took her paintbrush just to set her off. Oh it set her off alright! Oof!

'Night.

Dear Diary

Shame on me

I've been pretty wrapped up in myself lately. It's Saturday, so I have some time to gather my thoughts. Feeling kind of guilty about it because, you know, my grandma has been really sick and my mom has been running around like a chicken without a head trying to take care of her mom and her dad and also plan my Bat Mitzvah, and here I am worrying about my outfit each day and where to sit in the cafeteria. *Am I a bad person? Or am I only capable of selfish behavior because I am 12?* I've been so preoccupied with my newly discovered self-confidence and life goals that I've lost sight of what is really important—studying for my Bat Mitzvah so I don't make a fool out of myself in front of all my friends. And I don't even have a dress yet. *There won't be a Bat Mitzvah if you don't learn the material. The party isn't a rite of passage—it is a privilege for all of the hard work you are supposed to be doing. I guess if you don't find a way to put down your phone, we won't have to worry about dress shopping after all.* I kind of resent that tone. Like, let me be hard on myself—I do enough of that already, but can't my mom at least try to believe in me so maybe I can start to believe more in myself? I get it. But when she says things like that to me, it makes me want to do even less. I want to prove to her even more how worthless I really am, because it is exactly what she is saying to me. *I don't know why we are making ourselves so crazy here with this Bat Mitzvah—she can't even get her head out of her little diary or off her phone.* Well, when you put it that way—perhaps shame on YOU, Mom, for having so little faith in me.

Dear Diary

Phoebe and balls

Sometimes I write in you every day, and sometimes I just get so busy. So sorry, Diary. Thank you for still sticking by me and being a true loyal friend. A book. Stories, rants, and some cartoon drawings—this is my one true friend? (Maggie don't be so hard on yourself.) It's better than therapy—you don't challenge me or question me or make me dig deeper or do homework (although I guess I end up doing that to myself all on my own…interesting…self-inflicted therapy).

I've been thinking lately, did you ever notice that when we have too many options it actually makes us feel more stressed out and, sometimes, even more unhappy? Even something as simple as what to eat at a restaurant can sometimes make people so overwhelmed. *Is it so lame that sometimes I just want my mom to make a decision for me?* Sometimes I will have more than one option of where to go on a weekend or I will have to decide between two friends for plans or something. Like the other week Bree texted me for a sleepover and Hallie asked me in school to come over the same day. I didn't know how to decide?! (Don't get me wrong—many times I don't have any weekend options at all and I'm miserable with no options, but it always seems when it rains, it pours.) But making decisions between two or more good choices is so hard to do! At least for me. Then I sometimes end up telling a convoluted story to one friend because I don't want to hurt her feelings and end up screwing up all my plans in the process. Phoebe has it all figured out. "Friends" is the answer to everything (I've been binge watching lately). I'm obsessed. When Chandler and Joey ask her if she wants to help them move furniture, she says, brilliantly, "Oh, I'm really sorry I can't help you—but I don't want to." *Why can't we all be decisive and honest?* It would be so freeing!

Maybe it isn't that we have too many choices, but more that we know what we want to do but are afraid to say it because of the reactions other people will have. And I'm not even talking about the big life-altering decisions like changing friends or not inviting certain people to a Bat Mitzvah—things that will really last—I'm talking about moving furniture when you'd really rather watch a movie. *It's nice that you are always so considerate of everyone's feelings, Mags, but if you keep doing that you will forget to take care of yourself and learn what makes you happy. Your needs are important, too.* Is that what she is really saying, or is she saying make a decision, for once, and stop being so passive?!! ~~Maybe she needs to think about herself first sometimes, too, and remember that her kids need her after school and not just her mom.~~ I take that back. I wish I wasn't using a pen.

Or sometimes I don't like to sleep over at parties and my mom will give me all these options like "I'll pick you up at 11." Or "Text me if you want to come home but TRY to stay." Or "Just stay and don't doubt yourself so much, you can do it." And I feel like I'm old enough to want to be able to make my own decisions, but I need help! I can't decide! So lame that I want my mom to just limit my choices and cut out the stress for me. Also, to be honest, when it comes to sleepovers, I'm gonna let you in on a little girl secret… They stink. We all hate sleeping in someone else's bed (I mean, really? eww. gross) while they are all fast asleep and stuff. Or sleeping on an air mattress or on someone's floor. We all like our own beds! So I guess I want my mom to be the bad guy so I don't always appear so lame by not wanting to stay over. My mom usually gives me those "outs" for situations where she knows I don't want to have to say no. I know I can always blame my parents. (They are good for something :)) A sleepover is like helping someone move furniture—it sounds good in theory, but the reality just isn't enjoyable. I want to learn to be honest and say "I don't really want to. I'm sorry, I don't like sleepovers." I wish I could just always have the clarity to figure out what I want to do and the balls (gross) *courage and self-awareness* to make the decision to just do it without worrying about the consequences. A true friend would understand anyway, right? (Wait—that is exactly NOT the point—the point is that I need to do what works for ME, not a friend). I think the pack leaders do that. Kaia, Josie, Nicki, even Switzerland (sometimes). I think the little dogs follow the big dog because the big dog makes the decisions (and plans) for them so they don't have to make any decisions on their own.

My parents had to be in the city tonight, so they left us with a babysitter. Part of me feels like that is so annoying, but another part of me loves when my parents aren't on my case all night. Before she left, she said to the sitter **Charlotte needs to be in bed by 8:30—she has her reading to do for school and should have her lights out by 8:45. And for Maggie, please make sure she leaves her phone and computer downstairs before heading up to bed—they suck her in like a vortex. Between that stupid diary, Amazon, TikTok, Instagram, and Netflix, I don't even think she hears a word I say at all any more. She will listen to you because you are young and cool.** (Omg that is so embarrassing! Now the sitter thinks I think she is young and <u>cool</u>!) Now I officially am going upstairs early. I don't even need a babysitter.

I do like her, though. She is a senior and she is pretty chill and she lets us order sushi and watch tv and whatever. Tonight she was playing with Charlotte and painting her nails and giving her a pretend makeover—Charlotte was thrilled and I got to play along and learn some key contour skills. Charlotte was covered in makeup. I felt slightly glamourous (and Chelsea was cool and made me feel cool) so I feel good at the moment.

After Charlotte went to bed and Chelsea was downstairs doing homework (lol she was on her phone the whole time), the phone rang and it was my grandma (no one else uses that line except her, practically). I tried so hard to be upbeat on the call and tell her where my mom was. I have to give her credit—she is a class act. She was so confused but passed it off as though she just called to say hi to Charlotte and me (even though she kept mixing up our names and it was after 10 p.m. and, of course, Charlotte would be in bed). I decided to try to keep the conversation going a bit—I wasn't sure if that was more for my grandma or for me, but I started talking about art class and my new friend Neha and all of the drama with Sarah and the cafeteria. At one point, my grandma started to tell me this story about a *fight your mom and her friend Diane had when they were your age, and how upset your mom was (Maggie, you know how stubborn your mother can be)* and how my mom talking to Diane on the phone after their fight and how they worked through it. It was the craziest few minutes ever—like suddenly there she was again, my grandma in all her glamour and glory—and I got to hear this glimpse of my mom and even of my grandma as a teenager's mom, and it was cool. Then she said *you're so smart and I admire your confidence in branching out and making a new friend.* She was right—I am confident! And then she said *I thought I was supposed to see your mom tonight and I couldn't reach her.* And then her voice got a little shaky and I felt like she was a little scared. I explained that Mom was in the city tonight and that she would call her in the morning and that everyone was safe and she was safe and should go to sleep because it was late. And I heard my grandpa in the background calling her and she said *Goodnight, sweetheart* to me and hung up. It was good to hear her voice, I guess, especially her old voice. And then when I hung up it made me feel sad all over again. I was even sad for my mom, wondering if my grandma interrupted her one night in the city with multiple calls on her cell, and how my mom, the class act, would have probably stepped away from the table gracefully a few times, even though she was embarrassed and frustrated by the interruptions, and then, of course, worried even more. And then she probably wished she hadn't taken this opportunity to go into the city after all if all it did was stress her out, ruin her night, and freak out my grandma. I texted my mom.

hi I spoke to grandma she called. don't worry she is ok I told her you are almost home and you would call her tomorrow. Charlotte is asleep have fun.

...Thank you, Mags. You have no idea. Sweet dreams go to sleep it's late.

Xoxo

Mom

(so funny how she still signs her name in a text sometimes)

Dear Diary

Can you wait for me?

Did you ever notice that girls never want to walk anywhere by themselves? We all are guilty of it. To the bathroom. Into a party. To the cafeteria. *Please. I get it. I was even uncomfortable last year when I had to walk into a FUNERAL alone.* (That doesn't give me much faith in my potential for growing up some day.) Maybe we do this for two reasons: The first reason is that the only thing WORSE than having no friends is having people THINK you have no friends. So whenever a girl is by herself, everyone always assumes she has no friends. The second reason is, we never want to have to LOOK for our friends somewhere if we are standing alone. Our hearts start to race, the whole room stares, we convince ourselves that everyone in the room is seeing us sweating and having so much anxiety. We girls are so crazy that we actually begin to believe that our friends have conspired against us and they have completely left the building and we will never find anyone to sit with ever again. So, what do we do?? We torture our friends and make them wait for us…while we pee, while we ask the teacher a stupid question after class, while we wait on the cafeteria line for lunch, change for soccer practice, walk into the auditorium for an assembly. We never do it alone. I wonder if boys do the same thing? Anyway, it is a great security blanket when a friend waits for me. Today I had to drop something off in my locker and Maya waited for me before Spanish class. There are two totally gross boys in Spanish class and it would have been so awkward to walk in alone. Phoebe wouldn't care, just for the record. All of them always walk into Central Perk alone. (Then again, they always know, at any given moment, their Friends will be there and there will be a seat waiting for them.) She would have no problem walking anywhere by herself and would wait for any friend as long as she had nothing better going on anywhere else.

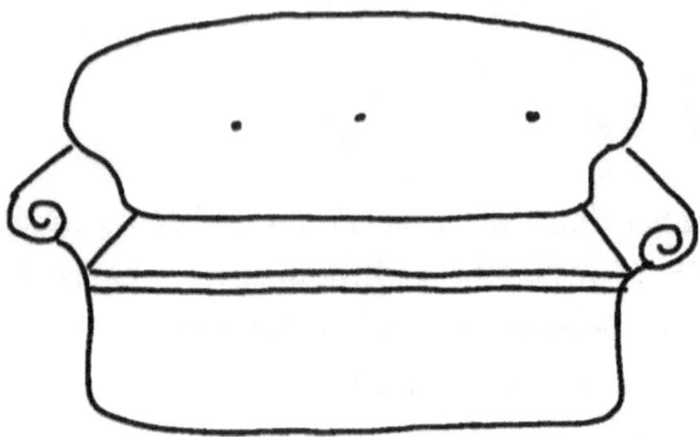

You should see my mom texting with her friends. It's actually pathetic. Whenever they have a party or an event or are just going out for dinner or something, there are a hundred messages back and forth. **What time are we getting there? Who is picking me up? What are you wearing?** I guess there is some comfort in knowing just a small part of being a 12-year-old girl is part of my genetic code and not just my insecure hormones. I get a kick out of sitting on my parents' bed when my mom is getting ready for a "girls' night" 'cause she is always telling me about all the drama and sometimes she doesn't even want to go but isn't completely honest or she will agree to go to a restaurant she hates or something like that. Uhhh, Mom…have some courage and pull a Phoebe and do what you want, where you want, and with the people you want! Give us kids some hope!

Dear Diary

The Insta-race

How many followers do you have? How many likes did you get for that pic? How many shout-outs did you get for your birthday? How many people say "ilysm" to you? How many people do you follow? Instagram is like the most insecure-security blanket ever. Like, any time I am not talking to anyone, I am on my phone. We all are. Look around any middle school and if anyone is standing alone ever after school hours, they are safely scrolling—looking very purposely busy—through their phones. The minute they get off the bus and begin their walk home, they (we) don't talk about our day with our neighborhood friends, we scroll. When we wait for our parents at pick-up or stand on the bus line—scrolling. When we are sitting at a restaurant or waiting for our Starbucks—scrolling and snapping. And I know it's stupid. I'm smart enough to know that, but it's not like I can stay away from it or pull myself out of the mix. You know I have tried. You HAVE to be on it and be a part of it—or you are just out. Social media is a built-in mirror—actually, it's a window with a screen and a tint and a curtain and a shiny new outfit, it's not a mirror at all. It's a window into the world of everything you are missing, at all times. All it does is show me how much cooler everyone else in the world is than I am. They are prettier, they have better clothes, they certainly have better plans, they are busier, their dogs are cuter, they have more friends, more followers, better filters, and more fun. Even food looks tastier. As if I don't already feel that way about everyone at school when I wake up in the morning—then I go on while eating breakfast and already my day gets worse before it even starts! Even when I am with my friends, we are sometimes scrolling on our own phones. Does that mean we are bored with each other? Or are we just incapable of a phone-free conversation? Even when someone lies to another girl to say she can't hang out because she has to stay home—she puts a video of herself with her friends on her story not even five minutes later. No longer is there any accountability or concern for someone else's feelings; it is more important to look busy and happy all the time. *Admittedly* I don't like it or support it and anything not actually genuine feels so weird to me, yet almost everything we do in middle school is just that—a game, and you just have to play along or you are left on the sidelines and are the last to get picked in gym class.

If all we want is to have plans, and then when we do have plans, all we do is stay on our phones, then how do we win? We don't even remember how to start a conversation or fill a conversation when there is a lull. We are always halfway focused on each other and halfway distracted by what and who we are seeing on our social media. Now all of our conversations are only about what we are looking at on our phones, or we are imitating the very TikTok which sets us up for self-hatred in the first place. The even crazier part is the race; the competition of it all; the unspoken rules. Did you know that you can't post more than one picture a day—or even more than a few a week—or you appear desperate for attention? Did you know you shouldn't post at 4 p.m. when everyone gets out of school because it makes you look desperate for likes? Do you know when the best time to post is? Between 5 and 6 p.m.—seems more casual, yet optimal "distracted from homework scrolling on Instagram" time. Did you know that if someone "unintended" latches onto one of the pics you want to post that you don't tag them at all? It is all orchestrated. Even the "spontaneous" selfies are taken and retaken and edited a million times. If something spontaneous and amazing actually happens and we didn't take a picture of it to capture the moment and therefore no one got to see it—it just isn't as great of a moment after all. **You poor girls must be exhausted from all of this work to maintain your image on social media. It's no wonder you are tired and can't finish your homework ;-)**

She is so full of it. (She is actually probably so right.) But she is on her phone even more than I am. She should put down her phone and realize she is ignoring her daughters and one of us is going to college in a few years and she will regret all the time she wasted! **I'm going to bed**. She didn't even say goodnight to me. She was arguing with Charlotte earlier over her math homework (I'm not sure which of the two of them was more frustrated with the word problems) and then I saw her cleaning up the kitchen and making lunches for us for Monday, but she definitely seemed to be in a fog. My dad started to help her with the pots and pans from dinner but she just got aggravated with him because he kept putting things in the wrong cabinets so he said something like **I was just trying to help, Julie**, and left the room. Sometimes it's best to leave the lioness in peace.

Dear Pathetic Valentine

Nice girls finish last

Warning, pathetic entry about to start. #feelingsorryformyself

Did you notice I didn't bother to write on Valentine's Day? One day I'll get a cute card from someone else besides my dad, right?

I am too nice. I need an edge. I want to be cooler, but I don't try hard enough. Maybe if I tried harder. I am neutral. I go along with the crowd. I dress like everyone else. I am a decent athlete and an ok student. I have a good enough singing voice and I can play an instrument. I go to camp in the summer and I ski in the winter. We don't go on a lot of vacations. My room is white and purple. My dog hates me because I'm too busy (alright, too lazy) to walk her, my sister hates me because I'm too busy (alright, too impatient) to hang out with her. My phone used to be a used phone. I don't have private lessons in anything and I'm great at nothing. Maybe I'm a good writer and a decent artist? I have friends and blend right in. I can dance—but in the back row. I can hold a tune—but in the chorus. I can ski but not race. I can run but not fast. I have boobs but they are a size B. What does this mean for my future?? *Am I destined for a life of boringness and averageness? Can I change it? (Do I want to?)* If I could change it—who and what would I want to be? Is it worth the risks? I know I want to be noticed—but *do I want to be noticed for who I am, or do I want to be noticed by trying to be someone completely different?* I feel like the not-so-nice girls are noticed—they have a reputation. They hurt people's feelings. They know how to give looks to people without saying a word. They have boyfriends. They don't wait for anyone—everyone waits for them! I know I want to be nice, and I know I would never be comfortable pretending to be someone I am not just to get noticed. I just wish someone would notice me for who I am now. I know it starts with the attitude I project out. I am trying. *But is finishing last better? Not causing any trouble and staying on the straight line? Always knowing what to expect and knowing everyone always knows what to expect from me? Or should I start taking some chances?*

That is so scary! I wouldn't even know where to start! *Do you think these girls know who they want to be, so they plan it more carefully and are more calculated?* Like they enter middle school like "I need to be the popular girl, so I need to set the stage." It does take skill and planning. It can't all be luck, looks, and the perfect personality. I know I don't have that in me. But if I decide not to be the nice girl for a change, people will be surprised and might not even like it. Maybe I can ease my way in. (Who am I kidding, I am not going to suddenly be rude and bitchy, that is so not happening.) Let me think about this and get back to you… I need to "Phoebe" it up a bit. *Phoebe is wacky and makes her living giving massages and she could never afford all of that coffee or that apartment on her salary. She is a total hippie and it's totally unrealistic. Is that who you aspire to be? Don't you want to be something, something real?* Sometimes she can be such a dream crusher. I didn't even ask her for her opinion. The funniest part is that this is just me hearing my mom's voice in my head! Now I am self-injecting my mom's criticisms and advice into my own thoughts?? Why does she feel she has to interject herself into my dreams and inner monologue. It does feel like my mom interjects more negative feedback into my life as a result of her own stress. It isn't fair. I doubt my grandma did that to her when she was young! My grandma worked as a writer when my mom and uncle were younger (I think she might have even taught a writing class at the local college or something, I'm not really sure, actually, I probably should have asked her more about it), so I think she was always home when my mom got home from school. And, anyway, who cares what she actually wrote or taught, that was, like, hundreds of years ago and life was so simple back then. They played games in their backyards and didn't have smartphones and got to play on any team they wanted and never had to compete for anything. Maybe when Charlotte gets older it will be her turn to be the dumpee of my mom's stress and I'll be free as a bird, living the life with my super hot high school boyfriend who looks like Timothy Chalamet, bouncing around freely from cafeteria table to cafeteria table and going for long drives with him every weekend.

Charlotte, sweetie, I'll tuck you in soon. Go brush your teeth. I wish she would take that patronizing tone with me sometimes, instead of always being in my business. Charlotte has it so easy. And she probably will grow up to be original AND popular. Little sisters are so annoying. She is just lucky I'm paving the way for her. I'll bet she will need a diary someday.

Dear Journal

The day was over before it began

I have been thinking about my big thought the other night about changing the world (well, changing myself), but how could I even begin to make plans like that when from the minute I woke up this morning, it was the worst day of my life? First of all—it was raining. Freezing cold rain. I mean, really? My hair is an absolute mess when it rains. Like a frizzball crazy person.

My grandpa was an artist, so you can see I clearly inherited his talent ^^

So that was awesome. Yeah, like I loved trying to braid and product and straighten and pin it this morning—that was a good time. Oh, and it was particularly awesome because it was 6:55 in the morning and I was already on track to be late for school. And here is the next best part—I had a field trip today. To a natural history museum. On a bus for an hour and a half each way. In traffic. In the rain. So—are you getting this? Raining, cold (did I mention cold??), bad hair, lame sucky field trip—AND I only had one pair of clean leggings and they were navy and I have a navy rain coat so I am in head to toe NAVY I am such a loser! I debated not going. (Well, in my head, of course. My mom would not have allowed that.) *Maggie, you act like your alarm surprised you—like it goes off at a different time each day. Why can't you just go to sleep on time so you can get out of bed on time. I swear you will walk to school if you miss that bus. I do not have time for this today.* Notice I just tuned her out and kept on panicking. The bus ride was SOOOOOO long and we had to take a regular school bus not even a more comfortable coach bus and we WEREN'T ALLOWED TO BRING OUR PHONES. *Can you imagine, all of us talking to each other for what felt like the first time in years without the escape of a phone in our hands for like two hours each way?* No bus pictures or posts, no videos to take on the bus, no music, nowhere to hide.

Thank god Neha was also on the bus with me so at least I had a friend to sit with. (Which was kind of nice because usually our bus talks are so short and we barely get to talk during art.) But when we got there, they divided us into groups and I wasn't with ANY friends. It was so awkward. I had Kaia and Katie, so I knew they would never talk to me and I would feel even more like a loser in my navy outfit. (Of course, they didn't even wear raincoats and they had black leggings on so they looked totally normal. And here I am in my 13 layers because my mom made me, and I look like Violet in Willy Wonka. Violet the big fat blueberry in a museum.) I decided to make the best of it and talk with Tyler and Andrew. I had to do it. I had to prove to myself that even dressed as an Oompa Loompa, I could say hi to guys. I felt like maybe in an ironic twist, it was evident (and freeing) that I clearly had set the bar so low for myself that day and expected to be ignored or laughed at, so, strangely, it gave me this bizarre boost of confidence 'cause I had nothing to lose. They said "hey" back (!!) (it worked??) and we all agreed how lame the trip was and how annoying our guide was. So that was cool. We got through the day (the one part with the dinosaurs was actually pretty cool and I have to give the guide credit, she really did her best to keep us interested, even after we giggled over her safari costume). No one really seemed to care (or notice?) my troll outfit, so I moved on pretty quickly and **rebounded** like a champ (spotlight, cue music). Neha and I sat together on the way home—she saved me a seat and we just slumped together and caught up on the long ride. It wasn't until after dinner when I was telling my parents about the day and told them that Neha and I laughed about the tour guides and the video we had to watch and the annoying boys cackling in the back row that I realized (this part I kept to myself) that Neha had saved a seat for me and it just felt so normal. (Diary, I'm actually smiling a little, I know you can't see it.) Come to think of it, I'm not sure why I didn't tell them the good part of my day, and only really ranted sarcastically about the absurdity and chaos of the whole (of course) terribly organized and uninspiring school trip. Why couldn't I just tell them I also had fun, amidst *amidst amidst amidddsssttttt (what a stupid word)* the rain and frizzy hair and gross boys?

She's exhausting me. I don't think she was referring to my grandma. Maybe. My mom is exhausting me, too! Maybe a girl shouldn't have to work this hard just to have her own mom understand her and be on HER side. ESPECIALLY AT 6:55 IN THE MORNING!

Dear Diary

Are you mad at me?

I hate that saying. I've said it before, regretfully, and I've been asked it so many times. It's like a rite of passage for girls my age. It's a way of avoiding real, uncomfortable confrontation. It's the middle of February and everyone is just cold and cranky. Everyone in the whole school has a great ski or beach vacation planned for February break—except for us. We never go anywhere or do anything fun. I swear the town will be empty. (I know that sounds so pathetic and snobby. I'm sorry. But this is my diary so I don't have to talk about how lucky I am to live here and all the war and starving people all over the world. I JUST WANT TO FEEL SORRY FOR MYSELF!!! 'Cause it's so unfair!) (ok. I feel better now :))

Anyway—getting back to what I was saying. I guess because the school knows we are all cold and having the winter blues, they decided to have a school spirit day. Just a costume day. So Ava (she is in my math class, have I told you about her before?), well, she and I are getting to be a little better friends lately. Anyway, she asked me if I wanted to dress up as Disney princesses together. So I thought that was cool (and I was glad someone asked me). It is like Halloween—it's like social suicide to dress up in your own costume alone. No one does that anymore (clearly I have learned that). Anyway, when we got home from school today we both went online and facetimed to pick a good costume. We both sort of wanted to be Belle—so that was awkward. (Don't worry, these costumes were, like, for teenagers, with short dresses and stuff, not like the costumes I used to wear around the house when I was three :))

Anyway—I had this idea that it would be cool and more fun if we did like a group costume and not just us. So I asked Ava if it was ok with her if I also asked Ali, Maya, and Georgia (Georgia is new here, she is a different Georgia than the one I mentioned before—she is cool) to also be princesses and she texted back like "it's ok. just do it without me." WHAT? I kept saying "Please don't be mad. Are you mad?" And she kept replying like "It's fine, I just thought it would be the two of us. You can dress up with whoever you want." I literally was freaking out. I did not understand??? I mean, I kept asking myself and then my mom—did I do anything wrong?? And my mom was like *You did not leave her out nor did you ever agree to have it JUST be the two of you AND it is a costume day, not a twin day, so the more the merrier.* (So much better when my mom agrees with me instead of lecturing me on how to treat people, and stuff.) So every time I would apologize and ask Ava if she was mad at me, she would text and be like "I'm not mad. I'll just dress up as something else." *Maggie—you do not have to ask her that anymore. If she wants to be mad, that is her choice and her problem, not yours. You didn't do anything wrong.* When my mom said that, I really did feel like a weight was lifted. Like really adult-like-freed from the childish guilt that it was my responsibility to take care of her feelings. Like, maybe for the first time—UNSTUCK. I can barely manage my own feelings, lol. It just feels so weird inside my stomach right now that she is mad and that I might have hurt her feelings—I just feel so bad! It was like when Sarah dumped me a few weeks ago. But, at the same time, I keep trying to tell myself that she is not being fair and she is being a little boring, right? *Maybe sometimes people are just lame and boring and it isn't our responsibility to fix them? Why should I feel guilty or responsible for a choice she made?* Phoebe wouldn't. Cher wouldn't, Fat Amy wouldn't, Blair wouldn't. Regina wouldn't. Total life goals.

So is this a glimpse of what it feels like to stick up for myself and do what is best for ME? It feels so strange! But I'm not gonna lie, it feels sort of good! I mean, I get to dress up in the costume I want with the friends I want to dress up with! I sort of took control of the situation and it sort of worked! Right? But typical that I finally try to branch out and make plans with a new friend and it backfires. I swear, not only is Maggie exhausting, but she exhausts herself. How did she get to be so old and so 12-year-old insecure? I am trying to remember her when she was Charlotte's age. She wasn't like this, was she? Where did the time go? I couldn't decide if she was sweetly reminiscing with my dad about how quickly I've grown up or asking him to convince her that he thinks I'm actually an angel and she is the one who is crazy. Neha told me this afternoon that she can't hear her mom talking about her through the walls so it makes her feel weird because her mom is just always nice and neutral so she never really knows what her mom is thinking at all. Come to think of it, is that better or worse?? How will I get through school tomorrow without asking Ava if she is mad at me or without being all insecure and weird around her?? I hope I can do it!! Keep your fingers crossed! I need to be like the other girls who do what works for them and don't waste all their time worrying about others.

I SO have to sleep. So tired…falling…asleep…right…now…

March 1st

Dear Diary

No offense (the only thing worse than Are You Mad at Me)

Dear Diary,

(sorry I haven't said that in a while :-)) Back in school after a long, boring vacation with nothing to do but watch everyone else's lives on the phone.

No offense, but you are super boring and unresponsive. Just kidding.

That's how in-betweener girls do it. We are not adult enough to be honest and we are not childish enough to be overtly mean. We say something nasty and spiteful, and then we think that if we say "No offense. I was just kidding" afterwards, then the person will laugh it off and pretend or believe it was all said as a joke. Um—yeah—try again. That is never the way it feels. Trust me. I've been there. If someone is saying something that needs to be followed by a "jk," then you know it wasn't nice. Well maybe you should ask Ava. Remember her? The girl who wasn't mad at me? (I knew she was pissed about the costume thing! Never trust a girl who says she isn't mad!) So today I walk into math, and she is sitting next to Dylan and Natalie and she goes "Maggie, that shirt is so cute! It looks like the one you wore for school pictures in 5th grade. Is it?" (I think I died of humiliation). So, of course, I totally laughed it off and sat at my desk. And then, she dropped the obligatory "I mean, no offense, it just looked a little small." As if I would wear that dorky shirt again in middle school?! She KNOWS that this shirt is new and she was just saying it to piss me off and to embarrass me. Well I guess she accomplished just what she set out to do. Payback in the form of a childish insult in front of my whole class. *Now am I supposed to pretend I'm not mad at her for doing it? Should I have chuckled and made fun of myself to act like it didn't bother me? Or do I have a right to be pissed?* Well I am. And I'm NOT going to pretend that I'm not mad like she did to me a few weeks ago. And I'm not going to say anything nasty to her right back because I won't stoop to her immature level. And besides, that would just be mean. *Can I do everything in my power (and believe me, this is new for me) to be ok with being mad at her and just deal with the gossip and the consequences of everyone knowing it? Why is it so hard for a girl to just be MAD and to be ok with feeling MAD?* Adults get mad all the time and they don't try to hide it. I didn't do anything to her and she was a bitch to me. In front of the WHOLE math class and EVERYONE heard. ***She embarrassed you in front of your whole math class? That's rude and unnecessary. What do you plan on doing about it?*** I'm so confused. This is, like, the second time lately where my mom has stuck up for me. I like it, believe me, but she always acts so angry with me so I don't get it. And now she is asking <u>me</u> what <u>I'm</u> going to do about it?? *Doesn't she usually just tell me what to do, and then I get mad at her for giving me advice, and then I do pretty much what she advised me to do in the first place??* It's like my world is being turned upside down. What else is new? "Well I don't know," I said to my mom. And—ready for this?—she said ***I know you'll figure it out, Mags.*** And she walked out of the kitchen. Just like that.

So I guess it's officially up to me to decide now. How do I want this to play out in this middle school horror movie that is my life? Let her deal with the new me! I'm gonna try to be like Josie and The Confident and not give a crap! I hope I can do it. Wish me luck! I have to stick to my guns. I can't cave, or I'll get walked all over and Ava will just get more people against me. She has made some *snide* comments on my posts lately and has been sending me snapchats whenever she is with other people like such a show-off. I'm hurt and I'm allowed to be angry. This morning when "the incident" happened I turned around at my desk and looked towards the front of the room. Then I started talking to Teddy and Andrew so that was cool. I didn't want her to see me get upset, but maybe

I should have? *Is it better to react genuinely and emotionally or do what we can to appear "above them" (though angry) and keep our reactions calm and clear?* I won't overreact—that is where we in-betweeners (hmmm <u>in-beTEENers</u>) go wrong. I thought for a second about whispering about Ava and causing a scene like she did, but then I thought again. That would have been beneath the new me. Looking back, I'm glad I reacted kind of neutrally—this way she didn't really know how I felt so I bought myself some more time to plan my next course of action. Operation Ava Confrontation was the core topic on the bus ride home today. Neha backs me up and we both agree that I should not let this passive-aggressive childish behavior slide and I should Bachelorette this nonsense and pull her aside. Sometimes, Charlotte, you just need to make your own decisions, like your big sister does. Something is definitely upside down in my house. Or is it finally right-side up? I'm having an Anne Hathaway moment. I guess there was a part of me who just expected that when I got home from school, my mom would tell me she was tired of hearing me complain but then would send me off in the right direction because she can't help herself. Like, I came home ready for the Mom rant and anticipated the challenge, but instead walked into my house to overhear her upstairs with Charlotte (who was upset about something juvenile, of course). Ironically, when I arrived in the kitchen for backpack-on-the-floor-phone-on-the-table-jacket-on-the-counter snack time to tell my mom I had made this decision, it was as if she already knew.

Dear Diary

Strength in honesty

As I write in you tonight, I feel satisfied. Relieved. For the first time in my whole life I didn't just pretend and ignore to make uncomfortable feelings go away or fade into the background. I didn't ask my mom for advice and I didn't need it AND I knew what she would say anyway. I didn't deserve to be teased. If I had done something to Ava, then fair play, game on. But I was blindsided. I actually facetimed her after school. While I was having a snack. My mom was even in the den. I didn't say "are you mad at me" and I didn't dance around the issue. *Sometimes I wonder if it is harder to keep the anger inside and pretend you are fine rather than to be angry and to actually talk it out?* I mean, the rest of the day in school yesterday, and all of last night I was an absolute mess—even though I know Neha and I had made a decision, it was scary. I was embarrassed and upset and trying to be confident with being pissed off but not sure what to do about it. I wonder if this just comes more naturally to Katniss or Hermione? Does Trinity have to practice becoming a badass or has it been with her since birth? Well maybe I am just a little more cool and confident today myself. I straightened my hair this morning and I put on a skirt—which I never wear—and tights with cute boots and a top that kind of shows my boobs but in a good way. I even slipped on some mascara—just little enough that my mom didn't notice. It's safe to say I felt cute and I liked it. *Did I feel better today because I liked the way I looked, or was I motivated to get dressed up because I woke up feeling differently?* Either way, I guess, it kind of worked. All day I walked around the halls feeling good. I just wasn't over concerned with what was going on around me, and was able to notice when people came up to me. When I saw Ava in math I barely said hello and talked to everyone else in class and then just did my work. Like, I didn't go out of my way to cause a scene, I just really didn't care. I think that was really the biggest difference. I didn't have to act like I didn't care, I genuinely did not. And the other kids in class were, like, into it. Like they looked at Ava and expected me to be all awkward and uncomfortable. But I wasn't. When I went to lunch and the other girls tried to stir the pot, like they do so well, I wasn't taking the bait. Even at Neha's table, my new friends were kind of into it—not in a drama-provoking way, but genuinely like Maggie what did you say to Ava after she humiliated you yesterday? I realized today that responding to them about Ava and this so-called fight was only going to make me look worse and make her stronger. I just wasn't having it. I told them "Guys, there is nothing to talk about" and I changed the subject. When I got home from school, I think she was probably really confused by my reactions today. So I jumped right in and facetimed her. She picked up right away. I didn't hold back. "Why did you purposely embarrass me yesterday?" She tried to play it off all casually, like it was a joke. She should have just admitted that she was being immature and was just trying to get me back for ruining her costume day, but she didn't. I didn't say anything lame like "It really hurt my feelings" because I didn't want to sound whiny, but I said "It was just mean. And in front of the <u>guys</u>? Was that really necessary?" I think that was the clincher. Like she knew that that was when she crossed the line. "Sorry. I don't know. I didn't mean it. I actually liked your shirt yesterday. Can we just move on?" So the new me and my new friend Ava—we moved on. My mom "conveniently" walked into the kitchen right after the call ended. *That must have been very hard for you, Magpie. I am really proud of you.* She kissed me on the forehead after that. So maybe that's it? I am raised? I am cooked? Maybe Charlotte is the new Maggie and my mom has to focus on her now?

I have SO much homework though so I'm sorry I can't write too much now.

She actually looked so adorable today. And happy! And she even put mascara on!! She noticed?! Of course she did! Is there ever anything my mom doesn't notice? And she let me THINK I was getting away with it. I guess that's actually kind of sweet. I didn't hear my dad reply, though. He probably didn't hear her and also doesn't even know that mascara is different than eyeliner. He is probably wondering if I wear makeup every day or just today…

Dearest Journal

Helicopter parents

I've heard that expression before and never really cared what it meant. But now I get it. My parents read all my stuff and are always in my business about school and friends. My mom just probably feels guilty because she is always so preoccupied with my grandma and doesn't even know what is going on in my life, so she thinks it is justifiable to cheat and just catch up by reading my phone? She has no right and I don't know why she doesn't trust me. It makes me want to hide things from her even more and not even tell her things; it makes me resent her for not being home even more than I already do. But I read her diary—was that just as much an invasion of her privacy? I think it's way different.

Sometimes my mom will pick my phone up off the kitchen counter and start scrolling and when I freak she'll be all bitchy. *I pay for this phone and if you aren't going to talk to me I have a right to know what is going on in your life.* I DO talk to her! *Maybe I'm telling her too much stuff and I should just be like all the other girls and tell her nothing?* Neha and her mom are kind of close, but… She doesn't tell her mom really anything at all (then again, I don't think Neha is even allowed to have TikTok so there's that…). *Is that why they think they can watch and control everything I say and do? Is it fair that my parents think they can know who I am friends with and what I post and who I follow? I am old enough to make the right decisions, right?* I mean—I know what is inappropriate when I see it. I know who to follow and who not to follow. I can't believe they are reading everything! I even know they are talking about everybody's business when they go out with their friends. That is so embarrassing!

So this one time when we had family friends over, I heard my parents talking about their friends' son's texts! They were like *Oh this is so cute. Max has a girlfriend and the girlfriend texted him to say she was upset that "they weren't communicating." And then Max texted back "ok."* (I'm not really sure why that is so funny, but my parents sure got a kick out of it.) But that's not even the point! I mean—now, not only are Max's parents reading his texts, but they are talking about them to their friends and now other parents are getting pleasure out of the humor of his texts! That is just wrong! Isn't it a total and absolute invasion of privacy? (If my mom knew I found…I mean read…her old diary…but that's totally different 'cause it is like an old movie from decades ago…right?) (shit.) And when I tried to tell my parents that I thought that wasn't fair or nice to be gossiping like that, they did the whole casual annoying parental

DIATRIBE

Diatribe

Diatribe

(great word)

where they laugh back and act totally carefree and insult me passive-aggressively like, *Sweetie, just because it bothers you SO much really doesn't mean it's bad. Stop overanalyzing and worrying so much. It wasn't even you we were talking about. This really doesn't concern you.* I hate when my parents do that—make light of something that is really important to me. *Well we are sorry you feel that way.* I HATE "sorry you feel that way, but…"!!!! *But we bought that phone, we pay the bills, and we can take it away if it isn't used properly.* (I feel like channeling Cher (pretending I have gorgeous straight blonde hair and young Paul Rudd as my cute brother boyfriend) and screaming "As IF!!!" right back to them.) Like they own me or something?! I would help pay for my phone bill, but I don't even get allowance! And if I watch my little sister

I don't even get paid for that, either! So, basically, I am stuck **STUCK** living here under their roof with all of their rules and I have no say? Now I have to be careful about everything I text or put on any of my accounts because my parents are stalking my private life. I don't want to end up like Max! I don't even have any privacy anymore. That is just so uncool.

It's fine, I'll just change my password and open up another account. (I should. But then they will catch me and then I'll be in so much trouble, I'm not even sure it's worth it.) I know I have nothing to hide, but I kind of would like the option. Lots of people have a Finsta but my parents are way too smart (btw, how dumb are some parents?? If they only KNEW what their daughters posted they would be horrified).

I overheard her tonight on the phone really late. I know she probably thinks I am asleep, but I can't sleep. I'm pretty sure she is on with my uncle. My grandma fell yesterday and she is now in the hospital. My mom and my uncle are taking turns spending the days and evenings in the hospital to give my grandpa a break and making arrangements (about what, I have no idea) for when she gets out of the hospital. It's so unfair! I wanted to make plans this weekend and we need to go shopping and now what? Am I supposed to just wait, like, an unclear amount of time until she gets home late at night so we can discuss it or does my dad have to take me? This sucks! I know it actually sucks for my mom and my uncle, and I guess it also sucks for my grandma that she is stuck in a hospital and needs hip surgery or something. But does she even realize she is hurt? I don't know if my grandma is even aware of this stuff anymore. God I really don't want her to be in pain. My God I'm an awful person that I'm worrying about going to the mall. But I need to go to Sephora before the face mask sells out and I can't get it online.

My reckless guilt (and inability to fall asleep due to online shopping and scrolling) began to simmer and I decided to waste more time and dig out an old memory box from when I was little that has been on my closet shelf for a while (my mom keeps adding "mementos" to it). I found old school projects (oh my I was so adorable—I remember thinking in 1st grade I wanted to be an astronaut during the unit on the solar system) and certificates (lol I won "best actress" at the end-of-the-year 3rd grade parent lunch) and class pictures from elementary school, some old "international" coins from my dad's dad, my grandpa Sean, and old birthday cards. I found one my grandma had written me on my 8th birthday… I suppose in many ways it was just your basic run-of-the-mill grandma-to-granddaughter birthday card, but it felt like much more than that tonight. Like she was telling me the future. And this is going to sound so cliché and dramatic and thank god nobody reads this diary, but it sounded like she was giving me wings. Things like *You have always been a ray of sunlight to me and you're beautiful inside and out… I love your fierce independent spirit, darling* (I love how only grandmothers can say the word darling since they are from the medieval times of castles and Shakespeare)…*My wish for you is that you always remember your love of music and reading…stay playful…and loyal to your friends and family…* and all of the other birthday niceties continue. It seemed a bit deep for 8-year-old me, but tonight, it was exactly what I needed. I closed the box, set my alarm for the ass-crack of dawn, plugged my stupid phone in to charge, and happily crawled under the covers. As I finish this entry I am now remembering that 8th birthday party—I hadn't thought about that in years. Both sets of grandparents came (they never missed a celebration or performance) and, since my birthday is in June, we had all of my friends come to the backyard and we did arts and crafts and had a dance party. I remember during the dance party that my grandma started to dance and even pulled my grandpa Sean (lol) out of his seat to dance the foxtrot or something with us. I was so embarrassed but also loving how crazy and *uninhibited* my sweet, cool grandma used to be. I think that was the year she gave me this silly little diary. Sweet dreams…

Dear Diary

Glinda the good witch

My mom is sleeping in the hospital tonight. She called to say goodnight before. She sounded like she was trying to be strong and together, but I heard her sounding tired. I should probably text her before I fall asleep— as long as it isn't too late 'cause then she will get mad. My dad was cute trying to get dinner ready and ask about our days and stuff.

Everyone knows Glinda. And I don't just mean from the movie or the show. I mean everyone knows "a" Glinda. She is strong. She is powerful. She is pretty. She is athletic. She is friendly. She is confident. She doesn't care. She can even be nice. She has a boyfriend. Always. She is rich. She is sort of smart. The truth is, she is even kind of average, but no one lets themselves think so. She is skinny. She has boobs. She has all the right clothes and never repeats an outfit—ever. She takes risks and doesn't get nervous about it (like I would). She is popular. (It is all about Popular, isn't it?) It really is this amazing thing. It's bigger than Switzerland. She isn't neutral—she makes a statement. I want just a little bit of that. I want to make statements. Anyone can blend. *What would my statement say about me? What do I even want to say?* I guess that's the first step. Glinda made her decision from the very beginning—she will not take a back seat to any girl and she will be the prettiest and she will get the most attention. And so she is and so we watch. *Who even is this Glinda in your grade or in your school, Maggie, that you spend so much time agonizing over?* I know that is exactly what my mom would say to me if she heard my inner monologue right now. If she were here she would tell me to go to sleep but she would get me thinking…

My theories about the different types of popularity continue to evolve. There is the <u>super-cool-untouchable-with-a-crowd-around-her-at-all-</u>

times popular girl. She has, like, 1,000 followers and gets hundreds of likes instantly. People "like" her pics just because they think 1) they'd better! and 2) if they do, they will be one step closer to her. She is the one where all the boys crowd around her at the parties and she just smoothly glides from group to group and there is always a circle to open up and let her in. She is never on the outside. (I mean, think about the reality of that for just one second—never being on the outside. That literally is like the answer to every middle school student's prayers. That is the bane of our existence. That is what we dread every day and what we try to avoid everywhere we go!) She doesn't stick with one crew. She glides "galides" all over the parties, the cafeteria, the fields, the dance floor. She doesn't want to be tied down or labeled with one particular group; that would be like settling down and then people would get to know her too well and get too comfortable with her. She needs to remain sort of like an enigma so she has like a mystery about her so everyone is drawn to her like bugs to a light. She can manipulate any situation to work in her favor. And does she ever?! She is Glinda. Like a queen.

Unlike Glinda, the girl-with-a-crowd-around-her-at-all-times, Switzerland doesn't so much glide and float from table to table in the cafeteria. She stays put and everyone goes to her. At recess, she is the girl who has a circle around her at all times. If she decides to go to a different place, people follow her. But remember, the key is, whenever she is with someone, she agrees with everything they say. This is the art of her manipulation. She doesn't really have her own opinions or individual personality, she doesn't take a stand. She just molds to everyone so she makes everyone around her feel special. She doesn't protect people or criticize or say what she really thinks. You kind of have to watch your back with her, but more so because she is so skilled at tricking you into making you trust her. She doesn't stir the pot or make waves—she waits for others to backstab each other and plays both sides. As much as I want that many friends and stuff, I don't think I could just not care about anything and not have an opinion. Even though she is so nice, it just feels fake.

There aren't that many of these girls in each grade, either. I would say there is usually only room for one of each. That's how they keep the power. They are each so good at what they do! The whole grade is like players in their show and they are running it. The funny thing is—they are not really good friends with each other. It's like they respect each other's role and have a silent agreement that they will not ever interfere with each other's space and friends. Like they virtually tip their hats to each other as they pass in the halls. Do they even deserve all of this attention and confidence? I am sick of always having to worry about the circles and which ones will open up for me and which ones won't. It's exhausting! And by the way—it's boring to always stay in the same circle because nothing ever changes in the circle. We just go around and around.

MOM. Sometimes I just text her in all caps so I know she will respond.

Everything ok?

Ya. Goodnight. Say hi to Grandma for me. I'll bet my grandma Rose was a total Glinda.

Dear Diary

Maybe she's born with it

So last night's entry got me thinking… *Can we become confident? Can someone or something help us to feel more confident? Or are we born with a certain self-image and we just are who we are? Were Miss Neutral Switzerland and Queen Glinda the Untouchable born that cool and comfortable? Wait— maybe they fake it?* (Oh my god I never really thought about that before— maybe they are just the best at faking self-confidence just to be cool? I'll have to come back to that one.) *Maybe the smart people like me are always analyzing and overthinking and worrying because we know too much and think too much about other people's feelings and about who we are, so that's why we aren't so confident? Maybe the confident are too dumb to think much about it at all.* I like my new theory that popular people are stupid! I mean—they spend all their time focused just on being cool, right? And I'm over here debating my role in society. I feel like I just figured out the secret of life! I guess that is what "ignorance is bliss" means. So I was born complicated (I mean, smart ;-)).

Can you imagine what would happen to middle schools all across the country if everyone found out that all the popular people are actually just stupid?? The uproar! Middle schools would be turned upside down! We're talking "Hunger Games" and chaos everywhere! Mayhem! Losers taking over! People laughing at the popular people in the halls! The crowds and circles breaking apart and nerds taking over! Fingers being pointed, "You mean all this time I stuck by you and wanted to be just like you because I thought you were cool, but now I find out you are really just stupid?? I wasted years on you!!" I'm picturing "Mean Girls" and Regina George just being the laughing stock—but not because she got fat, because they found out she was just plain dumb. (I think I'm having way too much fun with this.)

Anyway back to the original question (anything to avoid my math homework right now)… My mom picked me up from school (finally!) today (she probably felt guilty that she wasn't home last night), which I guess was kind of nice of her to make the effort, but I was going to ask Neha on the bus what she thought about Glinda and we didn't have time to really get into it during art today. I think we are born a certain way, for sure, but I have to believe that with the right support and the right teachers and friends and stuff (and the right parents?)—wait—there is no way that my parents actually have an impact on my supporting-character role, or do they? But I think they are just background noise, the grown-ups we are forced to live with until we don't have to anymore…cue "Law and Order" _dun-dun_—what if they are the very people instrumental in shaping us and we aren't born with it after all? Does that mean that we _can_ learn to feel more confident? That we can begin to feel better about ourselves and, perhaps, even reshape where we fit in in school? Change circles. Get bigger circles. Maybe we are all on our own journey to find our best confident self as we try to figure out who we are—but maybe some of these girls just figure it out faster…or are just doing whatever it takes to get there even if they don't like themselves very much. Who knows… _Maybe confidence is a lifelong pursuit?_ **_Honey, even I feel insecure sometimes. Even the moms in town have cliques and layers._** And before she got sick, my grandma used to always talk nonsense about her circles of friends and how she was clawing her way into some of the popular bridge and canasta games at the club. And even how they don't like to include certain "girls" because they don't play Mah Jong as well as the others! Can you believe? So does this mean I'll be dealing with this shit my whole life?? My head is spinning. How am I going to fall asleep with all of these unanswered life-altering questions whirling in my head?

MOM I texted her again, even though she's down the hall.

MOM

She is probably asleep. *(Shut it down Maggie, think happy thoughts and go to sleep!)* Clearly, I have to parent myself right now.

Oh my god. Goodnight.

Dear Diary

Flirt

That whole batting the eyes and tossing the hair and giggling at boys and playing hard to get thing—yeah—I don't know how to do it. I need a "How To Flirt (and not look like a jackass)" handbook. CAN SOMEONE TEACH ME, PLEASE?? Is there any other way to get a boy to notice me? When you are living in the in-between upside down, in order to get noticed by a boy you need to be popular and pretty, and, according to my new theory on popularity, pretty stupid too. I think there is this art to making boys feel good about themselves by acting less smart around them. So because I'm smart and sort of pretty (but not really) (it depends on the day and on my outfit), no one will ever ask me out. The boys probably know I will never be satisfied (just call me Angelica) and will hyper-analyze myself out of any potentially new and fun relationship or activity until I am miserable and alone once again. I think if I had a boyfriend, then maybe I could <u>get</u> a boyfriend? Because if some boys notice that other boys noticed me, then, like, I'll sort of be legit. Like I will actually exist in school, not just blend into the wall. But the thing is, I don't like anyone right now. My mom always asks me, because she said she always had crushes at my age (and she is a freak because she used to tell the guys she liked them), and I don't. I need to like someone. *Can you make yourself like someone just to like someone?* I do think sometimes it is just a decision a girl makes; a commitment—to pick a certain guy and decide he will be the one she likes. I mean, of course there is the more natural like/love, but that probably only happens in the movies. In this situation I am talking about the goal or idea of conquering a crush, not falling in love. I mean, some of the guys are cute, but not really. But what if that someone decides to like you back but you don't actually like them? I know there is a guy who likes me but he isn't cute. How can I like someone back who isn't cute? He also isn't that popular. If Mike was popular but not cute, then maybe. Maybe even cute but not that popular. But neither? I don't think my social status is strong enough to withstand that. My mom got back late last night. It didn't take her long to get the truth out of me and insert her words of wisdom. *Maggie, once you really like someone, they become cuter and cuter to you. You have to open yourself up to it, though. There you go again closing doors before you open them.* I can totally see that Ali and Kaia and Josie and all those girls totally flirt with the boys. They are seen as leaders to the girls, but with the guys they just act sort of "girlie." It's like watching a bunch of professional actresses. Like these girls act one way with each other—strong, bossy, smart, savvy—and then with the boys they become silly, naive, stupid, lame, and, well, flirty. I should really get my flirt game on. I'll talk to Andrew tomorrow. **She won't even say hi to a boy.** (My dad didn't seem too unhappy about that. Maybe he wants me to wait for Prince Charming, too?)

March 8th

Dear Diary

(not a) group text

I didn't talk to Andrew or Mike today. Too weird. And my hair looked awful today 'cause the gel I put in this morning froze on my way to the bus so I was a freaky mess.

If you are in a group of friends and then you find out they all are in a group chat without you, what is that about? It feels like they are all doing it on purpose, deliberately talking about you behind your back. There is always one person who starts the chat and decides who is in it. So who knows how long it has been going on?? But when I found out who started it, I was like, of course she did. She is a bitch anyway so I don't care, but still. When I called my friends out on it they all denied it, but then one by one they all apologized. Juliet is a wannabe and doesn't even know where she fits in. She sort of wants to be in the more popular group, but instead, she is stuck with us. She is on my rec soccer team and acts like she runs the show, but really, we all know she is just a fake. But, incredibly, everyone was still afraid to tell her to end the group chat and include me. People even wrote "um, wait, Maggie isn't on this text" and she was like "yeah, whatever" and no one stopped her! I don't know why she feels like she has this power. *Who gave her the right to pick and choose?* **Who needs her? Start your own group chat—who cares? You don't even like this girl.** I get her point—why do I even care? If I am secure enough in my friendships with the others then it shouldn't matter. It just stings so much to know there is a conversation going on without me. What if I miss something? And why is it such a big deal to add me into the chat? It all just feels so deliberate.

And we aren't even getting into the other group chats, each named something else with a key player missing. Perhaps each had been started to discuss a birthday plan or share dangerous gossip. "Without Maya" has been a hot mess lately, since Hallie wasn't careful the other day and texted something like 'Ali is being so annoying' (which, to be clear, was a careless rookie move on Hallie's part, but she was distracted and her head was not in the game). Of course, Ali never reacted to that comment, but she didn't need to, because everyone must have hurriedly texted Hallie on the side and said "WRONG CHAT" "DELETE your comment about ALI" "You sent that text to ALI"... so she instantly tried to cover her ass and replied to her own text instantly like 'jk Ali'... but we all know the damage was done.

It's mean. I'll start my own group chat and play dumb. I'll even be the bigger person and include that awful useless manipulator. **She should just start her own group chat and move on.** She was particularly frustrated this evening and unloading on the phone to her friend. Too late, Mom, I'm already on it. I can take care of myself!

Dear Diary

Sluts and other inappropriate showoffs

It's so obvious. We all know what they are trying to do. They have boobs—even if they are small, and they squish them together so tight just to show them off. My mom always says *boys don't even know what to do with all that information* which is quite funny, because, really, who are these girls doing it for? Not their friends…they are doing it to get noticed by the boys. Literally, you should see this. First of all, some of them do it in their posts—like they scrunch their arms together to push their boobs together and act like, in the pic, they aren't really trying to do that at all, just casually lying on their beds. Oh my god, are you KIDDING me? And then there are the bikini shots—the "I'll just angle my selfie just so—there—the perfect cleavage shot." Then there are the girls who dress like total sluts to school? WAKE UP, MOMS, CHECK WHAT IS UNDER YOUR DAUGHTER'S SWEATER! I mean, the most revealing, low-cut, inappropriate cut-out tee or tank (or a bra disguised as a top) with everything showing! Really?? And wait—you should see what some of the girls wear to Bar Mitzvahs and other fancy parties. SLUTS! (Quite frankly, I'm not even sure we are allowed to say that word anymore… So it's slut-shaming to call a confident 12-year-old that word, and there is the confusing message that 'a girl should be able to dress in any way she wants and express herself through fashion'…yet it is totally cringy when they do and they look like 26-year-old try-hards in a 10-year-old's dress… I'm so confused.) The highest platform shoes ever and the shortest dresses ever!! (I hate quoting my mom on this, but it does secretly make me laugh… She said to a car full of us last week when she dropped us off at a party **Their vaginas are hanging out.** My dad won't even drive me there anymore because he is so uncomfortable.

I do love their shoes and their dresses ARE cute, don't get me wrong, but they really look so inappropriate—so desperate for attention. But, here is the kicker, of course, they get ALL the attention they want! And me, over here in my flannel and jeans…me over there in the corner, in my boring circle of friends, in my semi-cute 3" platform wedge sandals and skater skirt dress… I'M RIGHT HERE CAN YOU NOTICE ME??? So, basically, if I dress conservatively (i.e., boring) just to fit in, then *does fitting in mean blending in*? Oh my—I think I need a vagina dress. I actually don't think I stand a chance without one. I can try to convince my mom to get me one of those dresses—or, better yet—since I know she will say no, I can trade with someone and get dressed at their house! Who am I kidding? #1 I would never be able to break the rule and, even if I were brave enough to do it, I would get caught. #2 It would be so obvious that I am trying so hard to look different and everyone would make fun of me! Then I'd be the ultimate try-hard. Alas, the status quo remains.

Dear Diary

Secret Self

I may not be allowed to wear the slutty *(freedom of self-expression through bandeau corset tops disguised as a dress, excuse me)* dresses (and I don't think I want to?), but I know I'm pretty bored of doing and wearing the same conservative things every day. I think it's time I take some chances. I did feel my peak self when I wore the skirt the other day and straightened my hair—does that count? Maybe I start with funky shoes? Rebellious makeup? Wacky hairstyles? Coloring my hair or my nails? I would shock the middle school crowd if I suddenly broke the mold. <u>Nobody</u> breaks the middle school mold. Molds might bend or break in high school, but not at 12 years old. What's even funnier than imagining the reactions of others is the fact that I'm going through all of these game-changing options in my head as if my parents would even let me out of the house dressed like a rebel. I should probably just start subtle and wear mismatched socks—ease my way in. But my social life is just so lame, I want to SCREAM!!! Even my parents let me go to the mall without a chaperone, and yes, Ali's mom and Mandy and Georgia's moms do, too, but Neha's mom said she only will allow her ('cause the world is so scary dangerous and there are literally predators lurking on every corner) if she follows us (discreetly, lol) 20 steps behind…so…no thanks. I mean—there are guys and girls who hang out with each other every weekend as a group (I'm sure there is hooking up going on), but all my friends and I do is have sleepovers and go to Starbucks. I think I am letting my youth slip away without being social enough!

I am going to start hanging out with edgier people—I will seek out those under-the-radar mold benders. I feel like I can morph myself a little bit—I just have to be cautious or it is social suicide. I'm not going crazy, don't worry. Even if I were brave enough, the real outcasts and rebels wouldn't accept me as one of their own even if I tried. I'm way too nerdy and rule-abiding and mainstream for them. After all, what happened at "The Breakfast Club" stayed at "The Breakfast Club" and didn't dare flow into the daily happenings in the cafeteria. But there are layers here—I'm just looking for the next layer of cool—a step further away from the circles around the popular crowd. The layer just far enough away that they aren't clawing their way in, but close enough that they are still accepted as normal. Alternative-ish.

Will they see right through me? Will they laugh at my attempt at rebellion and mold-breaking? Can a girl be true to herself if she still keeps a part of her life secret or private? Is that being fake or dishonest? Or is it ok to try to have more of an "outside" self and an "inside" self? Maybe it is all just another part of me—the way I dress and the way I act—it's still just me. Deep down inside I am still just overanalytical Maggie. I want to believe that as long as I stay the same on the inside, I can experiment a little bit on the outside. I guess the next question is… Where do I start? How do you change yourself? Maybe it isn't my "self" that needs to change, but the choices I make. Maybe if I do things a bit differently, I will actually be more true to myself than I have been all these years? I can play the game a little better—be a little more "political." Work the crowd a bit. First step is to stop overthinking. *Maggie, stop watching the mind-sucking Kardashians and be original. These brainless celebrities are all air-brushed cartoon versions of themselves and are destroying the self-confidence of girls and women everywhere. We have to embrace our flaws and be ourselves!* I don't know that wanting to change the color of my eyeliner means I'm ready to embrace all of my flaws, exactly, and what does she mean anyway—which of my (million) flaws is she referring to? Suddenly I feel more flawed than before! Or maybe she can relate to this dilemma (as every woman probably can) and in that aspect, maybe my mom will support my new sock fashion or eyeliner.

She always tells me to be true to myself, so maybe she does want me to take some more chances with fashion!

I think my first step should probably be studying my Torah portion because I think I might actually fail my Bat Mitzvah. Hebrew School is so annoying and I still need to find a dress.

Maggie has been talking a lot lately about taking chances. I'm nervous. What if she does something dangerous? Or what if she wears black lipstick or cuts her hair? I don't know what she sees on TikTok and I can't control it and monitor it or she will hate me, but it is so scary! How will I support her and be a good mom even if I think she looks ridiculous? I was about to cry myself to sleep—feeling so betrayed by my mother's never-ending mixed messages of support and criticism—when I heard my dad chime in for once. Honey, Maggie needs to figure some things out on her own. Sometimes that means taking chances. She won't do anything dangerous and that's all we need to concern ourselves with. What she does with her hair or clothes or makeup or whatever you are so concerned about—that isn't permanent. Remember that talk at the middle school we went to when she was in 6th grade? These kids need a little freedom sometimes. Let her just BE!

I'm not sure why he thinks I won't do anything dangerous—maybe I just WILL!! But, for now, I will sleep knowing my dad is on my side, and deep down, I know my mom cares, even if she might care about my hair just as much. I guess it comes from a good place. Let's see if she can let me BE and keep her mouth shut! Let the games begin…

Dear Diary

Prince Not-So-Charming

I know it's so cliche, but you know how I always said I wanted a boyfriend, for, like, ever? Well—Matt told Kaia that he likes me, and Kaia (!!) randomly texted me and was like "hey, Maggie" (I literally don't even know how she got my number) "…if Matt asked you out would you go out with him?" I totally screamed into my pillow—you might have even heard me ;) but I didn't know if I was more freaked out that Kaia texted me (like now one of the more popular girls in school) or that someone actually liked me?? (It's as if Matt sensed my new outlook on life and he must have picked up on my newfound vibes of change-making.) So, obviously I texted her back and was like "um, yeah." (I mean what does she think I am, crazy???) And she was like "ok, cool." And then like a half a second later Matt texted me and was like "hey, do you wanna go out with me?" And, even though I was shaking and freaking out, I was like "um, sure." And he was like "ok, cool."

Um—and then I cried. Like a total loser. I freaked out and couldn't handle it. This is all I ever wanted, and I couldn't even handle it! Why?? *Why is it that when you hope and dream and wish for something that sometimes the hoping and the dreaming and the wishing are more fun than the actual reality of it happening?* It's like the reality is sort of a letdown. Could the reality ever live up to the dreams in my head? The vampire kisses and the magical moments? The simple dreams of middle school love? Hooking up in the basement or at the beach? Will there be a crescendo of music in the background when we finally make out? The dim lights and starry nights of my dreams? Maybe I didn't really want this in the first place. Oh shoot…he just texted me again!!! He actually asked me if I want to go to the movies this weekend!!!!! OH MY GOD!!

um. sure, I texted.

MOOOOMMMMMMMMMMMM!!!!!!!!!!! Holy crap I'm actually terrified. What have I done? She actually ran upstairs she thought I was dying. *MAGGIE MY GOD what is wrong with you??! You are screaming like you are bleeding to death you scared the CRAP out of me!* I couldn't tell if she was actually happy for me or just relieved I wasn't dead when she finally calmed down after I told her. She smiled and even chuckled a bit. *Wow! The movies, huh? What a nice idea! How do you know this boy?* She might have even been a little passive aggressive. Unfortunately for me, she wasn't too up for giving me advice on this one—or at least right now. It is, after all, 10:45 p.m. right now, so she wasn't too thrilled with my boyfriend emergency and the whole waking up of the younger sister and scaring of the parents. She just kissed me goodnight and told me we would talk about it in the morning. IN THE MORNING???? How am I supposed to sleep now? My WHOLE life just changed, and she doesn't even CARE!! One day I decide to wear some blue eyeliner and that night I get a BOYFRIEND? It is all happening so fast!

She got asked out. That is what she is freaking out about. I'm too exhausted to deal with this right now. So inconsiderate of her to scream like that and wake the whole house. Harry, where is my Tylenol PM? Honey, she is excited. She just wanted her mom and wanted to share this moment with you. Maybe you are being a little harsh because you are just tired? I didn't realize I had done that—now I feel badly. I mean, I didn't say that to her, just to you, but maybe she overheard me (I do think she can hear us, Harry).

I CAN HEAR YOUUUUUUU! I decided to scream from my bed.

And I accept your apology, I mumbled to myself under my breath.

Sorry, Mags. I really do want to hear more about this boy. I'm tired and I took it out on you. Sorry.

I had to document that for posterity.

Dear Diary

The breakup

I know what you're thinking… "Well, that lasted long." Don't judge me, Diary. You are my only judgment-free zone. I couldn't go through with it. I wasn't ready. I don't like Matt. Should I just go out with him just to go out with someone? Or should I wait until I really like someone (which could be forever)? *What if my first kiss is with someone I don't really like—won't I regret it? Isn't a first kiss supposed to be pretty magical? Or, at least, memorable?* I don't want to kiss him and be grossed out and never want to kiss again. I take this stuff seriously! This really isn't working with my whole "I'm ready for a change" attitude. I think I take things too seriously. It's what separates me from the sluts (sorry—*young middle-schoolers who are unashamed about their feigned self-confidence and ability to flirt freely and kick ass in a tight super-short 'dress'*). I care too much. Can the new me be cool enough to break up with someone before we actually even go out? I feel like I don't have extra energy to take on a relationship right now. I have to focus on moving slowly to the outer layers of cool. I wore a cool jean jacket today and boots instead of sneakers. It felt good. *Well, look at you, all cute and dressed for school! Someone trying to impress her new boy?* She obviously doesn't understand my new plan for social action and a new fashion identity. And I saw this outfit on a TikTok. Ironically, maybe this whole Matt thing did come at the right time, just when I needed a little boost of validity and confidence. Just being noticed helped! Maybe he noticed me BECAUSE OF (!) my recent obvious new "I am trying to give a little less of a crap" attitude and that's why he asked me out?

I just texted him and said something like "I'm so sorry, I am so busy this weekend." And he was like "ok." So I guess we broke up. Today in social studies we didn't even speak. We never really spoke to each other before yesterday anyway, but still, it felt so awkward and everyone was watching. Should I regret my decision? Is there any turning back after a breakup? Can you learn to like someone after you already decided that you don't like them??

I'm so tired. I actually exhaust myself. It was actually more relaxing to listen to my mom talk about me on the phone than to think about myself. **Mom, did Mags tell you about her new boyfriend? She was so cute and was freaking out, but she got all gussied up for him today at school.** I am beginning to appreciate the way my mom tries to keep my grandma in the loop of our daily lives, even though I know my grandma doesn't even realize it. I should really call my grandma. Maybe tomorrow. I'm way too tired now.

I need a vacation. Hopefully everyone will forget this ever happened. Including me. My mom better not judge me for ending my relationship. ~~I know my grandma won't care because she won't even remember tomorrow.~~ I shouldn't have said that.

What should I wear Monday?

Dear Diary

Shopping heals all wounds

Monday morning…

My mom knew I needed a distraction after my traumatic week. New boots should do the trick. I've actually been dying for a new pair of boots. I literally only have two pairs and they are SO old and beaten up. There is this new kind of boot that is so cool—but they are sort of dark and "goth" and have a platform so it took me a while to get up the courage to buy them. But I'm finally ready. It's the new me, remember? These boots are the first step! I got them and I'm OBSESSED! Felt like a rock star all weekend. Wore them till my feet were bruised and blistered and sore—but I felt awesome! Casually checked myself out in the mirror at home and in store windows a few times and felt like a million bucks. She even had me Facetime my grandma and show her (she said something like *it will be good for Grandma to see you smile, Maggie*). My uncle is with her this weekend, so he helped with the Facetime (my grandpa doesn't know how to use "these devices," as he calls them). She looked… old. It made me feel sad and uncomfortable. Like after her fall and when she was in the hospital, she just, I don't know, changed a little. She said, *"Oh Maggie, you look so grown-up and beautiful. I can see you are really changing—it's in your smile! It's like there is a confidence (I always knew you had such confidence). I love your new boots, but are they comfortable? Are you having fun at the mall with Mom? I'm sorry I haven't been able to visit you lately, I was in the hospital but I will see you soon."* "I'll see you at Passover, Grandma," I said. *"I look forward to it very much, Maggie."* And then she drifted off a bit and started to talk to my uncle Robby and then I handed the phone back to Mom. Do you think, for just that moment, she really did see the change in me? She always calls it like she sees it, so maybe she did? Diary, when I looked over at my mom, she was smiling, but I saw there were tears in her eyes, but she didn't admit it. *Grandma is having a good day* she said to me, but I felt like I knew the truth.

Other than that depressing Facetime, I felt amazing…until this morning. Today is Monday. It is 6:45 a.m. The reality of the new chance-taking me suddenly seems too bold for my own good and I am starting to doubt my new goth boots because everyone will think I went freaky and dark. I have ZERO time for journaling at this moment, but I'm totally freaking out and needed to vent. I changed my outfit, like, seven times, just to water down the image a bit. I know—if I show people in school that I am nervous to take fashion chances, then they will sense it like a pack of wolves and they will destroy me. If only I can go into school acting like "Hey. What's up? What? Oh *these* boots? I dunno just thought they were cool" and act casually, like they are no big deal, then the middle school vultures will believe that I am confident enough to wear them and they will be intimidated and surprised by my confidence and risk-taking behavior, and they will retreat. My god, it sounds like the Discovery Channel or Animal Planet. Sometimes I wish I weren't so scared of my own shadow. It is definitely easier for the dumb. The dumb and the shallow. *Maggie, hurry up and come downstairs!* Business as usual. If she knew I was busy writing in my diary it would send her catapulting over the edge.

Is this what it all comes down to? All we "tweens" really are is a pack of animals? A herd of hunters and prey? The cafeteria is our jungle? Only the strong survive? It reminds me of the hyenas in "The Lion King"—those are the girls that surround the King (uh—Queen) of the jungle. And they just giggle at everything she says and does and follow her like a herd. I will face those hyenas today and head out into the tumultuous jungle with my almighty jungle goth boots. Perhaps I will start a new pack of hyenas and they will gather around me in my new chunky, strength-instilling, fierce, ahead-of-the-trend boots and I shall lead them down the path of fashion trend-setting and confidence building—against all odds. Hear me roar!! (I'm so late for the bus—gotta go!) I'll just throw a pair of sneakers into my backpack as a backup just in case. I'm sure my mom will have a mouthful for her friends at the office today—all about how frustrating I am and how afraid I am and about my pathetic love life and weak ego, and, of course, how I'm always late for the bus and I drive her crazy. At this moment, I'm glad to give all those ladies a little distraction. You're welcome, magazine-office ladies.

Dear Diary

Those hallway looks

I got stares. All day. Like—who gave Maggie the right to wear *those* boots? Those are only for the fashion forward, or those who live in the city, or those goth girls. Who does she think she is, Wednesday Addams? Boots like those are only for girls either so confident they don't care, or so unhappy that they want to go against everything trendy and hide in their darkness and pretend they want to be there. Boots like those are NOT meant for Maggie "she-who-blends-in-with-the-crowd." In art, thank god, everyone was so distracted by Rory, and Neha whispered to me "You see, Maggie, nobody cares" and I couldn't help but smile as I remembered that message loud and clear. Can you imagine if I didn't throw in "a hint of color"?? Thank god I had on my pink scarf to counteract the vicious (non-verbal) attacks. I know what you are thinking… How do I know they were hating me? Have you ever seen a toddler girl in a stroller look another toddler girl up and down as she passes in another stroller? I know it sounds insane, but we are wired this way from the start! Toddlers, girls, tweens, teens, and even (shocker!) our mothers and grandmothers! We all give the look. Is that so sad? *Does this mean women never evolve or grow up? Does this mean we will be stuck in middle school forever?* The middle school hallway is just like the office or Foodtown or the gym or the hair and nail salon? Women/girls everywhere sizing each other up in an instant? We are skilled! We can draw 100 conclusions about a female within one second of seeing her—we don't even have to meet! I dare you to try us! *Is this a survival skill or a terrible curse of **girlhood**?*

It is awfully uncomfortable when someone else is doing the looking and I am the one on the receiving end (wearing incredibly ugly, but once thought to be super cool, new boots). I hate to think I have subconsciously and instinctively given these same looks to other girls. Maybe I'm not as ready as I thought I was. I don't think I will be changing females of future generations, but I don't have to like it, right? I mean, I have spent a lot of time with my own mom and aunts and grandmas and great grandma—I'm pretty sure this shit is in our blood. Part of our genetics. It's in our code. On the X chromosome. We are girls, we give looks. We make decisions and judgments about others based upon what we see. Then we share those opinions, of course, by whispering it to our friends, or we just text them to others, and just like that, we are labeled and it is viral. I walked around in blistered feet all day to prove a point—but to whom? To myself or to others? I proved to myself that it was scary and very uncomfortable to take a fashion and image risk like that. Will I be brave enough to wear them again? Maybe each time I will slowly be carving out a new image for myself and the looks will just move on to the next girl. Or maybe if I never wear them again, all I am doing is letting the hyenas win. *I think these boots are too small on you, Mags.* She saw my blisters—but that wasn't the point. She is either embarrassed for me, knowing these boots are ugly and I am going to get teased and she wanted to protect me, or, maybe worse, she is embarrassed herself by me and she just wants me to dress like a normal person and blend in because my middle school years are hard enough on her.

(Clearly I need new boots.) I'm destined for failed relationships—with shoes and with people.

I need to see if I can return those boots. I tried to be supportive and let her buy what she wanted, but I knew she would regret it. Maybe I'll wear them again tomorrow.

Dear Diary

On the right side of the crowd

I can't believe how quickly I lose sight of my new goal in life. I guess I just get distracted. Like, today, in school, for once it felt like everyone was on my side, or at least that I was on their side—because we all are so annoyed with Maya. She is SO annoying and is driving all of us crazy. I mean—the thing is she is SO nice, but she hasn't changed at all since elementary school. We are all dressing more grown-up, taking subtle fashion chances, we like to shop in town or at the mall, go to Starbucks, have our own Instagram accounts and straighten our hair, and Maya just still doesn't really get it. She is going to get left behind if she doesn't keep up with the changes. She still acts so immature and silly and we have all totally moved on from that. We are more independent now, we are allowed to make plans on our own after school and just text our moms. She isn't interested in meeting new friends from the other schools and is so hurt that some of our old friends have met new friends. Selfishly, I am sort of loving the fact that everyone is sick of her because it makes my position in the group a little more secure, you know? *That's quite a callous move on your part, Mags. You and Maya have been friends since you were little girls—and you now don't feel any sense of loyalty towards her?* I hate when my mom points out flaws in my character—it makes me feel even more guilty than I am allowing myself to feel right now. Just a few weeks ago she told me to embrace my flaws, and now I should stop being flawed? I'm confused. The truth is, I do feel badly that we are all talking behind her back (sometimes we have a group chat about it, but she isn't on it, so she doesn't know) and that we are collectively making decisions about Maya's place in our group. Maybe I am not being true to myself by just joining the masses on this, but *isn't there some value in self-preservation? Don't I have a right to choose to hang out with friends I actually enjoy? Or do one's past friendships always have to be honored just because we were young together? Is the moral thing always right, even if social advancement is also important for survival?* Hang on, Diary, wow, I need to let the gravity (I FEEL LIKE THERE IS AN ALIEN SPACESHIP HOVERING OVER MY HEAD) of that thought sink in.

I can't figure out why I care so much about still having all of my old friends on my side, even though I want to break free from them a bit and also enjoy my new friend group at Neha's table. I think it is all subconsciously part of my bigger plan to have everyone like me so when I truly become my real self and branch out with my style, my new boyfriend, and my new circle-around-me friend group, no one will hate me. *Maybe part of my survival and sanity, no matter how hard I try to shake it, is always remaining on everyone's good side? OMG am I turning into Switzerland?* She will figure it out. She may hurt some people along the way, and she will get hurt herself, that's for sure, but this is middle school. We all survived it and so will she. There definitely is an alien spaceship. So this is just what growing up is? Figuring it out?? My mom just sounded so…callous. Like mother like daughter, I guess. So it is all her fault ;-) Like, not callous about me, in fact that was strangely empowering and cool, tbh, but callous like she casually admits this is just a part of life and figuring it all out…(just felt like I had to clarify, I have no idea why).

Dear Diary

You don't know how much you love someone until it's their birthday

(and even sometimes how much they might love you until it's yours)

It's Maya's birthday. I feel bad now, 'cause we have had so many great times together. Obviously I had to post a huge shout-out to her on her birthday with all our private jokes and quotes about us and hashtags about our friendship. It's funny how, when you think about it, even though I have only known her for, like, six years, we have made so many funny memories together and had a lot of laughs (like that time in Mrs. Dobler's class in 4th grade when Tyler farted and everyone heard and she laughed so hard and spit out her juice all over Andrew). (To us, it's just Juice Day, so no one really knows.) It sort of bums me out when other people write long posts and they aren't really even good friends, though. So many people post shout-outs and they haven't even known Maya for as long as I have. Our families have vacationed together, too! But that was way back in the day when we used to take actual vacations. Now we just drive places or "stay local" (my parents love to say that, as if it is purely by choice). At the very least we used to go to Florida to stay with my grandparents, but now that they are back up here, we don't even do that anymore. I shouldn't really complain, I mean since my grandma has gotten worse we really can't leave her, but for real, it does suck a little. Sometimes it's like a contest who can post more stuff. And the pics—I have so many cute pics of the two of us together from so many years in school together. What's the point of posting pics from just this year? Now I feel bad that I was so annoyed with her the other day. *Is it ok to be so annoyed with a friend one day, but to remember how much you really like them underneath it all when you finally think about all the time you have spent together?* Is it weird to think about all my elementary school memories as being shaped by and with Maya—but to be annoyed with her for not changing and growing up? Maybe she is the smart one and we are all just fooling ourselves? Maybe Maya has it all figured out and she knows exactly who she is, and we are all just frantically bumbling around trying to change and fit in and set fashion trends and meet boys and hook up and find the best cafeteria table and straighten our hair, and there is Maya, just happily with her same five friends from elementary school, confidently and comfortably seated at the same table, oblivious to all the changes and drama around her. *Is she missing out or is she the smartest girl in the room?* **The thing is, we can't just give up on a long friendship before giving it some real thought. There is value in each of you changing and evolving at different paces—but is that reason to throw everything you have shared away? Remember, not every friendship is perfect.** She says that all the time, but when you are a teenager it just feels like if it isn't perfect then it takes too much energy and I am using all my energy just to get out of bed every day and just function! I don't have time for all this extra effort! I feel like every time my mom gives me advice lately, she is barely looking up from her own phone and texts, and she is so distracted by my grandma I don't even know if I should trust her judgment! And when she does look up, she is just rolling her eyes, so obviously bored or exhausted by my daily sagas. I'll just leave her out of it. **Sometimes I think I am just talking at her and she doesn't even listen to a word. I should just stop and see how she functions without me.** To top it all off, after that nasty comment (that was so unnecessary, by the way), she told my dad, **Harry, I have a missed call from my brother—that isn't a good sign. I'm afraid to call him back.** And then all I could hear was soft mumbling and my heart started to pound a little faster. What if something really bad happened? I had to stop my mind from racing and focus on the task at hand… Maya's birthday. Focus, Maggie, FOCUS!!

It made me wonder (since I was already distracted by overhearing my mom about Uncle Robby's missed call) if my mom still keeps a diary of some kind. Or did she just stop after the one I found from when she was in high school? Maybe, somewhere, there are 10 more volumes… maybe in her nightstand drawer, underneath stacks of papers, there lies her "adult diary" (would it even be called a diary at her age?). And, if so, would she write in it how sad or conflicted she is (or must be, I assume) about my grandma? This whole thing is just so confusing. To be mad at your mom and also need your mom and also be sad about your mom suffering.

Happy birthday, Maya! My mom hates me so who cares.

Dear Diary

The invite got lost in the mail

This morning I only saw my mom for a few minutes. She was all business-as-usual as she tried to get us out the door and get herself ready to go to work, and she hurriedly (and randomly, casually) said my grandma had a rough night, or something, and that Uncle Robby was going to bring her for some tests. Then she kissed me on the cheek (a big smooch, I might add) and I wiped it off with an EWWWW MOM and raced out the door for the stupid bus.

So, here I go again feeling sorry for myself and angry at myself for being so stupid. Just when I feel good about something or confident with my friends, someone goes and has a sleepover and decorates a locker and I look like the fool. The answer is always "We didn't do it on purpose, you just weren't there when we made the plans." But it always feels so "on purpose" and it is so in my face. Everyone loves to get their locker decorated for their birthday and the same is true for decorating a friend's locker—we all love to do it for someone else. But even for locker decorating (omg this sounds so pathetic when you actually think about it), there is like a hierarchy of who is in charge, who invites everyone to help out, and who decides what will go on the locker, and how early to get to school in the morning to do it. And then there is me—not getting the memo at all that "we" were decorating Maya's locker this morning before school. It is so annoying. Just when I thought we were friends again and I was feeling good about Maya again. But, truthfully, it isn't Maya's fault. She didn't plan the locker part, at least. I can easily blame Ali for that. And Hallie said she had my back and told Ali to include me. It certainly comes as no surprise. She is out to get me or something. And they were supposed to be the ones who didn't like Maya anymore in the first place! So my day started out so shitty when I got to school and Maya was so happy about her locker and I felt like a big fat loser. Until lunch. Just when you thought things couldn't get any worse. It turns out Maya is having a sleepover this weekend for her birthday, and I wasn't invited. They were all talking about it. So I bravely pronounced—"Wait, what sleepover?", 'cause, really, how rude could they actually be to talk about it in front of me—even middle schoolers aren't that stupid (we are much more manipulative than that). So that's when Maya's like "You were invited, Maggie. Didn't your mom get the email?" So, Diary, I texted my mom right away and she was like "no. sorry." (you KNOW what she really wanted to say was *Well, sweetheart* (in that condescending tone) *maybe Maya didn't think you guys were friends anymore.* So was I really invited and the email got lost (can emails get lost even???)? Or was I invited and her mom forgot to email my mom? Or, did she really just not invite me and now she is lying to pretend she did? *Is an invite an invite no matter how it comes?* And I thought everyone was hating on Maya just a few short days ago. I guess I'll never know the truth—but who cares. She is so boring anyway. Oh, don't get me wrong… I'm GOING to that sleepover! If I am not there, that is like open season for them to talk about me behind my back. A girl's got to protect herself. And it all starts with being there—whether I was invited or not and whether I want to go or not. And whether she wants me there or not ;) It is self-preservation. Survival. Elle Woods dancing in that stupid bunny suit and refusing to back down to humiliation!

My invitations for my Bat Mitzvah are going out soon, so nobody better mess with me! *I just hope she doesn't stick her neck out where it doesn't belong,* she whispered to her friend Jenny on the phone tonight. I am such an embarrassment to my own mother. I looked at Bear lying sideways on my pillow, all hunched over and exhausted, as if to say to him, "You and me both" since Jenny was the one who got him for me when I was a baby. He would probably be ashamed to represent one who supports such negative Maggie energy.

Dear Diary

We are how others define us

The sleepover this weekend was fine. I had an ok time. Glad I went 'cause I didn't miss out or worry about private jokes or Instagram posts or pics that I wouldn't have been there for. The only thing worse than not being invited is having everyone else know you weren't invited because you aren't tagged in any pictures. Even though we all know I wasn't really invited. I think it was just easier for Maya and me to just pretend to make it less painful and less awkward. I actually was kind of bored and silently was uncomfortable at night and was texting Neha and wanted so badly to go home, but I was way too embarrassed to tell anyone, so I tossed and turned all night feeling like the sun was never going to rise. I kept thinking I heard noises in her playroom, too (even though I've been there a thousand times) and everyone else was snoring, sound asleep next to me, sprawled out on the couches and air mattresses and blankets. I went purely for self-preservation, really, so I couldn't dare leave before it was over. And, on top of that, how could I call my mother, who would chastise me for ruining Maya's special day and for being selfish and immature, etc.? I didn't want to hear it from her. She usually offers me a way out, an escape clause, for every sleepover, but this time she did not, so it was my job to act like I didn't need it (or her!).

Anyway—I really wanted to write about what happened in school today. It got me thinking, *if someone describes us or categorizes us TO our faces (totally different than what others say behind our backs), do we have the confidence to challenge or dispute it at just 12 years old, or do we automatically believe their opinions to be true? And I mean it can be in a good way or a bad way. Is our self-image that fragile and our self-confidence that delicate?* Clearly, through my 12th year of life I have been doing some valuable research on confidence—some of us are born with more than others, and some of us spend our lives in search of more validation and confidence. Some people have more confidence because, well, they are simply better looking than the rest of us, others gain it because they are really good at something, and others become more confident because of the positive vibes they get from others (maybe because of their incredible personality :-)). But I think for most people, it changes minute to minute and day by day. One thing I know for sure is that each positive experience we have builds us up, and the more negative things we believe about ourselves, the more our starting confidence gets chipped away. *It makes me wonder where I will actually end up—or, more specifically, will my "confidence," like my growing body, just eventually level off and stop changing?*

Self-image, I think, is how we define ourselves, and what holes and categories we fit into (like, I'm an athlete, I'm a nerd, I'm a singer, I'm a writer, I'm an artist, I'm a dancer, and so on). *Maggie, you are such a bad listener. I said go to BED!* (a bad listener, a failure…) The point of all this rambling is that I did this project in 2nd period art today and I actually nailed it. Like it was really, truly good. And I thought I sucked at art. But I did this portrait thing and it was really amazing. I was SO proud of myself and I really surprised myself! I like to draw and doodle all day in class (and, clearly, in my diary) but, believe me, nothing is ever good. THIS was good! My art teacher not only complimented me, but she held it up in front of the class. It was like whatever good stuff she was selling about me, I bought it! I could feel my little inner ball of confidence growing inside my brain. I sat up straighter in class at the art table. Maybe I should be an artist when I grow up, I contemplated. So I was feeling pretty awesome about myself for the whole day. Like I felt like I smiled differently, walked down the halls a bit differently. And the point of my story is that later on, in science, suddenly I'm talking to these popular boys and they are TALKING TO ME! Not only did they notice me, but I was comfortable talking to them and they actually responded!!

I think, and don't quote me on this, I think I actually flirted!!! And I guess it worked! Could my sudden burst of artistic talent have given me enough confidence that my behavior in front of boys even changed? (I mean, for the day at least?) Will I be able to keep this up? Will I be able to spread my newfound confidence outside of the art room and into tomorrow? If the next art assignment is something I suck at, will it all go away? Like a dream? (I wonder how much artists make for a living? I could get a loft in LA and live by the beach… I digress.) I wonder if the boys in science think I'm pretty. I'm going back to my cool boots tomorrow! Artists wear cool boots.

I'm going to frame that portrait. Wait—even my MOM thought it was good?? How come she didn't tell me? The land of the Upside Down continues…

Dear Diary

What goes around comes around

The weirdest thing has been happening for the past few days… Josie has been, like, talking to me. Sort of friendly. This is the same girl who said my Bat Mitzvah wasn't *really* a Bat Mitzvah (because all of the popular people wouldn't be there). And suddenly she compliments me on my sweater, she asks me for help in class, she even smiles at me in the halls. Was it my boots??? Like suddenly I'm a person to her. I exist. (Do you think she heard about my art project? LOL.) I really don't know what to make of it, but some people say she is jealous of me and my confidence and that she thinks I'm pretty. That would be so awesome, but I'm not sold. Why would she be jealous of *me*? She is the popular one and I'm so middle class. *Maybe she has been dethroned and, on her way down, she wants to take me with her?!* Is she really, deep down, just as insecure as the rest of us? I don't think she wants to be my friend or anything—don't get me wrong. But I'm not gonna lie, I am enjoying it. Is it pathetic that it is sort of a confidence boost? Hearing myself actually say that only confirms that it is. I am giving her so much power that she can actually have an impact on my fragile self-confidence just by saying "Hey, I like your sweater." And only a few weeks after she so deeply insulted me. I should get her back for the awful thing she said about my Bat Mitzvah—actually meaning that I am not even a legit person if my party doesn't even "count" amongst the guest lists of the mainstream Bat Mitzvahs. And now, here I am, psyched that she is acknowledging me, after I wanted to punch her in the face before. I need to have more of a backbone. But I just can't help it—this attention from her, and yesterday from the boys, it really makes me feel more confident. I guess it is just being noticed by some more people other than my teachers and my six boring friends. It is nice being a girl and getting attention for girlie things, like how we look and how we dress (god! another totally pathetic admission! I sound so shallow and boring. I sound like a popular girl!!!!!). Honestly, I really don't care about Josie and she is a bitch, but if she is gonna lay some positive vibes on me, who am I to pass them up? That's my game and I'm ok with it. I will not sell out and become her friend because she was mean and so rude. I'm gonna wake up early and straighten my hair tomorrow—it might actually be worth it for once. *Maggie, have you called Grandma lately? It would really mean a lot to her, and actually to me. God knows you are on that phone enough that you definitely have the time. She is stuck in that horrible rehab place and now she has a cold and they had to switch her room and she is so lonely. Would you? I think you should.* I was totally expecting her to yell at me for being awake, but she came upstairs sort of dazed. I will, tomorrow, I told her (omg Diary, remind me to call her I am the WORST!). She's been stuck in that gross rehab place for a few weeks now. I don't even think she knows she won't be out before Passover; it really sucks. I guess my mom keeps rambling about needing to get her 24-hour care when she goes back home. I don't know. How did this even happen? What if this is something genetic and my mom is next? And then Charlotte and me? I know falling isn't genetic, but I do keep hearing the word dementia all over the house, and I don't know if that is Alzheimer's or what either of them really mean, but I probably should call my grandma, whatever she has.

Please, honey, make sure she calls her tomorrow when you get home from work. (That's a lot of pressure for my dad, which is probably why I heard him just agreeing to help and encouraging my mom to calm down—she probably loved that.) *I will be with my mother all day and I don't want to call Maggie and pretend she called my mother—even though I know my mom won't know. I can't bear to hear Maggie's excuses when she forgets. She is just so wrapped up in herself.* (I wanted to SCREAM I AM TWELVE GIMME A BREAK!) *Just leave me out of it,* she said. I'll be damned if I let her win this one. I will call her as soon as I get home. I'm big enough to remember, I just hate when they nag me.

Dear Diary

I'm a Barbie girl

I was thinking about what I wrote last night (not about my grandma). I continued to feel a bit like a rock star all day—which is good and surprising considering that after I wrote in my diary last night I had a nice, spontaneous, total family-disrupting and house-turning-upside-down pre-teenage meltdown. I'm not sure why. Maybe I should have been doing my homework instead of writing in my diary or getting my hot iron ready for tomorrow? (That's a start.) We just got bombarded with work this week and I freaked out last night. Parents screaming at me, little sister crying, me slamming doors, Mom saying *Well maybe if you just spent less time on TikTok…* blah blah blah. You know how it is. Classic. It shouldn't be my fault that my parents are so stressed out and they just take it all out on me!!!

Anyway, I feel like for many (most) girls, we do spend a lot of time trying to look and dress a certain way, and we scrutinize ourselves in front of the mirror each morning before school—and then change our outfit and hair three times because the first and second ones just didn't work. *Is it really wrong that we do this because our image is important to us? Does that make us shallow?* I know there are girls that don't care about how they look—I just haven't met any. Even the girls who **pretend** they don't care by rebelling against girlhood and dressing against the norms—<u>even they are doing it to make a statement</u> about themselves and to get attention and to create an image. Don't be fooled by their "I refuse to conform to the social pressures of fashion trends"…believe me, I am onto them. They have their own fashion trend playbook and it is simply a different issue of the magazine.

I mean now we are all experimenting with fashion and makeup (I'm really good at it, btw), and straightening our hair, and curling our hair, and doing our nails. Do we have to feel guilty about that? I keep seeing these new stupid-looking Barbie dolls with bodies and faces that look more "real" and "natural" but I don't really think girls are going to want to play with gross or ugly Barbie dolls—sorry to say. Deep down, girls want to be pretty. I think all the moms are the same. They all get manis, and work out, and get their hair done, and shop, and dress nice and cool each day (even if they are just in gym clothes). They care, too. So call me boring and unoriginal. Hate on me for being basic. Maybe girls into their looks are old-fashioned, but I think girls like to look and feel pretty—and middle school girls might actually care more than any girls of any age, ever. That's why it's so hard for us! We have to spend so much extra time working on it because we are so UGLY!! We are gawky and awkward and we have big ears and small noses and braces and little boobs and zits and no waist and skinny feet! And we are also moody and temperamental because our hormones are always raging unpredictably and no grown-ups ever understand us, so getting dressed to feel pretty takes, like, three times the amount of time it does for a normal person. But I'll tell you one thing—when we DO find the right outfit, on the right day, in the right mood, at the right time of the month, in the right weather (so the jacket isn't necessary cause it ruins the outfit), with no humidity so our hair looks good, with the right new boots, we feel like Barbie or Cinderella at the ball for just a few minutes and it is glorious. Usually until, like, 5th period science, and then we feel awful again. But what a great morning it was :-) I feel ready to go to sleep so I can face the day with a Barbie grin tomorrow! Goodnight.

She never called my mother. I asked you ONE thing, Harry! To JUST remind her.

oh my god. I am actually the selfish piece of shit my mom said I was that I hated her for calling me and was determined to prove to her that

I wasn't. *What is wrong with me???* I was wondering why she didn't text me or speak to me at all when she got home tonight. But there I was, all wrapped up in my stupid Barbie world (how apropos) and I couldn't even manage to make one phone call to my stuck-in-bed grandmother. The very same grandma who never once forgot my birthday and always tucked a check into a card for every occasion and said "get yourself something special" and even when I was too cranky to want to have dinner with the grandparents, she always hugged me and told me I was beautiful and smart and talented. Yes, that grandma. That very one. Yet somehow I can manage to set up a donation box and collect money and sports equipment to send to kids in Africa. I can't even use the very cell phone in my own two hands to make my grandma's day and call her. I feel like such a failure. Epic. What is the meaning of all this energy of self-improvement if I can't even do one simple thing for someone who I actually love? I'm debating getting out of bed and going downstairs to talk to my mom and say I'm sorry. But I'm too scared. And what if she punishes me and takes away my plans to go to the camp reunion this weekend—then I'll just die. I'll talk to her in the morning. I opted for shameless silence in my bedroom. I'll have to go to sleep, or at least pretend, just to ensure I can avoid any potential late night confrontation. Lights OUT.

Dear Diary

The final meltdown

Ok…a lot to cover here. When I look back on today it's like I have lived nine lives and experienced the entire spectrum of emotions any 12-year-old girl could smash into her complicated brain and awkward body (let's see…rage, shame, joy, pride, sadness, guilt…shall I proceed?). Sometimes it doesn't take much to set us (well, me) off and cause a total freakout (and sometimes it is a necessary, warranted explosion). Last night was pretty bad, but tonight was just fighting over stupid stuff and I really didn't want to fight, for once, because I knew my mom already hated me and I didn't want to give her any more reasons to freak out. The day started out on the right foot. I was determined not to screw it up. This morning I made sure I got out of bed on time and was ready to make the bus. (Neha never takes the bus in the morning 'cause her dad drives her—which she says is kind of nice but kind of awful all at the same time. My dad only drives me if he is randomly going in late and we just listen to music and he lets me just chill and be groggy, but my mom thinks the morning drive is quiz-and-catch-up time, and I'm not exactly over-caffeinated at my age so it's rough.) Anyway, getting up and making the bus (and being…cheerful?) was a small miracle, I know, but that's how thin the ice was that I was skating on. Thank god I had a little extra pep in my step because it's finally Friday. Ready for this? I didn't even straighten my hair. Something had to give. Ponytail and sweats (and a touch of mascara) and my backpack was packed, and I was in the kitchen with a minute and a half to spare. *Here's your…* before she could even say "lunch" I interrupted her and said I was so sorry. That I knew I let her down and I knew she was right by knowing I would be too selfish to remember. *Thank you, Mags. I'm just so tired. I feel like…*

I interrupted her again—mostly because I didn't want to miss the bus because that would have been a catastrophic end to my very carefully planned morning, and, secondly, because I just wasn't in the mood for a lecture. I was wrong, I know, but did I have to hear a whole lecture about my mom's lack of feeling valued by her whole family all before 7:13 a.m.? I wanted to go out on a high note and to run out the door after giving her a quick hug and a kiss. The crazy part is, instead of yelling at me, she actually lingered in the pre-bus hug and squeezed me so tight—I wasn't sure if it was more for her than for me, but I felt her take a huge slow deep breath and squeeze me even tighter as she exhaled. It was a lot for the wee hours of the morning, but it made me feel both good and bad at the same time. I had a lot to think about on the bus ride to school this morning. Like, maybe I can avoid all of this guilt and selfish-shame if I just do more for her and call my grandma, and better yet, maybe calling her will make _me_ feel good because I will be doing something nice for my sweet grandma and not just doing it 'cause my mom told me to. Hmmm having a "you just had to learn it for yourself" Wizard of Oz moment and my heart felt all warm even looking out the dreary school bus window dreading the long day ahead.

My grandma and I used to always watch "The Wizard of Oz" when she visited—and I had forgotten about that until this morning. Right then and there I set a reminder and an alarm to call my grandma as soon as I got off the bus this afternoon. And I did! And even walked the dog while I did it. I'm so glad I remembered, and I felt better after we hung up. It was a quick call, but she told me it was _wonderful to hear your voice_ and I said I missed her and loved her very much. I salvaged my mom's faith in me for one more day and even was proud of myself that I did it…until now. Tonight, it kind of blew up all over again, but for no real reason and in a way that makes it even worse. And now it's 10:53 p.m.

I don't know what is wrong with me lately, but I am soooo stressed. My parents are so strict. We have this swim class at night on Fridays (it's so cold and I don't know why I have to swim in the winter even though, I suppose, it's technically spring, it is freezing out and dark after school—but my parents want me to be more "active" and they say swim is a lifetime sport, or some nonsense like that). (Thankfully it is only 4 weeks long). I met two other girls there that I am becoming friends with, but I don't know them very well. On the bus line after school today, a few of us (it's kind of random—it's girls I probably haven't even mentioned) were discussing what we were going to do for dinner at swim because we used to bring dinner to eat in between both classes (there are two sessions, don't ask), but then we started to walk next door to the ice cream place and have dinner there, but now the ice cream place closed so we got a ride from one of the moms last week down the block to a deli, but the mom didn't drive us back, so we walked back for our 8 p.m. class at the Y. It felt sort of cool and independent, but I knew deep down it wasn't so safe. So tonight before class my parents told me I wasn't allowed to walk back but that they weren't going to drive me. So I feel so stuck with these girls I barely know, their parents who I don't know, rules I hate, and decisions I can't make. And I think I told them I would bring them dinner tonight in case we didn't get a ride to the deli. (I have no idea why I even offered that it was so weird, but I did.) But then before swim when my parents were asking me about dinner and walking and driving, the other girls didn't text me back so I didn't have any answers for my parents so I got so frustrated and they got so pissed and I just felt like I was waiting for a decision that I couldn't make and I felt so stuck. STUCK. *What do you do when you need answers and people don't text back?* Why don't they text me back?? I KNOW her phone is in her hand! It is SO annoying and so hard not to be in control of a situation and to have your parents jumping down your throat for immediate answers. I felt so dependent upon the other girls and their stupid moms, like my hands were tied, and I hated it. The conversation in my kitchen before swim with both my parents was not a pretty one. When I got home it was fine, but before I left, my dad was screaming and my mom was trying to calm him down. **You are not being reasonable, we need to allow her some independence but also keep her safe!** (that was kind of an interesting turning of the tables…my mom calming my dad down?!) and I was crying because I was so stressed about dinner. And all the good grandma stuff went right out the window. Why can't they trust me? I know how to make my own decisions. I mean, sure I forget to call my grandmother when I promise to and I forgot to finish my social studies paper last week and I hate practicing my Hebrew and I showed Charlotte a really inappropriate (hilarious) TikTok the other day, but still, how can I learn to be trustworthy if they don't trust me?

I don't think I was meant to swim. I suck anyway and I hate the way I look in a bathing suit.

Dear Diary

In case you were wondering…

I got my period in my pajamas last night after my super complex 12-year-old-almost-13-year-old day. Today should be awesome—I just had to rant for a second. Already running late for school and I have a nice new zit on my nose and my mom won't ever buy me the cream I ask for. And she is making me take the bus because of my "behavior" last night and I have nothing to wear because everything is dirty and in the laundry and my mom hasn't done the laundry in, like, forever, because she is literally never home so I have to go into her closet to find something semi-normal.

Ooh wait, new cute leggings—these will do. Gotta run!

Dear Diary

That's the spirit

It's Friday and it's Spirit Day and it's THE DAY BEFORE SPRING VACATION!!!!! Today everyone had to dress in their team colors. My team is the green team. I had a green tutu, green face paint and eye shadow, a green sweatshirt, green socks, and green hairspray. I looked fierce! But then this morning I thought I looked TOO green, so I took off the tutu and the green face paint because I didn't want to look like a freak. But then I tortured myself and was like—it's Spirit Week, I have to go big! What am I afraid of? Why do I always doubt myself? Is it a Barbie complex? Even when I feel like I look good, why do I have to second guess myself and then change my outfit? *Am I afraid to look too good because it will appear that I care too much about what I look like? Am I afraid that my outfit will show I put too much time into its preparation, and it will make me seem weird?* Is that worse than looking good? Maybe it all has to appear effortless. No one likes a try-hard. But then again, it's a costume, so different rules apply. This is not an average day and it certainly isn't an average outfit. I'm still slightly scarred from Halloween. So I decided to compromise my spirit a little to take a safer risk—I still wanted to celebrate and I allowed my campy/wacky side to shine through a bit, but I didn't want to look like a lunatic. All of this indecisiveness and the costume changes made me late. **You look adorable. I'll drive you—don't worry.** It's like—just when I think she hates me the most and that I have mastered the ability to predict her behavior and to keep myself out of trouble, she shocks me. And what's worse is, as much as I hate to admit it, my day was actually better because of it. I didn't start my day apologetic and guilty and defensive, I just started it relieved. And my mom's compliment actually stuck with me and I did feel cute all day. *Maybe all along I've been waiting for my mom's approval and not my peers' at all?* That theory changes everything. My dad even called us in the car from work. **You should see how cute she looks. She should win the spirit contest for sure!** My dad was speechless. All he could muster was **Really? Oh! That's great! Have a good day, girls.** Well, the land of Upside Down has spread to my very own home.

Dear Diary

A lot of build-up

I'm happy to report that my mom still seems to like me. Maybe because I like her and I'm on break from school so I'm relaxed? She went to see my grandma again today because the rehab place called and said she got pneumonia or something so they had to admit her, so she dropped me off at my camp friend's house on her way to the hospital. We've been planning this camp reunion for weeks at my friend Eliza's house. I was so excited to see everyone, but here I am, up all alone at night again for what feels like another failed attempt at a sleepover. I always get myself all psyched up to go and then when I finally get over the initial excitement of seeing everyone, I just kind of get bored and want to go home! It's like 1 a.m. now and almost everyone is asleep. A few girls are whispering and giggling on the couch with their phones in the corner, but I'm surrounded by so many sleeping bodies I can't move. So I decided to write with my phone as the light. At least my camp friends don't judge me if I'm writing in my diary. They so don't care, and for that I really am grateful. It's nice to be away from home friends for a bit. I don't think I'm in my head as much with my camp friends, but maybe I am. Maybe I should be thinking about my mom visiting my grandma and not about whether I am in my own thoughts but I can't stop thinking about it… Maybe I can't sleep because I have anxiety. Everyone has anxiety so maybe that's what this is? What if it's anxiety?

I think my Bat Mitzvah has to be all girls. I literally have no guy friends. I mean, I have like seven guy friends. Why would any of the girls want to come to my party if there are no guys there, though? I am trying to convince myself that if it is all girls then the party will be like camp—no boys to inhibit us or to dress for, so we can all just be ourselves and I can still be the star!! Right? Yeah—I don't think so. The reality is, I need a long list of guys to go with my too-short list of girls-who-aren't-even-my-friends so my Bat Mitzvah can be better than all the others—or, at least, a little different. I don't have much time to spare, either. *Is there a crash course in being social and savvy and flirty that I can take?* I had a boyfriend once for less than 24 hours. Maybe because it's like one of the last parties of the year, people will actually really want to be there? Invites go out soon, so I need to finish my search for soulmates and real boyfriends very quickly. I need to build up a solid list for my collages and speeches so I'm not the only loser who doesn't get them. This is what happens to me—I finally put my head on the pillow at night after a long day and my mind starts to wander and worry. *Anxiety.* I texted my mom—I have no idea why—she is asleep I am sure. *...night night. Sweet dreams.* I couldn't believe she replied. I asked her why she was still up. *Just got home late from seeing Grandma and wanted to watch some tv to relax. Try watching something instead of being on your phone or stupid TikTok. Did you bring a book? It will relax you more. Maybe try writing in your diary?* (How does she always know?! I swear she has spies everywhere!!!) *Get some sleep or you will be a raging crank tomorrow. Love you xoxo* I feel bad she was up. What if my text woke her and she didn't want me to feel bad? I'm ashamed to admit it but I'm relieved she responded. In a weird way I just needed to hear her voice, even if it is over text. It's hard to explain, but I guess it's kind of like standing on solid ground, or being tucked in. Maybe she really is too stressed to sleep. Maybe she needed to hear from me, too? I guess she had a long day. Lately, when I'm up super late, I do hear her iPad from her room. I think she is always watching the same shows and movies over and over; maybe that's her way of relaxing. I wonder if she ever thought about picking up her old diary again. Maybe it would help her relax, too.

"Why is she always writing in her journal?" Just when I get a break from overhearing my mom's train of thought, I have to hear Jessica whisper that to Drew. As my heart sank into my stomach and I was flooded with more self-doubt (only this time it was more painful because I began to instantly question the very core of my closest relationships built on trust and acceptance), Jessica whispered louder with a giggle—MAGGIE GET OVER HERE AND HANG WITH US!! My worries instantly washed away and I felt so relieved. She wasn't talking about me. She was just talking TO me. What a concept. When we aren't worried about being judged or judging others, we can just be honest? I'm just gonna finish a few thoughts and then I'm headed over to the couch. I feel relieved and confident again. I'm upset with myself that I let my insecurities get the best of me. *Can't a girl just get a break?*

Dear Diary

I guess not

My grandma died. Last night while I was at the sleepover. My mom found out around 3:00 in the morning. She got a call, like right after she and I were texting. And I wasn't even home. I'm so selfish. I was at a stupid sleepover complaining about being uncomfortable. And she knew I was awake and she didn't text me or call me or come to pick me up. Maybe she didn't want to worry me or upset me? Oh my god—maybe she wanted me to enjoy my sleepover and it was a completely selfless mom trick, and I don't ever do anything selfless because I am busy and anxious and 12. And this morning when my dad picked me up I was a witch 'cause I was so sad to leave my camp friends and return to my regular existence and I was partly annoyed that my dad came to get me and not my new ally, my mom. And then my dad told me in the car. I felt simply awful. We sat there awkwardly in silence for the whole long drive home. He tried to be nice and offer wise words and *platitudes* but nothing really helped. I had such a stomachache. What happens next, I kept wondering. What happens to my mom? Will she ever be ok? What will I wear to the funeral? Do I have to make a speech? I should have called her more.

I can't sleep. I am so tired from last night—I should be sprawled out above my covers, fully dressed in my sweats from this morning, passed out with the shades still up and the streetlight streaming in, and instead I am in my pajamas under my covers, all washed up, sleepover bag still packed and dirty on the floor, and staring at the pages of my diary, lost in my thoughts, riddled with guilt, sad and all mixed up, and totally and completely exhausted down to my fuzzy socks. I'll never be able to sleep. Maybe some sheep…or I'll try a mindfulness app. Or maybe I'll study my

Hebrew (that ought to put me to sleep) (I just realized my grandma won't be at my Bat Mitzvah and now it will be ruined 'cause everyone will just be sad) or maybe I'll rewatch "Twilight"… How did this happen? It feels so long and so fast all at the same time. When did this all start? I keep opening and closing the diary and staring at the cover, forcing myself to remember when I got this book from my grandma. Maybe if I keep remembering it, then it will feel real or less sad or more sad or I'll cry?

April 7th

Dear Diary

Unclear

I've been feeling kinda hazy—like in a fog. I'm in a daze. Not sure how or what to feel or what to say in front of my very own mother (and uncle). People keep coming over to say "I'm so sorry" and I stand there like the awkward upside down tween everyone expects me to be. *You just have to say "thank you" when someone says that to you, Maggie. Don't just stand there with your hands in your pockets.* She also kept harping on me for something about eye contact and that strange thing where I keep smiling at the most random times. And all I find myself thinking about is "Where is my prince to whisk me away from this nightmare of my life?" How do I sign up for my own Maggie Protection Program—they can even let me out in a few years when this nightmare is all behind me and I wake up and I am gorgeous. *How do I close my eyes and coast through these next few years? How can I be invisible but not unhappy? What is wrong with me that I sat there at the funeral and stared into space, wondering if I picked out the right sweatshirt for my Bat-Mitzvah giveaway or if I had the right dress for the Spring Dance? Will my mom still have the energy to fight with me about planning my Bat Mitzvah? What if, actually, she has more time and energy now that she is gone? Maybe she will resent me 'cause now she really has to help me plan it and it will make her even sadder that she isn't with her own mother? This was the WORST time for this to happen!*

Obviously, my spring break sucked—but make no mistake, I suck even more for even thinking or writing that. I'm sad but it's so weird. Like I miss her, and I keep thinking about her. And sometimes my mom will just start crying, and I haven't even cried, maybe I need to cry? I feel like it would make me feel better but then I worry that I will feel like I'm faking it or being dramatic. I know she is also a little relieved. I really tried to behave all week. Thank god I had stuff to wear to the funeral and to shiva or I would have freaked out even more. Except for having to wear tights because it was still so cold, the outfits worked just fine. Back to reality right now, I guess. And back to school.

I guess my mom was too tired—or was she just too horrified by my behavior??—to even speak about me behind my back tonight. What's worse is that I feel even more stressed not being able to hear her horrid angry nightly truth rant before I go to sleep! It's as if it was my nightly closure—that which I focused on and channeled my energy to each night as I put my head on the pillow and contemplated my life—present and future—until I exhausted myself and fell asleep. Without her sharp words, without her truth, I feel even more lost than I did before! And now THIS feeling is overwhelming me even more and I don't know what to do. *How am I supposed to fall asleep if my mom is too upset with me to even tell me behind my back?!* Maybe I should make some noise in my room or slam some books on the floor so she yells at me to go to sleep? *Am I supposed to raise myself now? Is she washing her hands of me?* Oh my god I'm having a complete and total breakdown. And now I'm starting to cry! Hang on, I have to take a Snapchat of this!

Dear Diary

Virtual tween

I saw a few friends last week. It was actually nice when a few of them visited me when we were home after my grandma died. We just got to hang out a little, but it was really cool that they came—even if their moms made them. Hallie and her mom took me out for a lunch to give me a break from all the family stuff. It actually really meant a lot to me. Like it didn't take much on her part, but it made a really big difference in my day. I don't think I really thanked her, but I guess one day I will. Sometimes, I guess, true friends don't have to try so hard—in fact, maybe we all try too hard too much of the time. Neha came over, too, with her mom. I was glad our moms got to meet a little bit since she and I have gotten close and I think my mom really appreciated their visit. And they brought us flowers, which was so unnecessary but super sweet. It was funny seeing Neha and her mom feel a little awkward sitting in my house, but at the same time, it was a really welcome distraction for my whole family. Even Charlotte likes Neha!

I'm beginning to realize that I am a little selfish. Let me rephrase that—I have *been behaving* selfishly. I mean, how can I be psyched to go shopping or for a manicure when my grandmother just died. I am just too tired to behave any other way. We have state testing in school soon and the teachers are all stressed since they had to return from vacation and jump right into 'test prep' ('cause all that seems to matter to these teachers is our scores) and they are cramming us with work. My mom has been so out of it and so preoccupied she can't even be bothered with me lately. Her recent lack of doling out unwanted advice has really left me with a strange void I didn't ever think I would feel. *Do I really need her involved with every aspect of my day to the point that I can't function without her?*

Has my feeling of maturity and independent thinking just been a lie? Or, even worse, has she been **surreptitiously** *helping me through everything and making me believe I resolved these things all on my own?* This is all really a lot for me to process right now, Diary. After all, my grandma just died. I'm just going to close you for a second to sit with my thoughts and see if the tears come naturally.

Nope.

Recently I have been quite focused on wasting energy on counting my likes and comparing the number of followers I have with other people. I know—it's ridiculous. And I know it shouldn't define me, but let's get real—it does. It defines all of us. How can it not if I have, like, 245 followers and other girls in my school have 800? And it goes both ways—I follow so many people, people I don't even know, because I know it's cool to follow them. But if you think about it, even the word "follower" is so much different than on Facebook where they use the word "friend." I guess that means that even if we are all so busy taking selfies and posting stuff about ourselves, at least on Facebook the people looking at the pics are friends and not just hundreds of "followers" (strangers) who just look at a person's pics because they have heard they are cool. Instagram is so fake and so manufactured, so edited, though, you know? It isn't even real. I think our Finsta accounts and our Snapchat stories are more real—I guess because we are more careful about who follows us and who can see it. We can be truer to ourselves on our Finsta 'cause only the people we actually like know our accounts. If someone gives up your Finsta name to someone else, it is the ultimate humiliation. Sometimes, even, I have seen people be really mean on their Finsta accounts because they don't think others will see it—nor will their parents. Pretty sneaky. I know if my mom even cared, and if she knew I was obsessing over this all afternoon (instead of studying), she would tell me *you're being crazy and you should have more confidence than to base your daily dose of self-esteem on numbers and filtered pictures of strangers and celebrities.*

My grandma would be horrified by this, back in her cool grandma NYC days. She would shoot me a look about having more confidence and not wasting my precious time on nonsense, and I would have no choice but to shake it off. Instead I sit here upstairs and wallow. There was always a signature look she would give us—the look of approval or of disappointment—it said it all. I'll bet my mom is a little lost without those looks.

Isn't it ironic that a "fake account" is actually truer than a regular one? Something is very wrong with this world. No one even knows how to cope anymore. Everyone just wants to run with the masses and fit in. I hit rock bottom the other day, though. I actually was so concerned about hitting 100 likes for a picture I posted that I opened up two Finsta accounts and liked my own picture! How pathetic is that?? (Then I felt like such a loser that I deleted the accounts and the likes.) It's just that my phone is, like, always in my hand, so I just space out and open Instagram or Reels and scroll. I'm not too pleased with myself. My mom would surely be *mortified,* and she would tell everyone how pathetic I am. I just need something else to look at/read while my phone is in my hand and I am bored. Maybe I should get Twitter. Or read the news? I'll just play candy crush. Maybe my mom will come up to kiss me goodnight. I might have to go down the hall; she may already be in bed.

April 13th

Dear Diary

No time like the present

Self-pity is exhausting. Then again, so, I suppose, is the death of a loved one. I want to be patient, I do, but we've been eating donated food forever for dinner, we have no food in the house, I've had to buy a gross school lunch every day, and my mom hasn't even had the energy to fight with me in almost two weeks. The calm (and quiet) in the house is actually quite unsettling. I mean I know I can take care of myself; I just didn't think I actually didn't want to until now. And I'm afraid to complain because she will say I'm so ungrateful and self-centered, but also because maybe the old routine I am missing really isn't so much fun anyway. *Perhaps I should try to embrace this situation and relish my independence and freedom to do and think whatever I want (kind of)?*

I have had some extra time on my hands to think. Sometimes—well, let's be honest…this never is a good idea for me. Downtime and quiet makes me go into overdrive in terms of analyzing my social standings and my true friends. My art skills have sharply declined, and with that, my newfound goals for a loft in SOHO and a scholarship to a fashion college. My home friends are back to seeing me as normal—the novelty of my new boots and mascara, my surge in mad artistic talent, the boy who liked me, and the sympathy for my grandma's death have all worn off to everyone and I am back to (being) basic. So, naturally, this makes me long for a time when things were easier and happier, and I was noticed and appreciated. Since it doesn't appear that Prince Charming will be knocking down my door anytime soon or that my Bat Mitzvah dress will make all the boys fall at my feet like when Cinderella entered the ball, I'll go back to feeling like Ariel—"a fish out of water" (ha ha, get it?), longing for days as "part of (another) world" (lol I'm on fire now ;-) Well, it's either Disney, a world of magic and mystery, a madly scientifically strange universe, dystopia, superheroes, goblins, or camp. One of these, at least, is actually real enough to distract me so I can be hopeful and optimistic and escape in my mind. Instead of aimlessly scrolling and losing my mind.

I do LOVE my camp friends, but I am just not comfortable keeping in touch with them during the school year. I had such a great time seeing them at the sleepover, but it doesn't matter. I know it is so weird, and I should be so gearing up with my camp friends because camp is so soon. And so many of my camp friends live pretty close by. But it just doesn't feel normal to text them or whatever. But I miss them so much and I miss the way I feel about myself all summer. I just really like myself at camp. We can just look, act, and dress like total lunatics and we don't have to care at all. It is so awesome. So every time my mom is like *make a plan with one of your camp friends...* she doesn't understand why I am so resistant and awkward to do it. She didn't say it today; it's just that I know she would if she were to hear my inner monologue. It just isn't summer, so I am not my summer self—and *what if they don't like the winter me? What if I'm too boring or insecure and they don't recognize me and then it changes how they see me in the summer??* I would be so devastated if it changed the way they view me during camp. But at the same time, I get it, because my mom knows how happy I am at camp and so she feels like I will be happier at home if I see my camp friends. Sometimes it is just taking the first step for me that is the hardest. Like, if one of them texts or snapchats or facetimes me I am so psyched, but I always feel so awkward about starting it. I guess that sounds familiar, because I have been through that with my home friends, too. Always the follower. I am always afraid to take the first step when it comes to plans. You want to know why? Because there is nothing worse than these three things:

1. the three dots just flashing there when you know someone has read your text but they are contemplating and crafting their negative reply and haven't responded

2. the simple answer "sorry I can't"

3. the times there is no answer at all

4. oh and wait, there is a 4th—that time you asked them for a plan, they couldn't go, but then they never asked you to do something a different time. You feel like a loser. Just hanging there. Vulnerable. Out there in the open for all to see.

I need my camp self. Can I bring my camp self into my real world? But maybe I am only myself at camp because the setting is so different, and my annoying parents aren't there, and I am so free. No school, no homework, no social media pressure. Even though we all hate it so much when they take our phones away at camp, I know we all know deep down that it is a huge relief. Maybe camp is so great because we are just in the moment and not constantly staring at our phones, comparing our present experience or mood with everyone's else's virtual experience or mood based upon their pictures. As a matter of fact, we are so in the moment that we don't even want the time to pass us by—we savor the moments. *Maybe that is what we need to change—just learning to be where we are and have fun with whomever we are with. Maybe the only way for teenage girls to learn to live in the moment is if we are able to realize just how fleeting these moments are—even the difficult ones—and that someday we will wish we were young again and had our whole lives ahead of us?* In my mom's diary, she seemed to have so much of the same **angst,** yet never spent hours a day staring at a screen wasting her life away. Back in the olden days it still seemed painful to be 12, but it sure was easier to be 12 when you didn't have to see everyone else's life play out on a screen in the palm of your hand all day long. Maybe my grandma also had ANGST (such a weird word that adults overuse), but she wore old-fashioned clothes and went to dances and her world was in black and white and she had no idea there was life outside of New Jersey and tiny television sets. Life was so simple. Elvis was the biggest controversy in the whole world.

My mom was on the phone tonight. She has been on the phone a lot. All of her friends have been calling her. And she is on with my Aunt Iris and Uncle Robby every day. But this time, she wasn't talking about how stressed I have been or how I complain about not having a social life and I don't do anything about it. She didn't even mention me at all.

Goodnight.

April 14th

Dear Diary

Mirror Mirror

So I was getting dressed for school this morning and examining myself in the mirror in my parents' bedroom, as I often do for my morning ritual (my closet light sucks). I was wearing a new scarf, a cute cardigan, and new leggings. I had on my new lacy bandeau and a low cut T-shirt. Doing some twists and turns in front of the mirror so I could get a peek at every angle—even at the bright hour of 6:45 a.m. while I was exhausted, I scrutinized my outfit. It was still dark out, but I could sense spring in the air. I breathed in the opportunity for new beginnings and smiled at the thought of spring…then SUMMER and the feeling of freedom that it will bring to me. The only other thing that helps me to start my day with a smile and deal with the misery of school is feeling like I look good. And then my mom rolls over in bed (I guess she was going in late today) and says *Maggie, you look adorable. Pull up your shirt* (it was so close to being a compliment, lol) and my dad rolls over and says **Magpie, you realize the boys don't notice what the girls wear, right? They don't know if you wear the same outfit every day, or if you are wearing a new scarf or leggings or jeans.** (Even though it depressed me, it didn't surprise me.) **They might notice if you showed up to school naked. MIGHT** he said. Ewwwwww! My dad is so weird. But it got me thinking… *Am I wasting all of my time and energy trying to look good so the guys notice me when no one ever even notices me at all? Am I going through all of this trouble for nothing? Would they notice me if I looked different, if my hair were longer and I were taller and my nose and ears smaller?* And then it hit me…it isn't the boys that notice, it is the girls… So that's what I told my dad. "The girls notice, Dad," I said with sass and confidence—as if to say to him "Duh! As if

I didn't know that!" **She is right, Harry** my mom agreed. (My mom actually agreed. And it felt great! She was on my side!) Guys are just clueless sometimes. My mom and I actually had a good early morning chuckle at my dad's expense. Maybe my mom is always getting dressed so my dad notices, too. Or maybe that's what she tells herself—like we do—but really, she is just trying to look hot for all her friends at Trader Joe's, the office, or The Lunch Place—or, better yet, maybe she actually does it for herself?! My grandma always said she would put makeup on every day because *you never know who you are going to run into in the supermarket.* I really hope that isn't what I end up doing…but isn't that what we are already doing every day? I guess we always want to look our best for others—'cause ya never know. Other people's impressions of us are like looking in the mirror. I know it's pathetic, but let's face it. My future husband could be in my social studies class—I have to put my best foot forward! I think we are kidding ourselves if we think getting dressed up is for ourselves—we all know that if it were only to please ourselves, we would lounge around in fuzzy pjs and sweats all day every day.

In a way, my mother's reaction to me is also like looking in a mirror. When she smiles, I smile and feel good; when she criticizes me, I'm lost for the whole day. How does she not get that? How can she not be more careful knowing full well how fragile I am? It's as if she holds my self-esteem in the palm of her hand. *Is a girl's self-image really that tied to her relationship with her mother?* And then it hit me like a ton of "you are such a selfish dumbass" pile of bricks. Standing right there in my parents' room at 6:47 in the morning. Without *her* mom, who will my mother be? I didn't want her to see it, but it was there…the tear in my eye—it finally happened, and certainly not in the way I had expected it. It wasn't a sobbing movie scene, there was no background music or soundtrack, or faded scenery. Just me, in the wee hours of the morning, finally realizing I am capable of human emotion, thank god, and it was weird and felt super lousy—and I quickly wiped my face, afraid that my recent revelation would indicate my sensitivity and empathy and she might think I had gone soft. But I couldn't help myself, I was kind of overcome with this sadness and confusion.

"Have a good day. Bye, Mom" I said as I kissed her on her forehead in bed and ran out the bedroom door to make the bus. I haven't seen her much since I got home from school today—it was a crazy night of swim practice and homework and stuff, but as I lie here in bed, I can't help but wonder, *do I have to be my mom's mirror now?*

Dear Diary

I know you need a hug but I love my social life more

I actually said that to my mom today. I was actually pretty proud of myself. Feeling frustrated after another boring, average day of school. Neha and I were even talking about it on the bus—like that there just hasn't been much excitement lately, like everyone is in a bit of a holding pattern. Spring sports are starting, it's still cold out, summer is out of reach, it's just kind of blah. We still have so much homework. Even our art teacher called us out today for talking during class, but we were so bored! My mom was waiting in the kitchen when I harumphed and slouched my way inside from the bus. She wanted a hug when I got home and I just wanted to check my phone. I gave in—I'm not totally cold-hearted after all, but I'd be lying if I said I let her linger there as she would have hoped. I should have—she needed the love and she wanted to squeeze me tight, but I just was kind of in a hurry. Some of us are trying to plan to go to town so I am waiting to hear from everyone. (I know—I should just make the plan, but alas, I am waiting to hear.) With my Bat Mitzvah coming up, I can't afford to miss out on any social moments—I need to take advantage of every opportunity to make a memory. Just knowing I have the potential to have something fun going on is exciting and energizing. Otherwise I just come home on a Friday and do homework and scroll through my miserable existence. If I'm feeling wild and crazy, I will really let loose and catch up on "Pretty Little Liars" or "Gossip Girl" on Netflix.

Hopefully my mom will drive me and pick me up from town, and drive everyone to town and home, too. Sometimes she doesn't mind doing that (and it is easier for me because I always know I have a ride). I feel kind of badly asking her today, though. She really has been tired. But maybe getting out of the house will be good for her? Maybe she thinks *I need to get out of the house??* *Oh my god, am I a loser even to my parents??* I actually think that is rock bottom. I actually think my parents have a busier social life than I do. My god what do they tell their friends about me? My identity and self-esteem are based upon my social existence at any particular given moment? I do want to be busy all the time, and I do want plans and to feel active and included, but I guess I have higher standards than other girls. Like I want to be cool—but I'm not willing to sell my soul to the devil to get there. Even though the devil and her friend group seem to have SO much fun and they are SO busy on weekends, I know, deep (deep deep deep) down that those are not the friends I want and that I would not be comfortable with them. I'm just sitting here writing while I wait for all the texts because we talked about it at lunch today. Still, deciding on the group text if we should go to town and if we should get dropped off at Starbucks or Claire's or the diner is enough to put me over the edge. This should take another 25 minutes. It really does take a lot of time and a lot of energy to make a plan with a group of people. Everyone has an opinion, and no one takes charge. **My god, Maggie, what is the plan??** I give up. I texted the whole cafeteria table, and also added Neha's table—my new friends—'cause what the hell, I'm a risk taker—"My mom is bringing me in 15 minutes and dropping me off at Starbucks. We can walk around from there. Text me now if you need a ride." And they did! And it seems to be working! I don't even think it will be that fun to go, but I am just too afraid to miss out by not going. Even if it is just to take some pictures and post them, is that worth all of this hassle?

Hi girls! Look how grown-up you all look! She said shamelessly as we piled in.

I should never have volunteered my mom to drive. SO embarrassing! Why does she always have to talk to everyone when she drives? I felt like screaming, but then I felt guilty. I don't even know if they had cars or carpools when my mom was growing up, but I'm certain that if they did, and IF my grandmother ever did the driving, she would never have embarrassed my mom in front of her friends. She just would have put Elvis or the Beatles of Jazz, who the F knows, on the radio (CD player?) and driven on quietly. I guess I felt it would help my mom to get out of the house a little and stop feeling sorry for herself. But it will help people in the social media universe to believe I am social and fun—so maybe it was worth it as a political move to boost my social status. Isn't that why Instagram was invented in the first place?

Dear Diary

The elusive IT factor

If you've got "it," good things and attention just seem to come to you. She who has it doesn't have to ask for it or work too hard at it. She is like a magnet for all things cool. Girls with the IT factor are just charmed. Powerful. Magical. Kind of like Snow White—not necessarily the prettiest girl with the best clothes but adored and respected by all. Her special powers consist of just accepting herself and accepting others. That is her magic. (Now that is really something to aspire to.) Maybe you have to work at it, Miss Popularity, Miss In-the-Center-of-It-All, Miss Switzerland, but usually the people who have to work the LEAST at it are the ones who just have IT from the very start. It shows even in their smiles. Because they are just genuinely happy and they smile, like, all the time! It's like this crazy comfortable confidence. People have a combined fear (think about Snow White's stepmother!), respect, and adoration of those with the IT factor. It's celebrities like Jennifer Lawrence tripping and falling in front of crowds of people and not caring at all. I saw it happen on youtube. She was practically unfazed and unflustered. When I fell in the cafeteria, I think it scarred me for weeks. But how does she do it? It's her faults that make her even more loved than she already is. How do I embrace and accept my faults? Even learn to rock them? Maybe how a person feels shows more on the outside than how they look—so their feelings and attitude actually change how they look? If you have the IF/CF (the IT Factor/Cool Factor, just to clarify), you always have plans and places to go and people to hang out with (and Snow White didn't even care that those people were named Dopey and Sleepy and Doc). I'm sure Jennifer has a posse and is, like, partying with Taylor Swift all the time. And if a random fan wanted to be her friend, she would be nice and cool to them, too. Even when a girl with the CF decides not to hang out and do what everyone else is doing, people think that's cool and no one questions her. I recently had a brush with one of the Queens of Cool. It wasn't an actual "brush," it was an "Insta-brush" and it stung like a bee. And to make it even better—she didn't even mean to sabotage me.

I won (well my dad won) front row seats to the coolest concert ever last night—the Spring Fling in the city, and, like, every single star was within inches of me. Even Harry Styles looked right at me and pointed at me (and I nearly passed out) and my camp friend got a picture of that exact moment!! Even though I have periodically tried to fight the Instagram temptation and stop playing the game, because the constant rejection and negativity begins to feel personal, I felt this was insta-worthy and totally knew I would get tons of likes. I relished the joy as I watched the numbers climb instantly from 23 to 64 to 86 likes…getting so close to 100…and then, the goddess of cool posted a picture of her ice cream cone with rainbow sprinkles with a filter and in the artsy way, and my Harry picture was lost in the abyss of loser land. Her stupid, boring, unoriginal, inanimate picture of dessert got to 183 likes in nine minutes! That's what happens, I guess, when you have 1,200 followers. And when I say "followers," I mean that in the truest sense of the word. They follow because she is cool. It brings them one step closer to her IT factor. Not like me and, I dare say, most normal people whose followers are people they know and whom they mutually follow because they are all friends. Or we follow movie stars and celebrities like the Kardashians 'cause they represent cool and we can mimic them and they want us to. Like most people have 183 followers in total! I must turn off this 'like' feature—this contest is joy-sucking (I'll do it tomorrow). Here I was, at the pinnacle moment of my life, a brush with fame and Mr. super sexy hot man, and a melting ice cream cone steals him away—right from between my iPhone-holding fingertips. Long gone are the days when we would experience something and just enjoy it—now our experience is shaped by how many people watch and grade and like and virtually participate in that experience with us—even though they aren't even with us at all. The worst side effect of this, of course, is that even when we do have these life-altering happy moments and we do, of course, post a pic of it, when the likes are few and the comments are short, it can actually take away from the very elation we were finally having in the first place. This IT factor—if it were bottled and sold—would be the young girl's hottest commodity—flying off the shelves of Brandy Melville, Forever 21, Sephora, and Urban Outfitters. *Maybe it is the equivalent of my mom's wine?*

My dad the whole time at the concert was like **What are you taking pictures of? I don't understand why you are on your phone during the concert. This is supposed to be one of the best experiences of your life?!** It was useless trying to explain to him why, and even worse, to try to tell him I was sad during this awesome concert all because of the ice cream, and then my thoughts and dreams trailing off mid-concert to Snow White and how even with her ridiculous hairdo and red bow, she had seven instant friends and a Prince (Charming, of course)…

When we got home, I heard him ranting to my mom about my unappreciative behavior and my ungrateful immaturity and short attention span, and, much to my pleasant surprise, she defended me. **Harry—let her be. I promise you, honey, she will never forget this concert or what you did for her tonight, even if her behavior doesn't show it.** (Shit—did I even thank him??) **She is 12 and this was like a prime picture-taking moment—as ridiculous as I know it sounds, this is their whole universe—these posts and the number of likes…ugh it's just awful, but it is their—her—reality. Want me to talk to her?** I think even that was too much of a lecture for my dad—I know how he feels :-). By the time she was done with her wonderful daughter-protecting spiel, he was closing the bathroom door and getting ready for bed.

Dear Diary

Tag you're (not) it

Diary, did you realize that if you aren't tagged in an actual picture from an actual event that you were actually invited to or included in that a person actually cared enough to actually post a picture of—it's as if they didn't know you were there in the first place? Or they didn't want you to be. Or they knew you were there but didn't know your name. Or they didn't want other people to know you were with them. Or they just wanted to piss you off!! This happened to me a while ago, but I just remembered how pissed I was because it just also happened to Sarah. Sarah and I were going to Coffee Shoppe after school with a whole bunch of people, and then Ruby and Katie and Meghan came over to our table and there was a whole bunch of us and it was actually cool and fun. When Katie posted the pics, though, we were all tagged except for Sarah. She was like a ghost. Sarah didn't know why, like, if she did it on purpose or not. And then she had to decide if she comments on it or not. I said, "Screw it, just tag yourself—you were THERE!" So awkward. But now she is all self-conscious around Katie—and it may have even been a mistake and an oversight that she wasn't tagged! But she can't ask her, that would be even worse. *Why is it that to tag oneself, to make a statement that one exists, is actually more of a social suicide than allowing oneself to be ignored and ghosted altogether?* It's just that Katie has around 400 followers, so everyone will know that Sarah basically was left out. Being untagged is kinda like being invisible. If your name isn't there, it's as good as if you weren't even there at all. And it sends a message that you weren't wanted there in the first place. It makes me wonder, why do people invite others if they actually don't care if they are even there in the first place? Is it a pure numbers game? Are they just being nice, or is it, in fact, underlyingly MaleficentlyMalicioussss? I feel it is strange that someone would go through all the effort to surround themselves with people they don't really care about and then double down on the effort to NOT tag them. Katie is a bitch.

I got a ride home this time. I didn't want to ask my mom. I've even been a little worried about her. Like I feel like even though I miss my grandma so much, I kind of bounced back quickly to my normal crazy self. But when will my mom? Will she ever? I mean, how does she ever recover from this? She has so many years to live without her. Mother's Day is around the corner. And now at my Bat Mitzvah my grandma won't be there and my mom will be sad the whole time? That's even unfair to me. I want to be able to celebrate and not worry about my mom. There I go again. Why do I always seem to fall into that selfish trap? *Did you have fun today? Is this yours?* She just popped into my room, holding up a phone case I left downstairs, as if she were sensing my conflict. She is like a ghost lately. She floats around the house barely focused on me or on anything at all. Dare I say I miss when she was always all up in my business?? Now it's like she isn't even here. And at night it feels like she either goes to bed early or she and my dad just close their bedroom door (so I can barely hear them)! I don't like not knowing what she is really thinking! *Do I have to start taking better care of her so she can take care of me?!!*

I'm fine she always says on her nightly calls. Everyone is always checking in on her, which I hope makes her feel good, but I know it will never replace having her mom to say goodnight to. I feel bad for her. And what happens when all these nightly check-ins from her friends stop because they go back to their selfish ways? That's a lot of pressure for me and I'm only 12! I texted Neha to see if she would be on the bus tomorrow afternoon; I feel like I need to vent.

Dear Diary

To be a person is to have one?

It seems like everyone has their go-to person, their fallback, their best friend. But I think having a best friend is more than just the outside stuff we see in the movies, like two girls always laughing with each other and talking on the phone and whispering things in school. To have a person is to have security. Just knowing that person is there even when you are not together is comforting. As I lie here in bed and think about it, I realize that this might actually be one of the only things a middle schooler needs that does not involve followers, image, likes, grades, popularity, a seat at a cafeteria table, party invites, or a phone. It's like, we spend all our energy worrying about all of that stuff when, in reality, all we really need is a friend. A good, true, trustworthy, supportive friend. We need someone who has our back and someone who just really likes us for who we are. I really don't have a person. *I don't even think I know who I want to be my person; maybe that is even worse? Or maybe it would be worse if I really felt like I had a person, but they didn't choose me as theirs? I wonder if Neha could be my person? Or is it Hallie?* I actually think the beauty of having a person is that it's just an understood, mutual arrangement. It is an automatic two-sided deal. It is just meant to be easy and real—that's what makes it so special and so important. I am on a quest. A quest for individuality, attention, popularity, a boyfriend, followers, the ultimate fashion wardrobe, and to find my person. I sort of feel like that sometimes with Hallie, but I don't really think I ever let myself get too close to her because I guess deep down I don't really know if she thinks of me as her person. She has a lot of other people. Like, last week we had to do this stupid survey in school about safety and bullying (I really hate these stupid surveys) and they asked who is the friend you feel will always support you no matter what, who you can confide in (even the school climate people who make the stupid surveys know we need "a person"). I put Hallie on my paper and then I saw at the end of class that Hallie put down Juliet and Ali. I was like, whatever…but, really, that sucks. I don't know if anyone even put me down. It kind of makes me feel like no one wants to be my friend, even though I know that's not really true. It kind of means that *if no one thinks of me as really important to them, then am I actually important at all?* It was kind of cool 'cause on the bus home Neha and I talked about the dumb survey and how clueless the school is for making us take it—knowing all it will do is make us feel more like shit. We laughed about the insanity.

I asked my mom before bed who her person was. I think it was a mistake 'cause she started to get tears in her eyes. I felt like such a jerk. *Well that's kind of a good, but loaded question, I guess? I suppose I have different "people" for different stages of my life and different needs or voids to fill. Does that make sense?* Not really but I kept on listening. I felt like she just needed me to listen to her. I had so much homework to do and I had to write a skit for social studies, so I kind of hoped it wouldn't take too long for her to explain her people to me. *Growing up, Jenny and I spent every day together. We played in the neighborhood, carpooled everywhere, hung out after school, and giggled about first crushes and periods…* At this point in the story I'm not sure if her voice trailed off or if I tuned out because I already knew that about Jenny and I got bored. *I always loved my camp friends* She did always talk about Wendy, Tess, and Stacy. *When I got to high school, I think I kind of floated around. I guess I had lots of different friends but no tight "friend group," as you call it, and no person. I think I spent a lot of time fighting with Grandma and Grandpa and just being happy to hang out anywhere, I didn't really care where.* Interesting. *College—well you have met my best friends from college, Maggie, remember? God we had a blast.* Omg now we were having a trip down memory lane. One simple question! *But, the funny thing is, the closest people to me now are the people I met when you were born. Like just when you think you have made your closest friends, and you will, I promise, you have this beautiful baby and share every day and every mood with the people you meet in playgroups or preschool, and they are the ones you share all of life's ups and downs with because they are living them all with you every single day. There is certainly a sisterhood forever in camp friends because the special ones span childhood till forever, but those friendships take work because your lives take place in all different parts of the city or state. But these "mommy" friends, well, I suppose without them I would be terribly lonely. And they are the ones who really are getting me through this...* I told her I was so sorry I upset her by bringing it up. I can't believe I didn't even think it would also make her miss my grandma 'cause they were so close. So here is what I got from that... I won't meet my best friend until I get married and have a kid and I have a long road ahead of me until I do.

Ok, now I'm depressed. I need to go to sleep. **Go to sleep, sweetie. Give me a hug. You have your whole life to figure these things out. Rome wasn't built in a day. I love you.** Those were her inspirational words as she walked down the hall.

April 22nd

Dear Diary

Passover…

I'm super tired and just not feeling well tonight. I know I shouldn't complain, but I think I have a fever or a stomachache or something. The worst part about it all is that tonight we went to my aunt and uncle's for Passover and, as if it weren't bad enough without my grandma, my mom had to take care of me the whole night because I felt so sick. Is that the lowest of the lows? Or maybe she needed the distraction, and she was grateful for my neediness? *Nevertheless* (I love that word and have always wanted to use it in a sentence), the night was strange and awkward, and even though we talked about my grandma and tried to share stories, everyone knew there was something missing all night long. My poor grandpa; he was quiet but tried to be joyful and sweet, as always, but I got the feeling he was "somewhere else" all night. I mean, we know Jews are all about their suffering, and that's all we read about on Passover (it's so boring and so weird and there are plagues and frogs and blood and lice…and then we are supposed to eat…how does no one ever discuss that part?!) but tonight it really felt like survival and not suffering. No one was sad or crying, my aunt was racing all over the kitchen (she tried to make my grandma's soup and I didn't have the heart to tell her it was just not the same), and my Uncle Robby led the seder as he always does and all of us cousins had our assigned parts and, in a way, it was like business as usual. But I wonder if my aunt's soup made me nauseous? I had to excuse myself and lie down and my mom kept coming up to check on me in my cousin's room. I feel so guilty about tonight, but it wasn't my fault, I was sick! Maybe I was just sad and it made me sick? That would be so next-level crazy, so I think I'll stick with blaming Aunt Iris's soup. Even now, as I'm all tucked in and showered and writing-while-scrolling, my mom still came back in to give me another Tums and a cold washcloth for my forehead. She took my temperature with the back of her hand and with her lips pursed on my forehead, and according to those highly scientific methods, I no longer have a fever, so that's a relief. I think my mom really was relieved for my sudden-illness-onset tonight (you're welcome), as it was a guilt-free opportunity to remove herself periodically from a pretty awful evening filled with painful reminders that the aroma of my grandmother's soup was not filling the house, but in its place, the dense-rotten-chicken-too-many-onions aroma filled the house instead. Now I'm nauseous again.

MOOOOOMMMMMM!!

Dear Diary

The grit tonic

Maybe it's not the things that happen to us that matter or shape our lives—maybe it's the way we handle these situations and events. *Maybe how we handle what comes our way is what defines us? Is it the way we manage and recover from the struggle? Is it actually whether we RECOVER at all?* Maybe the IT factor is resilience. And resilience makes us confident because it gives us the distinct **distinct** motivation to overcome many of the (daily, mundane) obstacles we face. We feel better about ourselves because all of the stupid shit rolls off our backs because we know it doesn't define us (sadly an unfamiliar theory to yours truly). And how we bounce back, or not, sends very strong messages to others about our strength or "level of cool." How we choose to handle our daily setbacks—'cause a 12-year-old girl's life is friggen full of them—is determined by our grit. And in our middle school universe where everyone is watching all of the time, these reactions are an instant tweet or text or message about who we are as a person. Jennifer Lawrence, even when she isn't the "world saving" Katniss, isn't afraid to fall flat on her face in public, and, not only that, but these embarrassing falls actually bring her even more coolness. I mean, she literally falls all the time! Only the select few can do that! As you know, I've dedicated my 12th year of life to this stunning problem-solving research and these mind-blowing observations can help us with the formula for our tonic—our IT Factor tonic.

Here is the new mind-blowing theory of the year—the girls involved in the most drama are the ones that <u>appear</u> to be the most popular and together because they are always surrounded by other girls and are always whispering and attracting attention to themselves, so, therefore, they are always <u>noticed</u>…but I'm beginning to think that those of us who are not always causing a scene are actually better off. However, the "in the long run" might be the missing piece here. The whole concept of "struggling now to be better off later" is a tough one to swallow at my age. If I weren't so awkward and overly philosophical, then I wouldn't even need this diary! I mean, I can't imagine in the world of grown-up moms that the most popular moms in the town are the moms who are always whining and complaining and crying and whispering and competing with each other to look the best and to go to the best parties and on the best vacations. I'm pretty certain, at the ripe age of 12, that confidence and grit are related and that those of us with more of both will be happier and more successful teenagers and adults. So I have to…WAIT??

Is this why adults are always saying to us "Oh, middle school is the worst, just wait till you get older and it is so much easier"? Which also makes me wonder…is it? Is there actually a way to enjoy middle school now? Aren't we wasting these years as young girls because we are lost in our struggle for coolness? Won't I look back on being 12 one day and wish I were young again? (That does sound ridiculous—I don't think any woman would ever long for the days when she had braces, frizzy unmanageable hair, her first periods and her first bra, cafeteria segregation, no boyfriends, skinny legs and no hips, oh, and body odor). I'm pretty sure when I'm old I may look back and want to be 16 or 18 when I had boyfriends and prom dates and tons of friends and gorgeous silky long hair and curves and the best wardrobe with a hint of individuality. That's where it's at. That must be the youth old people want to have again. Not 12. But maybe the less I let stuff get to me at 12, the better off I will be at 12 and then, ultimately, at 17! Sounds like a good goal to me. I can picture my football player boyfriend now…he is tall, and romantic, and he isn't embarrassed to dance and make a fool of himself because he is so cool. He drives a black Jeep and also plays lacrosse in the off season. Oh, and he plays the guitar—just for fun. He is Justin Timberlake, Shawn Mendes, Zac Efron, and Liam Hemsworth. *You are such a dreamer… I do love that about you. But Justin is mine* she always says with a wink. Like, EW, I am not competing with my MOM for future boyfriends. The crazy thing is, even my grandma had a mad crush on Justin Timberlake! How does HE have so much grit and coolness?? The dancing and singing skills don't hurt. I need to keep this grit goal. I need to meet my boyfriend and I'm on a tight schedule.

I was about to sit on the couch and call my mom. My heart just actually sunk a bit. I'm lying here in my bed languishing over my future brave self and my future husband, busy wanting my privacy and kicking my mom out of my room so I can be alone, and this is what I overhear from downstairs. She said it to my dad in the hall as she walked into the den. I think my bedtime (when I finally left her alone each night, I suppose) was when she could finally relax and catch up with my grandma on the phone. And now, just like that, she can't. I didn't feel like screaming her name—I knew she would yell at me for waking Charlotte—so I texted her "Mom, come up, I have a question." I knew she would come; she loves when I need her and ask her for help or advice. The problem was, I didn't know what I was even going to ask her yet and I only had 0.5 minutes to figure it out! All I knew is that I wanted her not to be lonely and miss her mom. I have a very important job.

Dear Diary

The battlefield

I feel like I work pretty hard and I know my parents feel like I do, too. And I think I'm a pretty decent kid (and I know my parents think that, too, most of the time). And I think I'm moderately athletically coordinated and have a fairly good singing voice and can mostly play the piano and I used to be a beast at the recorder! I can dance a little and I have a sense of humor and I can hold my own on skis and in a pool and with a basketball. I have friends, I get good grades, I'm nice to people, I sometimes study for my Bat Mitzvah, I give back (a little) to the community, and I even walk my dog—occasionally. I do NOT make my bed, I suck at doing the dishes, I refuse to do laundry, and I believe I am entitled to leave my clothes all over my floor because it is my room, but that is beside the point. So (gulp), I guess you could say I do very well at being average. Mediocrity is fine and all, but sometimes I want to be SEEN!!! But when I do really deserve something great and I worked really hard at getting it and it is my opportunity to stand out and excel at something—and get noticed—I really want it and I really believe I deserve it. *Is it wrong to feel like an average girl deserves to have her moment to shine every once in a while?* So when I tried out for the spring play of "Beauty and the Beast," I worked really hard at it. I ran my audition lines at home and practiced my **"there must be more than this provincial liiiiiiiffffeeeee"** solo all over the house. I was totally prepared for the letdown if I didn't get it (ya see, that's my grit… getting ready for my high school boyfriend already :)). *We all try our best and not everyone can make it. I just want you to be prepared— even though I think you are amazing and you have worked so hard… I* can handle rejection and disappointment. But it isn't easy to stomach that even my own mom doesn't think I'm good enough for the part. I can't decide, though, if I would rather that she lie to me and tell me how incredibly amazing my singing is or prepare me for failure under the guise of a faint compliment.

What I really struggle with, though, is when I DO get something and it gets taken away. Cue parents. *Is it ok to fight (ask) for something when you really feel entitled to it, or, better yet, to ask your parents to fight this battle for you?* Turns out, I DID get a part; not THE part, but A part. *Madame De La Grande Bouche.* Has a nice sexy sultry ring to it, right? Don't get too excited, she turns into the WARDROBE!!! Believe me—it was enough that I visualized my name in lights for a second. I tasted the fame (albeit, slightly less than Belle's). I heard the roar of the applause and saw all the smiles and congratulations in the school halls the Monday after the show. I envisioned journal dedications to me in the playbill, flowers being tossed onto the stage at the bows. I mean, I totally deserved this part and I EARNED it. (Doesn't every girl always dream of being a closet?) So I think I had a right to fight for it when they decided to give it to someone else. Right? I mean—they didn't exactly *give* it to someone else, they just wanted me to *share* it with another girl after they had already casted ME. They may as well have taken it away from me. I was so sad, I'm not gonna lie. **I'm gonna call your acting teacher Monday. I never call the school and, honey, I don't like seeing you so sad and it isn't fair that they changed the part after rehearsals already started.** At first I was so embarrassed that my dad was going to get involved and I told him no way, but then I realized it really wasn't fair what they did to me. I was mortified to think that I would only get the part back because my dad called or because I complained, but at the same time, as long as I get the part, who really cares how? It isn't as if I didn't earn the part in the first place. I remember when my old babysitter—who had been a dancer for years—finally, during her last year, tried out for a lead in the show (after years of never getting one) and she didn't get one. She felt like it was her last shot. She was devastated. *Are there times when someone deserves a part as a kind of recognition of their time and effort and not necessarily for their talent?* I don't know if her parents complained, but I bet they should have. She is an awesome dancer and she should have gotten her moment to shine because she was graduating and it's only fair. I know, what seems "fair" is not always what is supposed to be…but that's not fair. **I'm just saying, this whole life lesson about "fairness" is a very slippery slope. We have to be careful here. We can't fight all her battles.** One. This is one battle. And it's a dispute, not a battle. This isn't a Hamilton duel. It's a conversation. And maybe, just maybe, this actually IS a big deal. Maybe not in the scheme of life, but maybe it IS in the scheme of life.

What if this moment of stardom is going to open up doors for me as a future actress of the stage and screen—all because my 7th-grade acting teacher gave me the very shot I needed to acknowledge my hidden, unrecognized talent? And if it is taken away, I might never know the power and self-esteem boost it could have had on my growth and potential. I'm trying so hard to be a sensitive and caring daughter. Why can't she just be on my side for once? Goodnight.

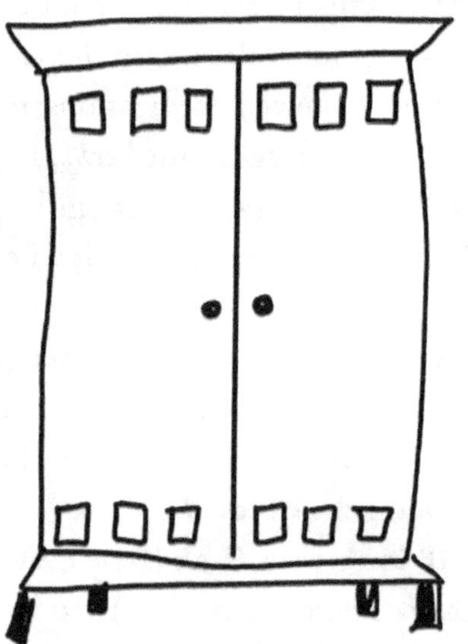

April 26th

Dear Diary

Stuck like glue

P.S. I found this on my nightstand when I woke up this morning. How cute is my dad?

Dear Magpie,

I know you'll think it is weird that your dad is writing you a note, but I just want you to know how proud I am of you and I sometimes find it hard to express it to you directly, and for that, I apologize. Maggie, you amaze me every day—you are unafraid to be yourself, you're kind to others, you are so much fun to be around. I think the best word to describe you right now is you have gumption. It's a great word, and it says a lot. Don't shy away from your gumption, even when the world and the school tell you that you have to look and act like everyone else. You remind me of your amazing mom, and I know sometimes you and Mom don't see eye to eye, but Maggie, that is because she sees so much of herself in you and she loves the spark in your eyes and in your heart. Maybe, come to think of it, Mom and I both should tell you more often, but know how proud we both are of you. I know it isn't always easy being your age, especially with all of the pressures of social media, but I remember being 12 and I am always here to listen if you ever want to talk. I can't believe my little girl is growing up so quickly. To me, you will always be the adventurous explorer who pretended to be Lucy finding her way through the wardrobe into the snowy wood and the sweet little princess dressed in blue pretending to lose her slipper on the stairs so I could pick it up and find you. Stay adventurous and never lose sight of your fairy tale dreams—it's the perfect magical combination that makes you, YOU!

I love you.

Love, Dad

If I <u>hadn't been</u> (using my best subjunctive, here) so late for school this morning, in theory I <u>would have</u> loved to process this note from my dad, but now the lifetime of a full day in school has passed and I have much bigger fish to fry. I should update you. The teacher apologized profusely to my dad. She said they hadn't realized the impact it would have on me, they only did it to balance out the blocking on the stage or whatever. Regardless, they switched it back and no one even knew what went on behind the scenes. Hollywood here I come…

Only in middle school would a person sit at the same cafeteria table day in and day out with people they do not want to sit with because they feel they have no other option. For three years. And who is to say that high school will be any different? *It's all so much better and easier in high school, Magpie* (she said as if in a movie dream sequence). She also thinks high school is all about cheerleaders and football players and singing in the cafeteria like in "Grease" and "High School Musical." So I'm not so clear that her judgment is the best. I just cling to my simple hopes that high school is the land of getting noticed, floating comfortably and fluidly between cafeteria tables, the demise of "friend groups," and making out and having too many boyfriends to balance with my homework.

I see it happen all the time, the middle school cafeteria paralysis. Girls like me sitting in the same exact seat every single day, even with girls they don't like or with girls they feel don't like them. Stuck. *Can you imagine as a grown-up constantly putting yourself in the same bad situation over and over again and expecting it to get better even if everything remains the same (except the outfits, of course)?* Is this yet another middle school phenomenon? Is this one of those miserable parts of growing up where "it will get easier, I promise" because no high schooler or adult in their right mind would ever feel so stuck? Here is the even more crazy part—even if us stuck girls were ready to change tables (though I did sit with Neha a few times), and even if we had a back-up option of another place to go sit (most people don't), and even if there was a spot at that table for us…leaving our existing table would be social suicide. Ripple effects heard all around the school. "Who does she think she is? Where does she think she is going??" "What right does she have to change and be someone else?" "Is she gonna dress all differently now? Is she gonna be goth, or sporty, or nerdy?" "Social climber."

And that is just from the spectators. Imagine the table chat at both the involved tables?? If this girl got up and left all by herself—well then, I would like to meet her, and she should be president. (Somehow my sitting with Neha doesn't feel quite as bold. Was it??) If a girl has that much IT factor to be brave enough to get unstuck, then, well you guessed it—she wouldn't have been stuck in the first place. Chances are, even in the fantasy world in which this stuck girl would break the stuck cycle, said girl would never go it alone. She would always have a partner in crime (girls always do: take note—they never act alone). The table chat would be insane! "How could they?" "That is so obnoxious!" "I thought we were friends!" And how would these two brave girls even explain the move? (By the way, they would absolutely, even under the valiant and heroic effort to change the face of middle school life forever, still say to their "original table" of friends "No, it has nothing to do with you guys, we just need to talk to these guys about something…" and make up some bullshit excuse because god forbid they ever hurt their feelings!) And we haven't even discussed how the <u>receiving</u> table would react! "Who are these two?" "We, like, don't even have any room." "What if their table gets mad at us?" And then the conversations at that table… "Oh my god those girls were SO annoying that's why we had to move here." And the bad-mouthing begins…but never to one's face. What are girls so afraid of that we choose to stay unhappy or in an uncomfortable situation because we have no option of leaving? The crazy part is, we really are stuck. There is no flexibility in the word "cafeteria," so let's just leave it alone and wait out the years of torture. Things can only get better, right? (Or so we are told.)

Her Bat Mitzvah is in less than two months and now she has play rehearsals every day. I'm too tired to fight with her, Harry. It's like she can sense my upstairs distraction and warped priorities. And the weird thing is, Maggie is just so busy now… And then I heard her voice kind of trail off as if she were processing that part. Maybe she wants me around more even if I drive her crazy? This is a lot on my scrawny 12-year-old shoulders.

Dear Diary

Caped Crusaderess

I am unique, I guess. I stick up for people—more specifically, for friends and for what is right. Call me a nerd. I am learning to accept it. I might want to look and act like everyone else, and only had a brief bout with individuality when I wore my new hardcore black boots to school, but I do try to draw the line when other people aren't being nice and I am there to see it. Even a simple "that's not nice" or "let's invite her, too" can go a long way. Like remember when that twin day happened, and I was worried other girls would feel left out? I'm glad I think about other people, but does that really help my social status and lack of popularity? You can pretty much guess the answer. The thing is, I guess I just hope others would do the same for me, but they don't! Even good friends! When some of my friend group is making plans and I am left out, why can't one of them just say "hey, let's include Maggie" or whatever? The kicker is, it happens right in front of me sometimes. Like "hey are you guys coming over after school?" and I have to pretend I don't even hear that? And where is Hallie or Ali to be like "shhh, guys, not cool, Maggie is right there" or "Maggie, we are all going out for ice cream after the show, why don't you come?" Nope. Nada. It feels like it happens all the time, even though I know it doesn't. Sometimes I wonder if being left out is actually easier than knowing no one stood up for you when you were. Are they all selfish Switzerland? As long as they are invited, who cares? I've heard it a million times since kindergarten—***Not everyone has to be included all of the time, Maggie.*** It makes sense, even when it hurts. What I am not ok with is when the invitation and plan-making happens right in front of me, and no one bats an eye. Isn't <u>that</u> what we learn in kindergarten? *Are all of those basic rules of "how to treat others with* *respect" thrown out the window because we are 12??* Maybe we are the next Mean Girls, Pretty Little Liars, and Gossip Girls—we are these dreadful characters that the world portrays all middle school girls to be. (Or are we that way because we are copying the awful girls on tv and in the movies??) Neha and I were having this very philosophical conversation during art today and when the teacher shut us down, we just picked up right where we left off when we got on the bus. Kind of a "which came first, the chicken or the egg, the movie or the behavior, the characters or the cafeteria"…and the list went on. We are so deep and <u>mindful</u>. The problem is, when one person is mean, it makes others want to do it right back, so the annoying cycle of exclusion and spite just continues. Why can't someone (besides me) try to break the cycle? It's that bravery thing again. We need a middle school superhero! (Clearly, I've been watching too much Marvel and "Stranger Things"). She (or he, I guess) would wear a sick, tight outfit (not a princess dress or anything like that). More like Wonder Woman but dressed more beachy with a cool California vibe (I'll get back to her outfit later). She would swoop into the cafeteria or hallway every time this stuff happens and take out her phone and post something mean about the other girl or take a selfie with the victim, which would give the victim extra cool superpowers because everyone would see it. She would be like a movie star, but with the power to take bad people off their pedestal. She would be like…Taylor Swift.

I'm sad for her. They all went to the high school show tonight and a huge group of them went out for ice cream after and only Maggie, Neha, and a few others weren't included in the plans. Girls can be so cruel. I would have driven her and those girls, but she shot me a look that sent shivers down my spine. That's why she was so quiet when she got home. She's right—when we pulled into the garage my mom got out of the car and just gave me a big teddy bear full-body hug and I was all for it. All she said was ***I'm sorry, Maggie. That probably sucked. I love you so much.*** I was silent but I leaned into the hug. I went straight upstairs to my room. I actually knew she wanted to save me so badly tonight—she practically witnessed the mayhem. I was so relieved when she got my signal to just lay low and resist the motherly need to protect her young. She was my superhero tonight. If I had to wait at the school for one extra second I would have literally died.

Dear Diary

The secret is out

Girls—we are all screwed. That bullshit that everyone has been feeding us about middle school being the worst part of their lives and that they promise everything gets better when they are older…remember that? Well, newsflash, it isn't true. It's life. I saw my great-grandma today (my dad's grandma, GiGi Violet), and let's just say she shared some stories about her card games and her senior center drama that were not too reassuring about the future. Here she is, at almost 90 years old, sharing stories about the girls (yes, that is exactly what she calls them, *girls*) that she has known for SEVENTY years, and she is gossiping about the one that no one wants to include in the game because she always tells boring stories, and the bossy one who always arranges the game at the house <u>she</u> feels like going to that week (the "queen," they secretly call her). Then there is my great-grandmother's closest friend, Meredith (I always remember her name because it reminds me of "Grey's Anatomy" because this Meredith was married to a doctor, which GiGi Violet was always so proud to share), with whom she always discusses the goings-on behind the scenes and they both agree that Penelope (poor sweet Penny) is losing her mind and she shouldn't be allowed to play anymore but no one has the heart to tell her, and that they shouldn't have to have the game at Selma's house because she has a cat and it doesn't feel clean, but no one has the heart to tell her, and that every time they meet at the club to play bridge, Esther always embarrasses them because she is too loud in the card room, but no one will open their mouth and speak up and tell her to be quiet. Seventy years of friendship based on holding back what you really think. Same games. Same girls in the same bridge game. "Why don't you switch games and play with different ladies?" I asked my GiGi. To which she shook her head and said *Oh no! I could never do that to the girls, and*

I can't leave Meredith alone to fend for herself with that flock of birds. Years of loyalty, my dear. (Her voice is a little different than my mom's, but when it comes to words of wisdom, it all sounds the same.) And then she jumped right into the fact that, actually, Meredith Grey (sorry I got bored) is a bit cheap and everyone always says (behind Meredith's back, of course) that it is uncomfortable to go out with her because *she never likes to pay or share a ride.* So even if they did switch games, the other "girls" don't want Meredith there either. I wonder what they say about my GiGi?? Maybe she is Switzerland and that is why she is stuck. For 70 years. Or maybe she just really loves these girls like sisters, and this gossip and complaining—I think the Jewish word is kvetching—is just what keeps things exciting at their age. I mean, how dull would just easygoing, happy, reciprocal friendships be? *Is she stuck or is it a choice to stay?* I guess I won't know till I'm 90. I think the other part of this girl code is that this is just part of who we are as girls. It is in our DNA. We all secretly thrive on this unsettled stress and, perhaps, a hint of drama. It all stems from our fear of being alone. We are just social creatures. The last time she came to visit us, she spent the entire time complaining about Phyllis (she is the bossy one who always wants to host). *She has no idea that we are tired of going to her house and no one likes the walnut brownies she serves, but what can we do?* When we got home from the obligatory, but comical, visit with Lady GiGi Violet, I just sat on the couch on my phone the whole time, chuckling to myself, watching my dad have zero idea of how to respond to my mom when she started to complain—not only did he not understand this complicated layer of secrets and suffrage, but we all know he just couldn't care less. Guys have it so easy. Such simple boring creatures.

btw—play rehearsal is SO boring. I mean, "Beauty and the Beast" is so preschool and cliché—as IF a princess would fall in love with a beast (as if a beast would love a bookworm) who cares? Goodnight.

Dear Diary

The Hunger Games

So, we are going to Boston. Sounds nice and simple, right? Well, dear diary, when you send 300 12-year-olds to Boston and put them in a hotel and ask them to get in groups of four for their rooms—it's like your biggest nightmare. Asking us to choose our favorite friends, in front of everyone. And everyone has to be included. And someone will be sharing a room and even a bed with the people who have NO friends at all! Can you imagine the pressure it places on 12-year-olds to strategically divide their friends so that, selfishly, they end up sharing a bed and a room with the people they like the most, but being very careful to ensure those people are also choosing them for their room! This is a very delicate and dangerous matter, and, as you can imagine, it's a breeding ground for deceit and secrets and lies and backstabbing and manipulation and **drama**. For real. Middle school at its best. We may all be girls who are afraid to make a change—but we are also girls who know we must survive—and that means it is also in our DNA to manipulate situations to protect ourselves from humiliation. We have officially been released into the arena, and we must carefully and swiftly select our weapons and run for protection.

Do the adults who work in our school who claim to know adolescents actually think this is a good idea—allowing us to select people for our rooms? Are they actually as clueless as our parents? Shouldn't the adults who choose to teach young teenagers how to be young adults have a better sense for what will throw these young teenagers over the edge? It's the Hunger Games out there. No one knows who will get chosen and no one knows who to trust and who will survive. This is actually, literally insane! I know I will *only* share a bed with Hallie, and I would love to also stay in a room with Ali and Maya and Juliet. In an ideal world (meaning: never and nowhere), those three girls will also choose me on their list, and we would all live happily ever after. But not only would that NEVER happen, I don't even have a way of trusting or believing them if they tell me they <u>did</u> write my name down because the forms are all confidential and they go to the guidance counselor and SHE does the rooms. So they would never tell me to my face that they didn't choose me (the same way GiGi's "friends" never tell each other the truth), so I would totally believe that they did and then, I know, it will all suck because I'm going to be stuck with the losers and dorks and kids who smell and don't shower and sleep naked, and sleepwalk and talk in their sleep and snore…with a teddy bear. It's a war zone out there. Leaving our fate in someone else's hands. My complete happiness and future existence as below-the-radar, averagely well-liked and accepted rests entirely in the hands of Mrs. Beetlejuice (I think her real name is Mrs. Beatle, but she took her life into her own hands by working with middle schoolers so that's what you get), who barely knows me and my insecure needs and my fears of being excluded. Maybe I should make an appointment! This is going to be a loooooong week. *Awwwwww, I remember when I went to Boston with my grade!* MOM!! This isn't about the 1800s! Things have changed! I felt bad. I didn't say that to her. I do know she meant well. Every time she tells me a story about when she was young, I can't help but think she is thinking about her young and healthy mom, too. I just tried to change the subject and brush it off. **I have to say, it seems like Maggie really has this one figured out. And this is a pretty big deal**! First of all, I can't believe she actually admitted to my dad that, for once, something I was worried about actually WAS a big deal, and second, I guess my lie to protect her from a trip down memory lane actually worked. I feel kind of uncomfortable right now in bed that she really doesn't know how stressed out I am—and how petrified I am about who I will end up rooming with. I'm not sure how long I will be able to fake it. I'm actually a wreck. I'll never fall asleep I just know it.

Dear Diary

I, like, totally, 100% forgive you

And so it begins. I knew this would cause drama. Ali got mad at Georgia because she told Maya that she saw her paper in homeroom and that Ali didn't write Maya down for her top 4 in her room for Boston. Ali, of course, lied and told Maya that she did write her down, so Maya was relieved because she wrote down Ali. But since Ali was lying, now Maya is screwed out of one match for her room (didn't I say this would happen?). This new girl Stephanie has been totally stalking me lately and wants me to room with her because she doesn't have anyone to room with because we have math and Spanish together and I am, like, the only person who even says hi to her. But even if she is cool, I don't want to be known as the one who took pity on the new girl and end up with just Stephanie and two other kids I barely know who also had no one to room with?! So we were all freaking out at lunch about the rooms and everyone is pretending to each other that they wrote everyone's name down (even though we are only allowed to write four names and we are only guaranteed one if it is a match and they wrote our name too). *What would have happened if we all told the truth*, you might ask? HA! I thought it would never happen. I thought it couldn't be done. I thought the sky would have been scorched and the seas would have dried up. Maybe it was a small step for us girls but a large step for girlhood…but I said, gulp, at lunch, after all this barking and clawing and growling and lying to each other—"Guys—we know we are all friends, but we know we each are closer to some of us than we are to others. We literally have to be honest with each other about who we put down, otherwise we will all get screwed and we will be rooming with Pete over there who picks his nose and eats tuna fish for breakfast" (I mean, since he's a guy that would obvs never happen, but you get the point) and, suddenly, there was silence. "We have to promise that there won't be hurt feelings and that we won't take it personally in order for this to work." (As IF that were even a possibility—it was still worth a shot.) And so we did. We shared who we wrote (and only two people wrote me down, which was so devastating and humiliating). Maya started to cry and ran off because she found out the truth about Ali (and only Sarah wrote her name down). Of course, Ali and Juliet and Emma were written down, like, three times each, but whatever. The bigger thing here is that Ali had to run off and deal with Maya. And now SHE had to be honest about their friendship—for the first time ever. They both went to the guidance counselor. (I'll bet Mrs. Beetlejuice is regretting this whole setup right about now :)) I kept glancing over at Neha's table to see if I could catch her eye during my groundbreaking, game-changing, history-rewriting cafeteria table conversation… She did look at me as if to reply "same shit over here" with a quick eye-roll and a smile. Truthfully, the two of us should just room together and skip all this nonsense, but I think there is a delicate hard-wiring which forces us to suffer through this that we cannot alter.

Maybe they both had this life-altering moment, who knows? Is it possible that honesty really *was* the best policy? Certainly not, according to GiGi Violet, but maybe that is because they weren't honest 50 years ago and it just go to be too late. I don't know. Sometimes I wonder if it really ever is, if it means hurting someone else's feelings. But the thing is, when there are lies, people's feelings still get hurt, so maybe it all depends on the situation. All I know is I waited for them when they got out and Maya said "I, like, totally, 100% forgive you" to Ali. So maybe it worked? Maybe she now understands that Ali doesn't feel as close with her as she does to Ali? That must hurt her feelings so much—but maybe in the long run it is better because Maya won't always be so disappointed in Ali always blowing her off? And maybe Maya won't try so hard to be her friend and Ali might actually like that and then Ali may want to be her friend all over again? I get this—but do you? So maybe I was right?

Now what? *Good for you, Magpie. Your friend group (as you girls call it) could use a good shake-up anyway.* I'm beginning to think that the way things have been going with my group of friends, we really could use a good shake-up after all. **Harry, I think I'm finally getting through to her.** In case you're wondering, I'm gonna let her think that is true. Julie needs a win these days.

Continuing on like we all like each other and faking it is not only exhausting, but it is really only making things worse. Boston could be the best city ever—and we haven't even gone shopping yet!

Dear Diary

Motels, puberty, and teacher chaperones

If she thinks she can text me from Boston and I will come get her, she has another thing coming she ranted before I left. My mom can be so negative at night when she is tired. As if I would have had my mom come drive to Boston and rescue me!! It's like she has no faith in me at all whatsoever. The funny thing is, everything I predicted would happen, did. But the funnier thing is—it was better than I could have ever thought! I did only end up with one friend, Maya. And initially I was so pissed and scared, too, because the other four (Ali, Hallie, Juliet, and Georgia) all ended up together and I thought they would have a much better time and have so many private jokes and Maya and I would feel so left out. But Anna and Lindsey, the other two girls we were matched up with, were actually really fun! Anna is in my science class and, actually, Lindsey and I didn't even realize we used to play soccer together and even had a random after-school art class together when we were in 3rd grade! We stayed up so late and ate so much junk and sugar and watched "Friends" and Jimmy Fallon and actually died laughing. All the boys were on a different hall, and they weren't supposed to come to our floor, but, like that would ever happen. Mr. Roland tried to take it so seriously and "set the ground rules because we are REPRESENTING OUR SCHOOL" (gimme a break) and said he and Mrs. Spengler (she is like 85 years old, none of us could even believe she came on the trip—and we think she is rooming with Mrs. Beetlejuice) were going to put tape on our doors at night so they would know in the morning if we snuck out of our rooms at night. Just another arbitrary stupid rule adults think is appropriate which everyone knows will be broken with zero consequences. I'm pretty sure a few people even hooked up by the elevator or in the stairwell when the teachers weren't looking. It was crazy! We were all running around getting ice and going to the vending machines and playing ding dong ditch with the elevators! (Everyone even said that Missy gave Billy Rudnick a hand job while they were in the back of the bus…not exactly sure if that is gross or cool or normal or whatever, but he is totally gross and she is a slut so who cares?) It was chaos at the Red Roof Inn but I'm pretty sure we won't forget it. Is it wrong that we went to Boston to learn about American history and all I remember is double stuffed Oreos and Billy Rudnick's hand job? Teddy and Alex were both on my bus and I don't know if I even like either one of them or if they hate me, but it was so awkward it made me blush to even think about it. Nothing really "happened" to me at all on the trip. Like I wonder what, if anything at all, I will ever even remember about my three-day trip to Boston, and when my daughter goes one day, what events or memories will I have to share with her? I'm not even sure I learned anything about the Boston Tea Party or Paul Revere or the American Revolution or whatever war it was, but I know I loved the fried dough in the food hall at Quincy Market and the penguins in the aquarium were so cute. But nothing really happened, unless "happening" means giving a hand job or making out or getting into trouble. I guess maybe the fact that it was just fun was the biggest surprise of all, and maybe that is all I will remember one day when my own daughter goes on her trip (I'm only having daughters, I know it).

You had a great time, honey, because, for once, you weren't expecting perfection and you just let things happen! I know what she means—that I lowered my expectations and it made me relax. I wasn't trying to live my life in a fantasy Disney movie or Hollywood's dumb portrayal of every middle school in America. *Maybe sometimes the best lessons of growing up are when we are distracted and uninhibited because we're supposed to be doing something else altogether?* It's kind of like when you are at an assembly or in class and you are supposed to be quiet, and suddenly you have a laughing attack or extremely important things to say to the people sitting in the row in front of you. When we are not trying so hard to make things good or fun or better, sometimes that is when the best memories are made. (Oh, and sidebar…Juliet and Ali fought the whole time, so, not gonna lie, that was pretty awesome.)

May 13th

Dear Diary

The girl with balls of steel

I didn't invite Ruby and Katie to my Bat Mitzvah. **She has to cut her list down. Look at this, Harry—she doesn't even like half of these people and some of them she hasn't even spoken to since the 3rd grade.** I don't think my dad really cared either way. Lately he just tries to stay out of my mom's way and keep her happy, just like I do. I was in no mood to upset her and make her cry even more—she has been so fragile these past few weeks since my grandma died, and I don't even really know what to say anymore so I just try to agree with her. I really had no choice but to cut them out. They aren't that nice to me, and last year Katie had a birthday party and I wasn't invited, so we are even. The only problem is that Ruby's Bat Mitzvah in the fall of 8th grade is going to be huge and awesome and I know she won't invite me now, so that sucks. I think hers is even gonna be in the city at a club or something. But we aren't really friends, so I have to realize that it's weird if they come to mine anyway. But here's the thing—I don't have, like, 100 friends, and I certainly don't have 50 guy friends! But I have to invite guys to my Bat Mitzvah, or the girls won't even want to come! So, I'm adding all these random people to my list to desperately try to make my party cool. *Is adding a bunch of strangers to my party list going to add to the "cool" factor and will people think I'm cool(er) if my party is more fun because it will just be the people who actually have fun together?* (um…YES!) (Somehow, I don't think this is what God intended when somewhere he wrote that girls should become a bat mitzvah.) I mean, really, this whole thing is a popularity game and all about the dress. And the pictures. And the countdown. And the posts your friends write before and during and after your party. It's a friggen contest. Oh, and a big milestone in my life, blah blah blah. Ironic, isn't it, that at the very moment where we are supposedly entering adulthood, we strip ourselves down to the most juvenile behavior? Who is the prettiest? Who looks the worst? Whose party was more fun? Who has the most friends? Who got a candle? Whose sweatshirt was the coolest? Whose hair looked the best? Curly or straight? Up or down? Short or long? Sweatshirts or water bottles? Did they dance or jump? Whose photos made the montage?

Anyway, I got off topic. Sorry. Katie just texted me and said, "I keep checking my mail and I didn't get your invite yet." WOW! That is insane! A girl who doesn't play games. A girl who (almost) just comes right out and says it? She was a bit passive-aggressive about it so she can't exactly move up to Phoebe status, but I was still impressed…and alarmed. It is actually quite inspiring—until I had to figure out how to answer her! *Could I be as direct with her as she was with me?* Should I play girl games instead and be like "What? You didn't? It must have gotten lost in the mail!" and then quickly beg my mom to add one more to the list just to avoid an awkward confrontation? So I ran to my mom and we really thought it out. Maybe this was an opportunity for me to be honest. I did it in the cafeteria the other day, I can do it again! *Why should you lie to her only to make her feel better and then be stuck having a girl at your party who you don't really like and who didn't invite you to hers?* I practiced with my mom. She smiled at me. I felt, in a way, like we were teammates and she was psyching me up for a big play. I sensed her faith in me… You can do this, Mags, I heard her say silently as she winked at me. I think she was proud of me and I knew I was proud of myself, but I was also secretly shitting my pants. I took a big gulp of my small, yet slowly growing bottle of Grit Tonic, I texted back, and then I hit send. Gulp. There it was. No turning back. "I'm sorry, Katie. I had to keep my party small and I didn't even really know we were friends because you didn't invite me to your party last year." Then there were the dreaded flashing dots on the phone…like she was writing back. Then the dots stopped, like she didn't know how to respond. Then the dots came back again… How was she going to respond to that? "Ok." she replied.

"Sorry" I wrote back, and I kind of was.

Dear Diary

Uniformity

My camp friend's cousin has a uniform. She goes to a private school. Schools have uniforms because the stupid grown-ups who made that policy do it because they want to eliminate competition and inappropriate outfits. But that's not how girls operate—in case you haven't figured that out by now. Most girls like me that go to a regular school spend a very specific amount of time and energy each evening and each morning deciding about our mood and connecting that to our daily outfit for school—what kind of message do we feel like sending that day? Are we showing confidence (jeans, boots, a tight shirt and a cardigan, hair blown out and straightened)? Feeling flirty and girly and seeking attention (a flowy skirt with knee-high socks and boots or converse, with a tight T-shirt and braids)? Feeling lazy and grungy—showing everyone that day that we don't care how we look, we woke up like this and don't need to put in any effort because we are tired and it's dreary outside (converse, leggings, a T-shirt and a flannel, hair down and wavy or up in a loose bun)? *Sometimes it really does amaze me how much you really do (think you) have it all figured out, Miss Mags.* I could go on…but my point is that just because you take away a girl's freedom to express herself through her outfit, doesn't mean she saves all of that energy and just puts it into her schoolwork. Turns out the teachers who make these rules underestimated us girls yet again, and our ability to waste incredible amounts of energy on how we look, dress, and act. It's like a secret power of ours. **I swear she could write a book someday** I saw her text her friends. (Did I really impress her for once?)

My camp friend and her cousin just facetimed with me this weekend and her cousin said she and all of her friends do everything they can to stand out even with their uniform. They switch up their socks. They wear all different types of makeup. They have a million pairs of shoes. They roll their skirt up higher than they are allowed to. They spend all morning ironing their hair and tweezing their eyebrows. They paint their nails obsessively. So instead of just spreading out all of that energy on their clothing (painstakingly planned to appear effortless), they channel all of that time into accessorizing. By limiting a girl's ability to express herself through fashion, you are inadvertently creating even more pressure for her to stand out as an individual and be more outrageous because she feels lumped in with everyone else in the same khaki skirts and boring monochromatic polo shirts. *Maybe uniform schools are creating more of the exact pressure and competition that their policies were precisely written to avoid?* A girl will be a girl no matter what limits are placed on her. Even in tan pants (sometimes I crack myself up).

I'm trying to fall asleep but my parents, for the strangest of reasons, have decided to get up off the couch and dance to the theme song from their Netflix show. They have been binging this sad, twisted, double-murder-about-town, turmoil-ridden sobfest show set in the early 1900s and suddenly, their wedding song plays in the background (Diary, I know this only because they, out of the blue, raised the tv volume to like a million and don't seem to care that they might wake Charlotte (and should, in theory, be waking me) and started to slow dance in the friggen living room!!) What is even happening right now?

I'm exhausted and they are keeping me awake!

May 16th

Dear Diary

American Horror Story

In the kitchen this morning, Charlotte and I were teasing my parents—for some reason they were both making coffee at the same time and they even smiled at one another (it was kind of cute—and a little like it must feel before a tsunami hits, so I was suspicious and very prepared). I whispered to Charlotte something like, we have to stick together, you and me, and she grinned from ear to ear (it doesn't take much to make a little sister happy).

Anyway, here's an old classic theme being dusted off…be careful what you wish for. I'm getting braces this week. I think I will look so ridiculous now on stage in the play and dressed to kill in my Bat Mitzvah dress… but I've been wanting braces for so long. At first, I wanted them so I could stand out and look older, because last year it was new and cool to be one of the first. Now, I'm one of the last and I feel weird not fitting in. Sometimes it really feels like it's hard to just reach a comfortable place in middle school. I kind of feel like once one thing gets resolved, then we just move quickly on to the next fiasco—the unliked post, the mean Snapchat, the bad hair day, the rejection, the cafeteria fails, and now the braces. I was just feeling inspired and invigorated by our Boston trip and new friends, and now this bomb gets dropped on me. I mean, it isn't like I didn't know it was coming, but how could I have prepared? Not only will I finally have a mouth full of metal, but no one will even notice because it's old news. *Is there actually anything on this earth worse than being old news?* I couldn't even complain to my mom again. **You've been begging for braces since the 5th grade and now you are crying because of it?? I will never understand you.** She kept shaking her head at me—with this crazy disappointed look on her face—a look that said-no, screamed-a thousand things to me with just one side eye and a head tilt. I wish she would stop yelling at me all the time! If she just took me to the orthodontist in 3rd grade when everyone else went, this never would have happened! It is all her fault! Why can't she just admit it?? I am not overreacting, I am not being ridiculous, I am responding to something very real and crappy and it could have been avoided. And she expects me to just go to sleep nicely with all my homework done and my backpack ready for tomorrow when all I really can think about is that if my mom didn't hate me so much, she wouldn't have put me through this nightmare of an existence. Mediocrity, second best, unoriginal, and now, old news. **She is impossible!!** This one she screamed so loud she actually wanted me to hear it! "THANKS FOR THE SUPPORT!!" It felt good to scream that right back at her. I HATE being 12!! Life is so unfair. I mean, not every second of middle school is a nightmare, but it feels safe to say that most of it is because we feel like these outside forces are controlling us. It's like we are all possessed and are helpless in our own adolescence. STUCK. Maybe this very helplessness and constant self-doubt are the forces that help us to be stronger adults, but the problem is, we are too young to care about how we will be as adults, or to care how we will learn from these experiences. So these painful, yet allegedly life-changing experiences are wasted on the young? All of the awfulness happens when we are too self-absorbed and depressed and hormonal to actually step back and be like, wow, that was a difficult situation and I feel awful but I know it is all happening to teach me a valuable life lesson and I will be a better, more evolved person tomorrow because of it. That's psychotic! We want to be happy and be cool and we want it now! And, for me, getting braces right before my Bat Mitzvah, it is too late!

I wanted to say to her something like, Mom, I know you miss Grandma and I do, too, but don't you remember when you were my age and you were mad at your mom like you wrote in your diary? Maybe she should re-read her diary so she remembers the suffering all moms inflict upon their children. Maybe I should suggest she does and give away my secret that I read her diary? Perhaps the unintended consequences would wreak havoc. I'll sleep on it.

May 18th

Dear Diary

We never really leave middle school

My mouth is in so much pain but I'm going to try to change the subject to distract myself. Plus, my mom got me a milkshake right after so I can't really complain that much right now. I didn't even have to eat dinner because the milkshake *was* my dinner. My afternoon with my mom got me thinking…she talked the whole time about when she got braces and the boy who liked her and *he was so adorable, Freddy, and he had braces and we had our first awkward braces kiss in Cameron's basement. And I remember right after Grandma made me go shopping for my Bat Mitzvah dress and she convinced me to get this fartsy dress…* Again, I lost her somewhere in between smiling and then seeming sad as she talked about fighting with her own mom about the dress. Anyway, back to me. I kind of felt like she was talking so much because she was nervous for me to get braces, and then there was a part of me that thought she rambled so much because she felt so guilty that she did this to me. Anyway— it got me thinking—through the endless storytelling and reminiscing of the glory days of her youth—ask your parents about their strongest memories of their past; they will always talk about middle school and high school. They always laugh when they remember the awkwardness and grin knowing they no longer feel that lonely or left out—but they always seem to smirk a little, as if to say *those memories, as much as I don't want to admit it, are still a huge part of who I am today.* Even though their brains were as chaotic and confused as ours are now, they remember it all so clearly. I know I am wise beyond my 12 years, but I can see it in my parents' eyes. It's in the reflection, like when they look in the mirror, they see their teenage selves sometimes. I swear if I had $5 for every time my mom looked at her reflection in shock and horror and stated something like "How can I LOOK like this if I still feel 18 years old?!" *If they remember all of the pain and suffering and the sporadic joys and plentiful awkward moments so well, then why don't they have more patience with us while we go through it?*

I actually don't think the grown-ups have it figured out at all. They just look better than we do so the stuff seems easier to deal with. *What if all the drama in middle school is learning how to survive and figure ourselves out, all because the drama never really goes away after all?* So the hardest part of life actually happens to us when we are too young and insecure to even know how to handle it—that doesn't make any sense at all. Things were so simple back in 2nd grade when all we cared about were what dolls we had and if we would go on the swings or play basketball at recess. When we didn't have phones and weren't glued to the sucking-in tornado of stupid social media. The most important time in our lives—the time when we have to figure out who we will be as a person, what our entire identity is and what is the meaning of our existence—happens, as it turns out, when we are only a teenager and our brains are underdeveloped balls of insecure mush. So the rest of our lives is determined by how we do right now?! I can barely get myself out of bed and to the bus on time and now I have just realized my entire prediction of adult success and stability and the level of my future happiness rests in these next few years! And I don't even have a boyfriend! The very core of all my adult memories is being shaped during these years of turmoil. I am just nearing the end of 7th grade, I am sitting in my childish room still covered in stuffed animals, dolls, and old photos of me with my parents and with my grandparents on special occasions, and from the comfort of my twin bed in the corner, I am trying to remember what even happened in September or even in December, and what life lessons I might have learned but apparently have already forgotten. Maybe it isn't exactly the remembering of the lessons or the daily suffering, but just knowing I'm almost finished with 7th grade, survived, made a new friend, took some chances, fell in the cafeteria, and even lost my grandma—maybe that is the big stuff that is shaping me even when I don't even realize it? I just wish I were popular or confident or some magical combination of both so I would be less moody and feel better and not feel this constant crushing weight of my very own future. And what's more, I feel pressure to solve all of this for my entire generation! That's a lot of pressure for a kid like me! **That's a lot of pressure for a kid like her. She is so busy climbing mountains, she is forgetting to brush her teeth and say "hi" in the mornings.** It's nice to have a little sympathy every once in a while—even indirectly and through the walls. Why can't I just be pretty? Goodnight. I'll surmount that little nugget during math class tomorrow.

I'm bored so I picked up my phone and went through my deleted pics to find the old entries from my mom's diary (god, that seems forever ago) and ended up finding one I thought I had read, but I guess I didn't.

Dear Diary,

I'm just so tired of being so young and I crave the time when I am 18 and am so grown-up and can make my own decisions. I want to be free to drive wherever I want and eat what I want and not have to always rely on my parents for rides and rules. Sometimes I feel trapped here... like Diane and I want to run off to college and experience the world and travel to Europe and live out our dreams. Not be stuck here in my little stuffed-animal-covered twin bed in a bedroom that feels frozen in my childhood. I want my room to be grown-up—like a proper teenager's room, and not with bookshelves stocked with sticker books, Judy Blume, and Sweet Valley High, and walls covered in Broadway posters and my ridiculous framed "best storyteller" award from the 2nd grade town library competition (which my mom had framed and still thinks is the absolute cutest thing in the world). Though my mom still does love to praise me (I suppose sometimes the praise can be quickly flipped into exasperation) for my ability to exaggerate or over-dramatize a story—which maybe one day will be a true life skill. For now, I think I should remove the embarrassing frame from the wall. Maybe I will leave the "A Chorus Line" vintage poster since it is still one of my all-time favorites (currently singing "Tits and Ass" to myself and giggling—the timelessness and irony is not lost on me at this miserably adolescent moment in my life). Tomorrow I will redecorate! Perhaps a cool Rolling Stones poster and a lava lamp from Spencer's (do I even like the Rolling Stones? I'll buy a CD and test it out). New room for a new me… I hope my mom will take me to the mall.

Xoxo

Julie

Dear Diary

SHE is so embarrassing

Hello Twelve, Hello Thirteen… Funnily enough I found myself humming that all day (now I know why my mom always belted that show in the car)! I love seeing Broadway shows (I'm sure you have figured that out by now, Diary), but I never got to see "A Chorus Line" because it closed a long time ago.

Anyway, hello almost-thirteen… I finally had some friends over after school. We were gonna hang out, do some homework, and then we had to write a speech for Juliet for her Bat Mitzvah next week. I had to make mine amaze because then she will write a good one for me. We were just pigging out on chips and making brownies in the kitchen and my mom came in. She has been working a lot from home lately (a flexibility I know she enjoys, but I kind of had gotten used to having the quiet at home so it is kind of annoying). She literally started cooking!! Is she actually annoying us on purpose or can't she help herself?? She had to make the chicken for dinner at 3:30 in the afternoon? She is so nosy! The worst is that she then started to make small talk with us— like casual, *hey cuties, oh my god have you seen the last episode of…* as if she were a teenager herself! My friends were being nice back and stuff, but they were probably thinking "Really? We came here to hang out and now we are stuck in the kitchen with Maggie's mom?" I kept trying to awkwardly and silently shoot my mom death looks across the kitchen, hoping she would read my subtle cues, but she just kept on chatting. Maybe she was trying to act cool because she was a loser at my age and was trying to relive those glory days. I couldn't tell if she actually thought that we wanted to talk to her—and it really threw me off that I couldn't read her as well as I normally can. Usually I am quite *astute* (as you know). But this casual "hey girl" chatter was out of character for her. Maybe she was pissed at me for my years of narcissism and was trying to get me back. Maybe she is still angry at the loss of my grandma so she wants to subconsciously inflict harm on those closest to her so we may feel the pain she is living with. Maybe she just missed her childhood self and wanted to feel that young again. Or maybe this was actually how she used to act in middle school and she was just (still) trying to fit in with the girls. (Omg I AM my mother???!!) Finally, we casually "had to go start our homework." I wondered, though, *was I really that embarrassed by my mom, or did I just feel like I had to act embarrassed so the girls would think I was cool?* Then it hit me before crawling into bed. **Your friends are sweet, Maggie. I had fun with them in the kitchen today. You girls are really growing up. It makes me happy and proud, but also sad, you know?** So straightforward, all of a sudden? She just wanted to be with me—that was all this was about. After all, I am her reflection, I am her. When she is sad, she just wants to be closer to me, I guess. I keep having to remind myself (often too late) that she isn't always this malicious monster I make her out to be in my head—I just don't understand why I can't admit it to her in person. Maybe today in the kitchen was just another way for her to try to understand me and all of my craziness. Maybe my grandma used to do this with her friends and she remembered those times and she wanted to create the same memories with me, or maybe my grandma didn't hang out with her friends in the kitchen so she wanted to be a different type of mom starting today…maybe she knows I'm about to be a teenager and won't need her around as much anymore (or want her around, either). It's a lot for me to wrap my head around. I'm so tired, and honestly, trying to manage my mom's emotions is a lot for me right now because I have a lot on my plate.

May 20th

Dear Diary

Don't ask me to talk and I will, don't tell me to listen and I will

I know for a while now I've been thinking about my mom—don't worry, I'm not going soft on you, Diary. I'm still utterly and completely focused on my self-image, social status, and friend groups, thank god. Otherwise, even I would be concerned I had fallen off the ledge into the abyss of adulthood and old age. I don't know, maybe it's because my Bat Mitzvah is in a few weeks; maybe it's because I'm starting to think a little bit like a grown-up. Believe me, all I care about is that everyone I invited RSVPs yes and that no one can believe how hot I look in my dress with just the right balance of heels and flats, princess and sophistication, and boobs and innocence. But aside from that, the grown-up, soon-to-be-a-woman part of me is reflecting a bit on my parents and their (over)involvement in my life. Sometimes I am so appreciative of all the work my mom is doing to put this together, and other times I feel as if I have to raise them both myself, or, better yet, teach them how to parent. *Why have I figured out so much of what it means to be an adolescent and my parents, who actually **were** adolescents, still can't figure out how to talk to me?*

We have already established that coaches, and bus drivers, and teachers and principals have no idea how to calm us down as a group or get us to show interest and attention. Last I checked, talking to teens or in-betweeners wasn't rocket science—yet the very people who feel they are expert enough to choose it as a career can't even figure it out. Why do our own parents, who are supposed to love and understand us the best because they have raised us, literally, from the womb, look like deer in headlights every time we approach them? *Oh, hi honey, are you ok? You look upset. Does your stomach hurt? Did you even start your homework yet? Is that dirt on your neck? What did you get on your new shirt??*

The moment they think we actually might want to talk to them, they fumble and stutter with their words, they don't know if they should help us or yell at us. And they don't know what to do with their bodies—like hug us or throw us a high five. It's so weird! Here's the deal, people—when you yell at us, we ignore you; when you demand that we listen, we don't; and when you ask us to talk and share our feelings, we won't. That's why in-betweenagers always hear their parents saying **UCHHGGHH she is so impossible!** But—and listen very carefully, confused adults who were broken as teenagers—we want to be better teens than you were and we certainly plan on being better parents than you are, so when we start to talk—about anything(!)—shut up and listen. I mean, put down your phone and look at us because I promise you the opportunity may not arise again for a very long time and if we have something to say then it must be important. We may be vague or indirect, but listen and you will probably (hopefully) hear the mixed and muddled message or question or fret or advice-seeking concern we are speaking of, albeit in a very roundabout and **circuitous** (like that vocab word?) way. If we are speaking to you, we need you. And we don't like to admit it. Don't miss this moment. It shows you we trust you. This is the sign of respect and love you try to demand from us but will never receive in the form that you wish to. It may not come in the way or at the time of day (usually around 10:30 p.m.) you prefer, but be patient and pay attention. And we will listen to you and be respectful of your terms and wishes, as long as you don't tell us to do so. We may need direction, but we don't like being told what to do—does that make sense? Parents have to find an indirect way and an optimal time, when our mood is just right, for implying that we need to do something. Believe it or not, we need to feel respected just like you do. I'm starting to respect my mom a little more because she hasn't been asking me to listen and she has been so busy planning my big day even just after her own mom died. I'll never tell her, but I do think it's pretty cool. I told her I'm really nervous about the RSVPs…and she listened.

Dear Diary

The food chain

Math class was so hard today. I seriously don't get this ratio and fraction stuff. I overheard Ruby telling Emma that she was annoyed that she wasn't invited to go shopping this weekend with Ava, Katie, and Juliet. I was relieved not to have been involved or to care that I wasn't invited either. I know it's a familiar tune; we just want to be included, even if the thing we are being included in isn't something we would want to be a part of in the first place…never mind, I'll get back to that. And sometimes, we are just relieved to be left out altogether because it is too stressful to deal with all the bullshit of actually being involved with the crazy plans and the plan-<u>making</u>. Sidebar—the plan-making is much longer in ratio to the actual length of time the "planned event" <u>takes</u>. So here I am, trying to solve a ratio word problem about "Mr. Smith travels from his daughter Amanda's house driving a car with three pounds of jellybeans and his wife rides a bike, taking a shortcut by the beach while carrying balloons" or something—I have no idea, because then I heard Ruby make Emma swear not to tell anyone and Emma said she wouldn't, she promised, because, Ruby said, she didn't like Katie anyway ever since Katie didn't invite her to her 11th birthday party in 5th grade and we all made our own pizza and sundaes at a spa. I saw Andrew (as per the usual, wearing his dumb jersey) watching all this silent drama while he was pretending to copy down the homework from the smartboard. He shrugged at Tyler and Tyler shot him a look. The teacher noticed something was up and she "shhhhhhhed" us. (I HATE being SSSHHHHHHHHED.) A minute later, Anna, one of my newer friends, asked me who was going to the mall and I tried to summarize it quietly—I mean, it was easy for me because I wasn't involved, so I didn't have to hide anything from anyone.

I faked my way through another word problem and the bell rang. On the way to lunch, I saw my acting teacher in the hall, and I told her I lost my "Beauty and the Beast" script. She said to meet her in the faculty cafeteria after lunch and she would copy another one for me in there. I did not want to go near the faculty cafeteria in the first place, but I was so embarrassed I lost the script that I smiled and thanked her and knew I had to deal. By the time I sat down to eat, Sarah asked if we knew why Ruby wasn't sitting with us. Katie shrugged but Maya chimed in that she heard Ruby was mad at them. Maya made the whole table swear not to tell because then Tyler would get into so much trouble. Tyler had hounded Emma after class, and she caved immediately. If Ruby found out she would die! I kept my mouth shut—I'm a good kid that way.

Then I had to go to the stupid faculty room, and I dragged Hallie with me (she's always up for an adventure and any teacher gossip she can get her hands on). I actually think she, too, was relieved to leave our annoying cafeteria table today. When we arrived at the sketchy faculty room, hidden down the hall behind the copy room (it's a little shanty place with no windows, a half-eaten birthday cake, an old fridge, and, like, 12 round tables shoved into it), I was shocked to see the most amazing sight. There was poor little Mrs. Hammerstein sitting at the back table with her packed lunch of a yogurt and half a sandwich in tinfoil, and she was all alone! At the front table, packed with 12 chairs that barely fit, were the popular, bullying, loud, inappropriate teachers. They all shot Hallie and me a look when we walked in. We stopped silently dead in our tracks. There it was, right in front of us—our very own middle school cafeteria but with underdressed oversized grown-ups playing our parts. It got me thinking… *Did these teachers become teachers because of their own unresolved middle school issues, so they came back to rewrite their middle school script—or is this what any cafeteria would look like in any office where grown-ups work?* Either way we are screwed. I thanked Mrs. Hammerstein and quickly left the room (secretly vowing to always be extra nice to her from now on). I couldn't wait to go to 5th period to see if Emma found out, or if Ruby knew she betrayed her. It was Spanish class and we don't do anything in that class, anyway.

Tonight at dinner, I actually couldn't help myself—at the dinner table I blurted out what I saw today. *That just breaks my heart to hear.* Initially I thought my mom's reaction was a bit dramatic, but I must admit, it really made me sad, too, to see how terribly these teachers behaved. *That poor woman has worked at that school for 25 years and given everything she has to that music and theater department, and she gets no respect from her peers because she doesn't teach a core class...or PE!* I was worried she was about to get up and write a letter to the principal or something. But instead, my parents and I actually talked about it. I guess since, for once, the topic of the day was not about me, we were able to have an actual 7-minute conversation and not fight. And we all agreed about how pathetic it was to see those teachers crowded around one table and leaving another teacher to sit all alone. *You see, honey? I told you we are doing something right. This kid is going to change the world. She sees the truth in people, aside from seeing the good in people. She's got real gumption, that kid.*

Clearly my dad loves that word lately. I'm not really sure what it means, but I guess it's good. Obviously hearing that made me feel a little better. It was a welcome distraction from the after-school argument about how I hate math and lost my script and wasn't invited to the mall and I hate my life.

June 1st

Dear Diary

It's not who I am but who I am NOT

I am not my parents. I can tell you that right now. I will not be them when I'm old, either. They don't respect me, and they are just cranky and stressed most of the time and then they tell me to study harder and clean my room 'cause it makes them feel better. I will be different. I will be better. I will meet my kids halfway and not make so many rules. (But maybe I need all of these rules because maybe they do it because I can't even decide what underwear to wear on some days?) (Shit—maybe they do know what they are doing?) I know that I am a nice person and I accept the fact that I am still figuring myself out. It will take me a long time to figure out who I am—I know that now. I'm ok being average, for now, and I know I shouldn't compromise my real beliefs just to fit in. I can, however, constantly change my fashion sense and makeup and hairstyle just to find the right look. Sometimes I'm a chameleon, sometimes I'm a butterfly. Even my unpredictability is predictable. I know that I am predictable and predictably unreasonable. And I know it's my parents' job to figure me out—they should consider themselves lucky that I am doing half their job for them. *You think you have it alllll figured out. Dad and I are doing the best that we can. You're just so confusing sometimes, Maggie!* I'm such a loser I am even making my parents' job easier. I even tell them about my days and how I feel. I need to rebel. They need to see just how easy they really have it with me. I'm going to go steal a car or smoke a lot of weed while talking on the (non-hands-free) phone in my stolen car. That oughta scare them into appreciating me more. Or maybe I will just come home from school and NOT talk. I will go right upstairs and slam my door like every other Tweenager In-betweener Upside Downer and my parents won't know what I am thinking or feeling or what went down today in class or in art with Neha or at lunch or on the bus or on Snapchat. They will just have to guess and assume and draw their own stupid conclusions like all the other useless parents out there. I don't understand why my mom took my phone away tonight just because I screamed at her when she yelled at me for not clearing my plate or studying for my Bat Mitzvah. It's not my fault!

GOOODNIGHTTT MAGGIIEEE!!! she screamed sarcastically through the walls and ceilings just to piss me off. I refused to answer. I know I AM changing and growing up every day, but I am NOT a pushover.

Dear Diary

My true self(ie)

I can't believe it's June. I'm almost 13 and, more importantly, it's almost SUMMER!!!! I can't even concentrate in school anymore. I've given up completely. I have, like, three finals, and I have like a million hours of studying to do and instead all I do is make a camp shopping list and dream about my Bat Mitzvah party and all of the speeches and toasts everyone is going to give me. It is finally going to be all about ME!!! (LOL, even I have to laugh because <u>I might be an underdeveloped 12-year-old but I know it is always all about me—at least in my house.</u>) I think it goes with the job description of being a teenage girl. I like the way TEENAGE sounds. I won't be In-Between anymore. If we weren't selfish, our entire existence as a species would fall apart. We females are supremely more evolved than boys (and I know moms are much more together than dads, so clearly that doesn't change), and that is because we are selfish, manipulative, conniving survivors. We are so focused on our projected image to the world that we sometimes forget where our true self ends and where our "selfie" begins. Our lives are kind of edited like our profile pics. We only see and remember the BEST and the WORST and nothing in between. It's funny—it's like my middle school self is a clear combo of my Finsta self (the true, uninhibited, youthful me for only a select few to see) and my Instagram self (the image for the rest of the world to see). *I wonder if the real me really lies somewhere in between.*

My mom just came in to kiss me goodnight. I slammed you shut so fast and threw you under the pillow like I was hiding drugs or naked pictures. She isn't stupid—I don't know what I was thinking. Clearly, she knows I keep a diary, she just better have NEVER looked inside. I realize, of course, that it is ridiculous that I am even hiding my "self" from my own mother. She actually is the one person who really would never judge me, and who really understands me, and now I even secretly know she was pretty much me when she was my age, so I know she gets all of my craziness. I'm pretty sure that even if I pretend to be super cool and rebellious and overreact a lot of the time, she still knows who I really am. She sees through me even when I really wish I could hide. I should probably consider actually telling her the truth more often instead of just hiding it and letting it rot in my diary. What good does it do in here? And besides, if I told her she would say *Oh, Maggie, I promise you things get easier.* The sad thing is she doesn't even SEE the truth, and that is that nothing actually really changes at all! I see it in her and she doesn't even know it! Even the teachers and the principal don't get it. They all think they have it allllll figured out. We are who we are and we will be who we always were. *Pontificating…* Not everything has to be everything all of the time.

But tonight, my mom actually crawled into bed with me. She is probably getting emotional about my grandma and my Bat Mitzvah coming up and she knows I'm leaving for camp soon and I am so outta here. She will probably miss me. I didn't get emotional or anything—probably because I am almost 13 and my hormones are totally leveling off. But I was happy to help her feel better on this particular night because I sensed that she needed it. (I'm so intuitive sometimes.) She, of course, had to go to the dark place of saying *shut off your phone, set your three alarms, tomorrow pick your clothes up off the floor, don't leave your hot iron on in the morning…* (I tuned her out after her first few senseless instructions). But the thing is, I know she didn't even want to say those things. It was like she was hiding her truth, too. Her truth is too sad for her to talk about sometimes. And I know she is lonely and heartbroken. My truth is too draining sometimes. And I know that she knows when I yell it is just because it is too hard for me to do anything else. Funny how we have this unspoken understanding. I accidentally let my guard down for a second—after she nagged me and I think my mind wandered from our painful true selves to my Bat Mitzvah dress or the possibility of a boy asking me to dance and I smiled instinctively—and she busted me and thought my softening up was for her. And she squeezed me tight and kissed my forehead.

I know, honey she said. *It isn't easy.* I think I squeezed her back after she said that.

Sweet dreams, angel. And she tucked me in, placed Bear under the covers with me, and turned off my light. Before she closed my bedroom door, I said to her "Mom?…"

I know, Mags. I love you, too.

Goodnight, Diary.

Until tomorrow.

Sincerely,

me